Totally Bound Publishing books by Jayce Carter

Dark Sanctuary

BOUND BY FEAR

JAYCE CARTER

Bound by Fear
ISBN # 978-1-83943-763-2
©Copyright Jayce Carter 2022
Cover Art by Fiona Jayde ©Copyright February 2022
Interior text design by Claire Siemaszkiewicz
Totally Bound Publishing

BOUND BY FEAR

Dedication

To my tarot cards, who never failed to kick me
right in the ovaries whether I'm into that or not.

Chapter One

"You don't look like you belong here, little fox." The man who spoke — tall, lean and dressed like a devil — was the epitome of everything Sunny had feared she'd find inside the BDSM sex club called Sanctuary.

Her breath sped, and her chest tightened as the large room shrank to nothing.

This is a horrible mistake. What was I thinking?

"Do you want to come sit with me and talk?" Devil-man asked, his lips curling into a smile below the line of his black mask. It wasn't a vicious smile, at least on the surface, but it sure felt sinister.

The desire to say no perched on her tongue, but she couldn't make it come out. She'd learned that saying no was dangerous, that it never got her what she wanted. The lesson was one that had stuck with her no matter what.

So, instead, she darted her gaze toward the crowd of people and pretended to spot someone she knew, waving in that direction.

The man stayed in his spot, letting her go, and she made a quick path for the bathroom. Once safely inside — the one place where no man would try to talk her into anything — she set her hands on the white porcelain sink and stared into the mirror.

Maybe a fox had been a stupid costume. She'd tried on a few different ones that radiated strength, but they had felt like a lie. Sunny was as soft as they came, so when she'd tried on the little white sundress, along with the fox mask that obscured her eyes, and some drawn-on whiskers, she'd known it was more *her*. Foxes were smaller than other predators, but quick and clever. She connected with that, understood it. At least, it had made sense until she'd walked into a club full of lions and tigers and dragons.

Suddenly, her fox didn't seem so clever.

One night. Prove that you don't want this anymore.

She nodded and straightened herself, pulling her shoulders back. She was here for a reason. She'd go out there, find someone to play with, and by the end of the evening, she'd know that she was done with all this nonsense. She could wake up tomorrow sure of herself, able to put this behind her. The plan helped her move forward.

The door to the bathroom opened as a woman in lingerie and a cat mask walked in, the music from outside deep and rhythmic. Her hair was blonde and beyond stunning, so pale it was nearly white. Even from behind the half-mask, her almost gray eyes shone brightly.

The woman approached, a smile across her pink lips, the color smeared as though she'd been kissing someone just before. "It's so much fun tonight, right?"

Sunny nodded despite not feeling quite so sure. "Yeah."

8

The woman glanced down at Sunny's wrist, at the cuff the receptionist at the door had placed there with a white ribbon. "Oh, you're new? Is this your first time?"

First? Try only. Instead of saying that, Sunny tried to smile. "Yes."

The woman stuck her hand out. "My name is Kat." She winced as soon as she said it. "I know — it's a masquerade party — it's supposed to be all anonymous. You don't have to give your name. I'm just not good at the whole secrecy thing. And *yes*, I know, Kat — cat costume — cliché, but why not, right?"

Sunny had trouble understanding Kat. She'd figured the sort of people in a place like *this* would terrify her. The men would be scowling brutes, lumbering around just looking for a victim, and the women quiet, frightened little things who cowered at everything. *That's what I was...*

Kat wasn't anything like that.

Sunny shook the offered hand, unsure how to answer, other than the fact that she wouldn't be giving her name. That would negate the entire point of her coming here on *this* night. Sunny needed to do what she'd come to do then leave — no ties threatening to trap her.

Kat chuckled, as if she could read the nerves that poured off Sunny. "Afraid of the big bad Doms? Come on — you can hang out with me. Safety in numbers, you know."

Sunny wanted to say no — it felt too much like putting herself into a life she was trying desperately to get out of. Still, having a partner next to her did feel better.

"That would be nice," Sunny admitted softly.

Kat asked her to wait a moment so she could use the restroom, then washed her hands before tucking her arm through the crook of Sunny's. It was an oddly safe feeling, as though Sunny had found a guide to this absolutely terrifying place. Sure, Kat wasn't all that intimidating, but at least Sunny wasn't alone.

They walked out, with Kat holding securely to Sunny's arm. "I love the last Saturday of the month. Something about dressing up makes everything more fun, plus it's the day we let the new folks come. It gets boring with the same old folk every weekend, and new blood is always good."

It also let Sunny move around the club with a sense of privacy, without feeling everyone was looking at her, could see her.

Sunny's gaze couldn't settle on any one thing. The bodies that moved on the dance floor, the groupings of people, the colors and costumes and activity, all fought for her attention.

And it all overwhelmed her. Sunny's world was quiet, calm. She'd worked hard to create a haven away from the craziness of everyday life.

So what was she doing *here*?

She turned her attention back to Kat, to the cuff around her wrist—identical to Sunny's except for the fact that it had a myriad of ribbons on it. Red, teal, green and yellow striped — they meant nothing to Sunny. She vaguely recalled the receptionist explaining it to her as she'd signed in, but Sunny hadn't heard any of it. Her anxiety had been far louder than rules or color coding.

"What do the ribbons mean?" Sunny asked, trying to find something to fill the silence with.

Kat held up her wrist to show the leather cuff with the colored ties. "For members, we use these to identify what people are looking for and what limits they have.

We still ask of course, just to make sure, but these make it obvious right from the start. If someone hates something you love, you know it may be a bad fit before even trying. Nothing worse than a hardcore masochist falling for a Soft Dom who doesn't like to even raise their voice. Makes everyone unhappy when people don't click."

Sunny frowned when the explanation didn't make any sense to her.

Doms never care what their subs want.

However, she kept that to herself. People saw what they wanted, and Kat seemed the type to let romantic notions blind her to the truth. No doubt she'd say the Doms here were different, that they were somehow exempt from the reality Sunny had experienced before. There wasn't any reason to argue over it, so Sunny let the topic drop.

They went to one of the tables set out with coffee and snacks, and Kat filled a small plate with items for them both. "I love your costume. You sure do fit in with the whole primal and prey thing."

And *that* made the damn panic creep up again. She hadn't thought of the fox as *prey*. It was a predatory creature, just smaller than some of the others. It seemed others saw it differently.

Kat looked past the table and locked eyes with a man across the room, one who wore a black mask with horns and a smirk. He crooked his finger to call her over. She let out a sigh full of want. "I'll be right back..." She pulled away before Sunny could answer, leaving Sunny with the plate of food and no backup.

A pit started in Sunny's stomach at the way Kat had followed the demand, at the memory of how many times Sunny had done the same thing, when she'd dropped everything she'd wanted and done as she'd been told.

She remembered a crooked finger, a silent demand that came a split second before anger, before violence.

It sickened her, threatened to drag her under so many worse memories.

"There you are, little fox." The devil-man from earlier came up from behind Sunny, his voice already tattooed on her brain.

She jumped, those overactive nerves of hers taking over, struggling to separate him from her past.

He's just a person. You're fine.

Right, because telling herself that made it reality... Saying it didn't make her safe, didn't do anything.

Still, she turned toward him, her shoulders hunched forward in on herself to make herself smaller. "Hello."

This is why you came. Don't chicken out now. Just one night.

He smiled, but she couldn't shake the way her brain screamed danger at her. Whether he was actually dangerous or not didn't really matter. Her body had decided, and it wasn't listening to her. It went off history, off what she knew to be true — men, especially dominant men, couldn't be trusted.

"Why don't you come on over to the couch there? We can have a talk, get to know each other. I've been watching you since you came in, and you look amazing."

Sunny tried to swallow down her fears, her doubts, but they stuck in her throat. She shifted her weight from foot to foot, unable to shake all the '*hell no*' swirling in her head. No matter how many times she reminded herself that she was here for this, she couldn't get herself to agree, to even want to agree.

He wrapped his fingers around her wrist, the one with the cuff, and tugged gently. "Come on, little sub, I don't bite too hard — at least not unless you beg."

Sickness churned in her stomach, the room becoming stifling, the air thinning.

He didn't yank, didn't tighten his fingers to the point of pain, didn't show any sort of violence or anger, yet she couldn't catch her breath. She couldn't stop herself from seeing him as the devil he had dressed as.

She followed, her body frozen and unable to fight back, to just yank and tell him no. What the hell was wrong with her?

Fear. It was what was always wrong with her, that beast she couldn't kill no matter what she did. Even when she thought she had it under control, it always reared its ugly, unwelcome head and turned her into *this.*

"I saw you the *second* you walked in," devil-man said. "You look like prey, and I am a man who likes to chase."

"I'm a man, Sunshine, and I have needs." The voice that haunted her dreams came back to her. It ran in her head as clear as if the monster from her past stood there right then, and the room blurred.

Just when she was sure she'd pass out, that she'd fall to the floor there in front of everyone, a large hand grasped devil-man's shoulder.

It wasn't violent, but it was a *clear* message of stop. "Hold up there, Jordan."

Devil-man — *Jordan?* — paused and turned toward the man who'd spoken, someone who made Sunny want to pull even farther back. This new man was tall, his body lean but strong. He wore a silver mask that covered his eyes, and his lips were pressed into a tight, unhappy line.

She did *not* want that sort of displeasure directed her way.

In fact, right then, going off with Jordan sounded like one hell of a good idea. His lean build would do far less damage than what this new man could dish out. It was like being faced with two monsters and picking the one with the smaller teeth.

"Yeah?" Jordan asked, his tone confused but not upset.

"Does she look like she wants to go with you?"

Jordan tipped his lips down, then took another slow look at Sunny, his expression lacking anger. "She didn't say no."

"Sure she did, just not with her lips. Come on now, take a better look at her."

Jordan peered down—as if just noticing the way Sunny were as far back as her arm would allow, how she leaned away and not toward him—and released her instantly. "I'm so sorry," he said, his voice softening and losing the sharpness it had before. It seemed he'd slipped from his Dom role. "Without the eyes, I have some trouble reading cues, I guess."

Silver released Jordan. "We'll talk about it later."

"Of course." Jordan looked at Sunny, somehow managing to have shrunk from the devil-man he'd been to a regular person, deflating before her eyes. "I'm really sorry, Miss. Can I get you something? A drink?"

Sunny shook her head, afraid her voice wouldn't work if she said anything. Even though he wasn't the monster he'd been moments before, her body had already thrown itself headfirst into panic.

"Why don't you go grab her something warm and sweet, Jordan, as an apology," the new man said.

Jordan nodded and rushed off, leaving Sunny there with only the man in the mask, the one who made Jordan look more like a cub. "Hey there, fox. Breathing helps, you know?"

The words struck Sunny as entirely asinine, until she realized…she wasn't breathing. She gasped in a breath, and right away her head cleared some. *Just how long was I holding it?*

"Better," the man said, then gestured toward a couch near the back, but one in view of the rest of the room. "You want to sit down before you fall down?"

I never should have come. She never should have tried to prove she was better, or that she didn't need this. Why couldn't she have stayed in the nice, safe little rut she'd spent years creating?

"I should go," Sunny said, her voice so soft that she doubted he could hear her over the music.

Yet he shook his head, that hard edge Doms wielded refusing to be argued with. Any thought that the man before her wasn't dominant fled. "Not yet. You can barely walk right now, about a mile deep into that panic attack you've got going. If I let you walk out now, you'll collapse in the parking lot if you're lucky. Do you have a friend here? Someone who can take you home?"

Again, she shook her head. There was Kat, but she wasn't really a friend. Just some girl she'd met in the bathroom.

She'd spoken to the owner, Toya, to get her invite to the event, but she wouldn't say she knew her either. Not to mention that the last thing she wanted was to talk to the one person who knew who she actually was.

Nope. She'd walked into the wolf's den all by herself, like an idiot.

"That's fine. Why don't you just take a seat? I'll sit on the other couch, give you space while you calm down. Soon as you get your wits about you, you can go. I'm not trying anything."

Sunny wanted to say no, but when she shifted her weight to her other foot, the leg gave out. It seemed her panic had taken more out of her than she'd realized, had snuck up on her without her knowing.

15

The man caught her, as if he'd been expecting it. "Yeah, not leaving just yet, are you? Come on." He helped her over to the couch, then pressed a hand to the back of her neck to guide her head down, to lean her forward. As soon as she did, he let her go and sat on the other couch, just as he'd said he would.

Which made her all the more suspicious. Men didn't do things to help for no good reason. They didn't give up what they wanted—*especially* Doms.

Still, she closed her eyes, focusing on the music, on the steady beat, going through the things her therapist had taught her. Focus on the now, on the scent of leather, of vanilla, of cinnamon. Pick five things she could hear—the laughter of a woman, the quiet conversation between two men, the music, the wind striking the sides of the building, the deep tone of a man—*no, not that one!*

She pulled herself together, piece by piece, until her chest eased, and she didn't feel as if she'd pass out.

Though, when she lifted her head, when the world didn't seem quite so scary, she wished she *had* passed out. Then she wouldn't have her savior in the silver mask looking at her so intently—the studying gaze of a man who knew too much already. That was perhaps the worst thing about dealing with Doms—they saw everything and were only too quick to use it to their advantage.

He held a drink, steam escaping the top. "Hot chocolate. Jordan brought it as an apology, but he figured you'd prefer if he was on the other side of the club when you looked up."

As much as she wanted to deny it, he'd been right.

He handed over the drink, and while Sunny should have thought twice about drinking it—it was from a stranger, after all—the warmth called to her. She sipped it, and the moment the sugar hit her tongue, she let out a moan. Then tried to silence it immediately. This was *not* the sort of place to make such noises.

Sure enough, the man's lips curled into a smile that made her warm in other, far less innocent places. And that reaction scared her more than anything else. She'd come here to prove she *didn't* want this, right?

She needed to sit her body down and have a long talk with it about good choices and bad choices, but that would have to wait.

"Feeling better?"

Sunny nodded, the cup in her hands like a leash for her own bravery. "Yes. Thank you."

His smile spread. "That's a pretty voice you have. It's a shame you don't use it more often."

She tried to tuck her hair behind her ear before remembering she'd braided it back.

"There you are," came another voice, one that made Sunny cringe again. A new man walked up—no, wait, two men—in metallic masks identical to the one worn by the Dom she was already with, except for the color.

The original man had a silver mask, the new one who'd spoken was in a black mask, and the third man had a golden one.

Friends? Lovers?

Sunny knew better than to ask, so she stayed quiet to figure it out on her own. Men didn't react well to a suggestion that they weren't straight, in her experience. It was like questioning their masculinity, and the last thing she wanted was to piss off these three.

"Sorry," Silver said. "I found a cornered fox who needed some rescuing."

Black lifted his gaze to Sunny, his lips sliding into a teasing smile. "So I see. Quite the prize you found yourself."

The words made her heart do that skipping-a-beat thing—not in a good way—but Silver was quick to come to her defense.

"She's jumpy, so give her some space. Jordan wasn't reading cues so well, didn't realize this fox isn't good at saying no with her words."

Gold turned his head, revealing long blond hair that had curls in it that reached nearly to his shoulder blades. He twisted as if to go explain things to Jordan, though *explain* probably meant *beat some sense into*.

Silver smacked Gold's arm. "It's fine. I told him we'd educate him later a little better—maybe we need another class on body language. He brought over some hot chocolate to help the fox get her breath back." Silver turned back to Sunny. "This is—"

Sunny shook her head. She didn't *want* to have their names. That had been her biggest rule when coming here, that no matter what happened, she could walk out, and no one would know it was her.

Well, no one except the owner, who'd marked down each person and their costume in case complaints were lodged later, but had assured her that information was confidential.

Sunny knew what happened when a person entangled their life with a Dom, when they welcomed such a person into their world—*nothing good.* Without names, without identities, Sunny could leave at the end of the night without worrying about turning into someone's property, without fear that she'd lose everything.

Again.

Silver huffed a soft laugh. "No names, huh? Well, Fox works well enough, and I suppose you can use mask colors for us. These are my friends." He gestured at the other two.

Black sat next to Silver, and Gold took a seat in the chair to the side of both couches. Strange that Sunny could feel so trapped even when none of them were right beside her.

There was something about the men that took up all the space, as if the rest of the world disappeared with them there. The music, the lights, the bodies of the other guests didn't matter anymore, not with these three surrounding her.

"So, Fox, is this your first time? Pretty sure I'd have remembered you if you were here before," Silver asked.

Sunny nodded, trying to act braver than she felt. She didn't want to look like easy prey, like something they could pick off with little work. "I just wanted to check it out."

"Doesn't seem your style," Black added, his voice not as deep, not as rough, and full of humor. "Sometimes this is all too much. No shame in being vanilla."

The tone felt condescending, as though Sunny were a prude who had never experienced anything in her life. She'd long dealt with her youthful face and sweet disposition making people think she was some naïve fawn, especially when added to her name. "I've done *this* before," she said, waving at the club to explain what she refused to say.

She'd done the whole BDSM thing. She'd experienced it all and knew exactly how badly it always turned out.

"Really?" Silver asked. Even without seeing the top half of his face, she could *feel* his lifted eyebrow.

"Yes." The word was short, but try as she might, she knew it held all the years of terror it brought back. How couldn't it?

None of them spoke for a long moment, until finally Gold answered. "And clearly it was a bad situation. Guess that explains why you're jumpy, don't it?"

Sunny curled forward more, staring into her cup as if the answer were somewhere in the swirling chocolate. Besides, not looking them in the eyes felt safer. "I don't want to talk about that."

Silver nodded. "That's fine. Not our business. A little advice, though? You need to learn to tell people no, to use that voice of yours."

Sunny opened her mouth to tell them that she'd *done* that before, and it hadn't worked. What was the point in fighting if she always lost? In her experience, 'no' only made it all the worse, only angered Doms.

Before the all-too-telling words escaped, though, she shoved them down.

What was it about these men? After her panic had ebbed, when she could think straight, she'd found herself willing to say things she knew she shouldn't. They created a wall around her, one that kept her safe from anything outside the small circle they'd formed.

And that was a dangerous thing to think and feel, especially because she should fear them more than anything else.

Will I never learn?

"You look like you feel better," Silver said. "At least, you don't look like you're about to fall down again."

Low standards.

"You want the front to call a cab? Or did you drive yourself?"

Sunny lifted her gaze toward the door, tempted by the thought of leaving. She could go home, back her little one-bedroom house, back to the quiet, the emptiness and the solitude.

And she could think about *here* more.

She returned to her dreams, the ones where she woke sweating and so close to release, with the memory of faceless men, with her wrists bound, her eyes covered and their rough, commanding voices in her ears, with her craving something she denied herself. What sort of life was that?

She'd come for one reason — to prove that *this* wasn't for her anymore. She'd get a taste, then go back to her real life understanding that the desire was just her own stupid brain playing tricks. It was nothing more than her mind wanting to relive her trauma, as if it could make sense of it if she tried again. She'd thought about it for months, looked at the website for the club and started an email to the owner over and over again. It had taken her so long to get to this point. She needed to be brave enough to face this, to prove to herself that this wasn't the life she wanted so she could finally let it go.

So Sunny shook her head. "I don't want to leave."

"Really? What is it you want then, little speechless Fox?" Silver asked.

Sunny swallowed and set her drink on the table before her trembling hands dropped it. "I want to try."

"Try what?"

"Everything."

Garrison had *never* wanted a woman this badly. He watched her through his silver mask and kept his hands folded in his lap to hide his body's reaction to her. While erections weren't unusual in Sanctuary, he knew the unsure little fox in front of him might just bolt at the sight.

Which was why his desire shocked the hell out of him. He was used to experienced submissives, the ones who would strip down at the curl of his lips, who shivered in delight when they spotted his flogger. He had never been the type to find much interest in the shy or unsure ones.

So what was wrong with his cock for wanting anything to do with the woman before him?

She wore a white sundress — was one of the most covered-up in the club — but damn if she didn't look like the best sort of bait. A white fox mask with lace details at the sides obscured the top half of her face, but it didn't hide her lovely, full pink lips or her auburn hair that was braided back and fell to just past her shoulders. It also showed off those big hazel eyes, far too innocent for the things he was thinking.

She was small, her shoulders looking downright fragile with the thin spaghetti straps the only thing hiding them.

And she'd said she wanted to try *everything*? 'Everything' was a lot, and the girl was startled by just a raised voice.

So Garrison sat back and studied her, taking in the way she shifted in the seat, the way she picked at the hem of her dress. She was anxious, that much was obvious. Beneath that, though? A flush sat on her cheeks and chest, and she darted her pink tongue out to wet her lips every so often — all signs the girl wanted *something*.

Garrison turned to his friends, to Connor in the gold mask and Trent in the black one.

A quick nod came from each — an agreement to see where it went.

Garrison had talked to her first, so it seemed his job to keep the conversation going. "Everything is a *lot*," he said. "And the lack of ribbons on your cuff says you might not be ready for that. So why don't we have a talk before we get started?"

She pursed her full lips but didn't argue.

Strange — the girl doesn't seem to say much for herself, does she? It was something to watch out for.

"You said you've done this before, and you didn't need to say it ended badly. How long ago was that?"

She sighed. "Do we really need to discuss this? I thought the idea of a masquerade party was to be anonymous."

"I'm not asking for your name and number, Fox, but if you just got out of whatever it was yesterday, tonight isn't a good idea. I don't get involved with anyone without knowing the basics about my partner."

"It's not *involved*," she said quickly, as if it were an instinct that bypassed her whole *don't talk* rule. "We wouldn't be involved."

Talk about commitment issues.

"If we get our hands on you, that's involvement." Garrison added a wink, and even with his mask, she seemed to catch it.

The time it took for her brain to catch up, to recognize the other part of what he'd said, was downright adorable.

"*We?*"

Trent nodded. "That's right. See the masks? Think of us like a pack. Sort of a three-for-one deal."

"If you're not interested in that, it's fine. You can walk out at any time."

Her throat moved as she swallowed, and it forced Garrison to think about how he wanted to drag his tongue up the fragile column, how he wanted to nip at her collarbone, how he wanted to pull down those teasing little straps and see her bare.

But she was nervous, so they would have to go slow.

She took another long moment, as if running logistics on how it would work — if it would work, if she was interested, what it would mean.

And when she took that lip of hers between her teeth?

Garrison was glad he was sitting down, because he'd have gone to his fucking knees for a chance to bite that lip.

"Okay," she said, voice soft. *Nerves? Sure. Uncertainty?*

He didn't think so…

More like wanting something but being afraid of it.

Trent leaned forward but didn't cross the touch barrier. "So, how long ago was it?"

She dropped her gaze, as if she wanted to hide. "Five years."

"And you've had counseling?" Connor asked, voice hard. It was easy to see that whatever she'd been through had left its scars, and none of them wanted to make it worse if she hadn't dealt with it.

She nodded, rubbing her palm over her knee. "Years of it."

"That what brought you here?"

"Sort of."

Garrison waved his hand for more information.

She blew out a long breath. "I wanted to prove I didn't want this anymore," she said. "I came here to prove this isn't for me."

Connor let out a snort, one that said what they all were probably thinking.

The girl was reacting like a Christmas light, turning on and off in the way that meant she might not *want* to enjoy this atmosphere, but she sure as shit *did*.

Still, Garrison usually had more tact, so he answered. "You were hoping you'd show up here, try it on for the night, then know you could wake up tomorrow with it all put safely behind you?"

She nodded.

He didn't love the idea of being some sort of disposable sex toy, and he hated the thought that she'd be gone the next day, but at least she was being honest about her intentions.

And he picked up the rest of the story she hadn't told. The asshole she'd been with had used BDSM to keep her under his thumb, had taught her that what he'd done was how it worked, and now the two were all tangled up in her head.

She didn't want to crave the dominance of another, but she did, and she hoped that one good try, now that she was better, would let her walk away knowing that whatever feelings she had weren't real. She'd confused abuse and BDSM, because for her, they'd been the same, which meant she had no idea how to let one go without the letting the other go as well.

Garrison rubbed his thumb over his jawline, seeing the girl sitting there, everything he wanted, and wondered how that would work.

Could he really offer her some fun for the night knowing she wanted it only because she wanted to prove she *didn't* like it?

"If you aren't interested," she said, her voice with a bit more backbone, "I can find someone else."

"Not if I go talk to the owner. One word from me, and she'll revoke your access if she thinks this isn't a safe place for you."

The fox nailed him with a look that said while she might be a bit damaged, she wasn't broken. "This isn't the only place around."

"No, but it is the safest."

"But if it isn't an option, I'll go elsewhere."

And she would. It was written there in her sharp eyes and the thin line of her lips. She had something to prove, and she'd find someone to help her prove it.

The thought of her ending up with another asshole, another fake-Dom to put that fear right back into her eyes, made Garrison close his hands into fists.

He couldn't let that happen. The girl was much too fragile to let her risk it, and *far* too tempting for him to let her walk out before he'd even gotten a taste.

"So?" She sat up, as if trying to look powerful, in control. "Will you do it?"

Garrison let out a dark chuckle, that tough edge of hers turning him on more than it should have. "You want to have three Doms for tonight to prove some idea that you aren't interested? Well, little Fox, we'll see just how 'not interested' you really are."

And he planned to prove her wrong.

Chapter Two

Sunny looked around the room, trying her hardest to lock down her nerves. She'd bet it was a losing game.

Still, they'd said yes. Silver's words came back to her, the promise in them, and she had to admit... It excited her as much as it terrified her, because she was afraid he'd prove the opposite to her.

After he'd agreed, he'd led her to a private room in the back of the club, the other two following close behind. They'd passed a man with a band on his arm in bright red that said 'security', who had checked with her before allowing them to pass.

She'd had to say she was going with them because she wanted to, that she wasn't intoxicated, that she understood the club safe word of 'red' applied and knew that she could use that word at any time and security would intervene if needed.

It made her feel slightly more comfortable.

Not that safe words had done anything for her before. She recalled trying them in the past with *him*, with the man who had put so much fear into her, and how it had only made him laugh.

Still, at least the security seemed to take it seriously.

The room had a flimsy pocket door, likely so it could be heard through.

Silver was still as intimidating as ever. When she'd walked behind him, she'd realized he had short, dark hair. Black was lean, similar in build to Silver but a little shorter, whereas Gold stood out as huge, his build reminding her of a bear.

Gold had a bag slung over his shoulder, and Sunny recalled the *bag* her ex had brought out when he'd wanted to play.

It had never meant anything good, and she struggled to tear her gaze away from it.

"Relax," Silver said, showing he was watching her closely. "You want to come see what's in here?"

Her ex had never allowed her that option... He'd liked to play games, to see how anxious he could make her, to let that fear grow and simmer and worsen.

Silver held his hand out, and after a deep breath, Sunny placed hers in his. He tugged her closer, sliding an arm around her waist. The touch was innocent, but she felt it through her clothing, through her layers of defense.

Gold set the bag on the bed, then unzipped it for her.

The reason for Silver's arm around her became clear when she tried to take a big step backward, as if the things inside the bag might jump out and bite her.

"Easy now," Silver said, grip solid. "Anything you don't like in there, we won't use."

She cast him a side glance. That hadn't been her experience. If her ex ever knew she hated something, that was the thing he'd end up going to the most. Weaknesses were the sort of thing a smart person kept to themselves.

Gold let out a rough sound, one of displeasure, but Sunny didn't bother to try and decipher it. "Take everything out. Anything you're okay with, put on the bed. Anything you're not sure about, put on the nightstand. Anything you don't want us to use, put back in the bag."

Sunny remained still for a while, unable to force herself to do anything. In the past, that would signal defiance, would enrage her ex. Instead, the three men stayed in place as though they had nowhere else to go and all the time in the world. Eventually, that gave her the courage to continue. She took all the items out first, not looking directly at anything as she dumped them on the bed. There wasn't as much as she'd expected, but that didn't stop the overwhelming feeling as she looked at them all.

Some were easy. The whip went back in, as did a flogger and a paddle. She couldn't seem to breathe right until they were out of sight.

When none of the men intervened, when they didn't immediately grab those things to use, she grew bolder.

The vibrator went on the bed. A dildo went beside it. Nipple clamps went on the nightstand, a butt plug into the bag. A silver tool that reminded her of a small pizza cutter but with spikes instead of a sharp edge made her pause.

Black reached for it, so she placed it in his palm. He held his arm out and ran the points over his skin. "Wartenberg wheel. It creates a prickling sensation but won't break the skin." He gave it back, and she repeated the same action on her own arm.

It was odd, a sharp feeling that stirred something warm inside her. Still, she pictured how hard it could be pressed, the damage it could do...

Into the bag it went, which had Gold making a soft huff.

Gold didn't talk much, but that didn't stop him from making his opinions known.

Sunny went through the rest of the items, placing them in the piles, mostly based on how much pain they could inflict. Anything that had the potential to hurt, she put in the nope bag.

At the end, only a few items sat on the bed. Cuffs, spreaders, vibrators, a dildo, a box that seemed to have some sort of strange vibrator in it, a mask, a gag.

Once she'd made her choices, she nodded and took a step backward.

Silver walked up and chuckled softly. "Not a fan of pain, huh?"

"I'd say more *'not a fan of trusting us not to cause too much pain'*," Black chimed in, as if the question weren't meant for Sunny at all.

Silver picked up the box, then *tsk'd* before setting it in the bag. "Made a mistake on this one, Fox. It's electricity play."

That got her attention. Electricity might have been the only way her ex hadn't caused her pain, and she didn't need to fill in the gap in her knowledge. She might have even lost her nerve if Silver hadn't already put that toy away.

Gold took the gag, then threw it with the no-go toys as well. "No way am I gagging you, not this time. Not that you say a whole lot anyway."

Her cheeks heated at the not-so-subtle reprimand.

Once they'd removed the few things they didn't want to use, Gold moved the remaining toys to the other nightstand, besides the cuffs, which he tossed to Black.

Sunny had kept out the hook and loop ones, putting away the heavier leather ones that required buckles. Even these thin ones made her stomach clench when in Black's hands. Somehow, they turned sinister.

And yet there was no doubt her cunt grew wet at the sight.

What is wrong with me? How could she want something so badly and yet be terrified of it?

Black crooked his finger, and she moved as if by instinct. She held out her hands, and he fastened the cuffs around her wrists, scooting the one from the club up so it didn't interfere. "You okay with taking off some layers?"

She frowned at the question.

"What?" he asked. "What's going on in your head?"

"Why are you asking me anything?"

"Because I don't know you. Don't know exactly where your limits are. So we're going to go slow, and I'm going to ask you a hell of a lot of questions."

"I don't want to answer questions," Sunny said, forcing the words out. She'd learned not to argue, *especially* with a Dom, and yet she made herself explain. "If I wanted an interview, I'd go somewhere else."

"So what, you think we're going to just fuck you and not give a damn about what it is you're wanting?" Black asked, a joke in his tone that said he was egging her on.

Except she didn't respond.

Gold cursed. "That's exactly what she thinks. This is a bad idea."

He's going to say no. They all are. That fear in her stomach started up again, over taking the lust, and Sunny grabbed Gold's wrist. "Please."

He stared down at her, and even with the masks, she felt as though he looked right inside her, as if he were

31

studying her. "You ain't ready," he said, then lifted a hand slowly to drag his thumb over her bottom lip. "I fucking wish you were, because there is nothing more I want than to strip that pretty little dress off you and taste every goddamned inch of you, but you ain't ready for all that."

His words coursed through her like flames, lighting her up in ways she hadn't felt in...she couldn't even remember. It was the way he said it, the absolute certainty that he could do it, that she'd enjoy it, the promise there that melted all the ice she'd filled herself with.

Still, she kept a hold of his wrist. When she spoke, it brushed her lips against his other thumb. "I *need* this," she said. "I can be good, I swear."

He dipped his thumb past her lips, and she closed around it, teasing him with her tongue. So she wasn't good with dirty talk, with saying what she wanted, but maybe this would convince him?

What man could walk away from such an offer?

His breath was warm when he exhaled. "You are a mess, ain't you?"

She didn't think he expected an answer, especially because the answer was obvious.

Yes, I really am...

Still, he pulled his thumb free, and just before she was sure he'd turn and walk away, he leaned down.

It was awkward, and he had to grasp her chin to tilt her head, so their masks didn't hit, but he managed to take the kiss he seemed to want. He tasted of electricity and sunsets, like thunderstorms over the desert. His kiss wasn't gentle, wasn't sweet, but that was fine by her.

This was the passion she'd wanted, the ability to lose herself to it, to get it out of her system and realize what a horrible idea it was.

Too quickly, he broke it and pulled away. "Okay, Fox. *Slow*, though. We clear?"

Sunny nodded, afraid of speaking and making them second-guess the choice. She reached for the straps of her dress, but Silver stopped her. His voice, rough and full of lust, didn't seem so scary anymore. "What's the point of a present if I don't get to unwrap it myself?"

He ran the back of his hand down her side, teasing the edge of her breasts through the fabric. She'd thought she'd have to white-knuckle this whole thing, but now?

Now she was so close to begging them to do more.

When Silver reached the hem, he crept his fingers beneath it, staying on the outside of her thigh, moving up until he reached the edge of her lace panties. He dipped beneath the waist, then moved along the front, teasing her lower stomach, making her feet inch outward on their own.

How could a man turn her mindless so quickly?

Another hand pressed against the small of her back, and she couldn't help but jump. There were more hands than she was used to, more to keep track of.

Black let out that laugh, the one that said he wasn't mad, before he grasped her braid in a tight grip and pulled. It wasn't hard, just the smallest of tugs, and yet her moan was low and wanton.

"Knew you weren't quite as proper as you acted," Black said, playfulness in his tone. "You tossed some of those things in the bag like a schoolmarm, but I knew better."

Gold came up behind her, his wide chest and hard body crowding her. He moved his hands around her, then cupped her breasts through the white fabric. It was such a blatant touch, the sort she used to love.

There was something unfailingly hot about a man who didn't hesitate, who didn't act as though he weren't sure what to do. Gold slid his large, warm palms over her breasts, teasing the nipples, as if he'd done it a million times before and knew exactly what she liked.

Which, to be fair, he seemed to.

Sunny let her head fall on his chest, a surrender, as she reached behind her to brace her hands on his hips, needing something to grasp.

"Fuck, you're something else," Gold groaned out, his voice rough. He shifted, slipping his hands down her sundress, moving the fabric so he could touch her skin directly.

If she was going to feel self-conscious about her breasts, it wouldn't be right then. It was impossible to wish they were larger, to wish anything were different, when his calloused fingers teased her sensitive nipples.

Black walked away for a moment, and when he returned with the clamps, those old nerves hit her again.

He held them up, loosening the setting. "Won't put them on tight. You hate it? I'll take them off. I'm pretty damn sure you won't hate them, though."

Gold continued to tease her nipples, to draw them into hard points desperate for more attention. He rolled them between his fingers, squeezed them, a mimic of what the clamps would do.

Sunny cried out when he pinched them, as though driving home the point, and Black's eyes brightened, as if he fed off that sound.

So Sunny nodded. How could she *not* say yes? Hadn't they proven their point?

Gold moved his hands to beneath her beasts, holding them up like a showcase. It was perverse, having one man groping her while another watched.

Then Black leaned in and took her left nipple between his lips, sucking hard at the nub, and Sunny nearly came apart. When he released her, he attached the clamp, closing it slowly over the glistening tip.

The pain was instantaneous and shocking. She'd used clamps before, had enjoyed them so long ago, but *this* was always that moment of doubt.

Black caught her chin, forced her eyes to his. "Breathe, little Fox. Give yourself a second to decide."

The safe word was on her tongue, but she did as he said. She breathed in, a whine on her lips, before exhaling.

The pain didn't lessen, but it turned from sharp to dull, to an ache that matched the throbbing in her needy, drenched cunt.

Gold continued to tease the other nipple, to keep her stimulated and on that edge. "Good girl," he whispered before flicking the clamp.

That made her entire body jerk, so close to an orgasm from the mixture of pleasure and pain.

Black kept a hold of her chin, then pressed his thumb past her lips. She obediently sucked it, then he lowered it to circle her other nipple.

It was torture, waiting, trapped and on fire and confused. Still, Black took the other clip and attached it, the same moment of pain hitting her, but this time without the doubt.

Gold shifted her dress down enough that the straps hung over her arms, then brought her wrists together behind her.

She tugged, testing his hold, finding it solid. It made her breath quicken but not in panic.

She felt like the animal she'd dressed up as, like a fox caught between three wolves.

And no matter how stupid it was, no matter how much she might kick herself later, she wanted them all.

Connor couldn't get enough of the little fox between them. Her nipples had been the color of peaches at first, but after a bit of attention, they'd darkened, grown stiff, and he wanted nothing more than to close his teeth on them, to watch her come undone.

Of course, seeing the clamps there worked pretty well, too. The tiny teeth bit in, and her reaction was what wet dreams were made of.

She was strung tight. He could see her thinking constantly, the way her brain never seemed to stop or slow. At least, until they got their hands on her.

Now she was mindless, just feeling, craving, *needing*.

She pulled against his grip—just testing his hold—and her breathing quickened, sending her farther down that hole, and he wanted to show her the whole damned thing.

Training new subs had never been his thing, but damn if this girl didn't get him going. She wasn't new, not exactly, but there was something damn appealing about showing a girl what she thought she already understand.

Garrison elbowed Trent out of the way, then fell to his knees. He glanced up her body, looking ready to devour some poor creature who had ventured off the path. He set his hands on the outside of her thighs, then pushed up her dress, slowly, letting her nerves get the best of her.

Ah, some games are worth playing slowly.

She trembled in their grasp, like something their pack had caught, something they'd enjoy tasting.

When Garrison pulled the dress up and over her head, showing what she wore underneath, Connor knew he needed to sit his ass down. She had on the sweetest little white panties — ones made of lace that had her looking like something innocent that had wandered into their little den of iniquity.

Fuck.

Connor moved the few steps backward so he could sit on the bed, then hooked the ring of her cuffs together, so he didn't have to hold her. There were better things to do with his hands. He pulled her into his lap, enjoying how she squirmed.

Garrison scooted forward, his gaze locked with hers. He didn't break that, not even when he curled his fingers into her panties and slid them down her toned legs.

Still, she kept her thighs pressed tight together, as if that were her last security, her safety net.

Connor reached around her and grasped her legs, noting how small they felt in the grasp of his large hands, and just how much he liked it. "Spread 'em, Fox."

She didn't, but each time he spoke, each time any of them did, that trembling started up. It wasn't the fear from before — that was pure need, and damn if that didn't draw Connor in.

Garrison cast her a smirk. "Come on. Won't be able to have much fun if I can't even reach the good stuff."

Trent let out a sharp laugh. "I think we've already gotten to some of that." He leaned over and tugged softly at one clamp, and sure enough, she let out the most perfect whimper, the sort a man could hear all his life and never get enough of.

Better yet, those thighs of hers went loose, and it let Connor pull them wide.

Garrison scooted in, just enough so that if she tried to snap them shut again, he'd be in her way. He placed his hands on the insides of her legs, thumbs a breath from her cunt, and offered one hell of a wolfish grin. "What a pretty little pussy you have," he said casually.

"You can't say that." She gasped, as though *that* were the most scandalizing thing happening. It seemed the girl struggled with the verbal, no matter who was doing the talking.

Garrison met her gaze, no shame in his expression. "I'm pretty sure I can." He ran his thumb up her exposed slit, teasing the folds there as though it were the most regular, normal thing in the world. "See, I have some experience, so I know what I'm talking about, and your pussy is beyond lovely." He pressed more, the thumb disappearing just a bit into her. "Soft, warm and" — his thumb sank in a little farther — "oh so wet." He used his other hand to pull back the hood of her clit, to expose it to the air, to all of them. "And this sweet little clit here is just begging for some attention."

As it turned out, their little Fox didn't seem to like being exposed. Or, rather, she *loved* it, even as she squirmed, as she shifted to cover herself again.

Too bad. Something about a squirming woman did it for Connor.

"Your lips may not say much, but your cunt speaks loud and clear. Be awfully rude to ignore it." Garrison leaned in and dragged his tongue over her clit, a hard lick that made her thrust her hips wildly.

It made Connor think it had been a while for the poor girl.

Not that Garrison seemed to have any pity for her.

In fact, none of them were known for mercy.

And while Connor had no idea how long it had been for her, he knew it had been far too long for him since he'd held a woman he wanted this bad.

He'd damn well make sure he enjoyed it...

Silver's tongue was magical, or so Sunny would have sworn. He slid it along her clit, holding her open for his assault, and Gold's hands on her thighs meant she couldn't do anything but accept it.

She threw her head back, grateful Gold moved so she didn't hit him in the nose by accident.

She doubted he'd take that well.

Silver pulled away for a moment, then nodded at the pile of toys. Black walked out of her line of sight. Silver shook his head, then nodded.

Black handed a thick, short, curved dildo to Silver.

Silver rubbed it against her cunt, the sensation teasing. "Are you going to take this for me like a good girl?"

"Yes," Sunny promised. Anything they said — *yes*.

Silver chuckled, then licked the tip of the dildo, tasting her from it, something that drew more heat to her cheeks at how filthy it seemed.

He pressed it to her cunt, then worked it into her with slow but insistent pressure. She was so wet, there was no problem, despite the fact that she hadn't had sex in years.

In fact, it shocked her that she wanted it as much as she did. How many men had she tried this with over the past five years? How many times had she kissed them, had she attempted passionate nights in the dark, only to pull the plug before the main event because she was as dry as the Mojave?

And yet here she was, beyond drenched, downright eager, and he'd slid the toy into her without the least bit of trouble. What was different?

The obvious answer was the one she refused to consider — that she wanted what she'd come to put behind her.

He pressed a button on the end of the toy, and it buzzed to life. It was thick, and the curve nestled it against the front of her pussy. It felt odd at first—not bad, just strange. She wasn't used to the sensation of something just staying there, of not thrusting.

Black sat on the bed beside her and brushed the clamps, even that tiny movement a reminder that made her cunt tighten around the toy. His grin widened, and he repeated it, never tugging hard, never causing any pain she didn't like, just teasing her by moving the clamps ever so slightly.

Gold's hands remained strong on her thighs, keeping her on display and open. It was some strange place between praise and humiliation, a line she'd never walked before. Her ex had enjoyed humiliation, but she'd always felt degraded during those times. Now? Despite being on display, she felt...cherished.

As if they looked at her like something of value, something precious.

Even with their filthy words, it didn't make her feel bad.

Gold's cock was impossible to ignore behind her, sitting in his lap as she was. It was solid and far larger than she was comfortable with. If he'd had a dildo this size, it would have gone right into the 'hell no' bag.

Yet, without even meaning to, she found her hands, still bound between them, twisting to rub against his hard length.

He groaned into her ear. "You're playing with fire, little Fox. Pretty sure you're not ready for me to fuck you."

And he was right. Or, at least, she thought he was right. It didn't matter then, though, because tomorrow didn't exist. Yesterday didn't. Only that moment and the demands of her body.

So she rubbed against his shaft, because she couldn't *not* do it.

Silver, still between her legs, grasped the dildo and tilted it as if searching.

When he hit a certain place, electricity surged through her, everything tensing for a moment. He let out a soft laugh before leaning in to latch his eager lips around her clit.

And it was shocking how intense it was. The vibration of the toy coursed through her, and when he sucked her clit, it added to the sensation.

Gold's fingers were tight against her thighs, and Black didn't let up teasing the clamps while Silver tormented her with the toy and his talented mouth. Before Sunny could even prepare, a powerful release crashed over her — through her.

She arched her back, leaning more against Gold, overwhelmed by the way her body tightened down around the toy, by the way it shorted out her thoughts. It was as though all that worry she'd had, all the fears, all the time she'd spent controlling herself so tightly finally snapped apart.

Everything that had weighed on her, the times she'd held back, the underlying tension that had become such a part of her she hadn't even realized it, drifted away.

She shivered as she came down, Silver having pulled the vibrator from her, leaving her exhausted and empty.

Black danced his fingers over the curve of her bare breast, reminding her that the clips were still on. The curl of his lips said he damn well knew it. "You're not done just yet, are you?"

Sunny sure *felt* like she was done. In fact, she hadn't felt this sated in…

Ever?

Maybe.

"I don't know," she said, startled by how sultry her own voice came out. She sounded like some sort of sex kitten, which was not what she'd ever been.

Black leaned in and blew a chilled stream of air over her nipple, and just that made her suck in a harsh breath. He smirked up at her. "See? You've got it in you. Ask me for it."

Really? He wants me to ask him to do it?

The words crawled around in her throat, but they wouldn't come out.

Don't give someone anything to use against you. How often had her ex asked her things, then used those same things to hurt her with?

Black caught her chin, so she looked into his eyes that were almost golden, then stroked his fingers over the clamps, shifting them. "I can see it in your eyes, little Fox. You know what it'll feel like when these come off. Such a deep ache when the blood rushes back in, and we both know you'll come hard again, don't we?"

She nodded. It probably wasn't a question for her to answer, but she did anyway, his coaxing voice pulling it from her.

"That's right, honey, so let me hear that pretty voice of yours. Ask me to take them off."

"Please," Sunny said, voice breathy.

"Please what?" He tugged softly at the clips, making her cunt tighten again, tearing away all her pride.

"Please take them off."

"You want to come again?"

Sunny nodded. She did want that, so badly. A moment before she hadn't thought she even *could* come again, but now?

She needed it more than she needed another breath.

"That wasn't so hard, was it?" He teased the clips, one in each hand. "You should learn to ask for things, or you'll never get what you want."

Sunny could have screamed right then, as he brushed the clips, as she was so close to the ecstasy that he seemed to be denying her.

"Come on," Gold rumbled, his chest to her back. "Stop torturing the poor girl."

Black laughed. "If only. All right, fine. You care to do the honors?"

Gold muttered, "*Sadist*," beneath his breath before he grasped the clips in his large hands. "Ready, darlin'?"

Am I?

Sunny nodded, not so much because she felt ready but because, for that split second, for the time until her brain started to work again, she trusted them.

Gold pressed his lips to her shoulder before removing both clips at once.

She had a moment of relief when they came off before it hit her, that deep pain as the blood rushed back in.

Black cupped her breasts and rubbed his thumbs against her poor nipples, driving the pain deeper, and Silver took that moment to dive back in, his insistent lips against her clit.

Everything exploded, more intense than the last release, shattering her. *This* was what she'd been missing the times she'd tried with other men, that edge of pain, the domination, the absolute need that grew inside her.

Every other time had bored her, and Sunny had stayed inside her own head so she hadn't been able to enjoy it.

That wasn't the case tonight, not when these three men touched her.

She wasn't Sunny, the broken girl who had been turned into a shell of her former self after her ex had abused her.

She was the fox of her costume. A costume wasn't just about wearing something else — she *felt* like something else, trapped between the wolves and never happier.

She twisted, her hands still bound, as the release tore through her.

By the time it eased, when she leaned back against Gold, the throbbing ache of her nipples had lessened, and the stroke of Black's thumbs helped. Silver pressed a kiss to her thigh, and Gold released his grip on her.

Gold's cock was still hard against her, and despite how exhaustion tugged at her, her pussy tightened, as if telling her it could go for that.

She shifted her hands, stroking against his cock, to which he groaned again, a deep, rumbly voice.

"So, pull a few orgasms out of you and you turn into a brat, huh?" The words were soft despite Gold's rough voice, but full of affection, as if it charmed him rather than annoyed him.

Which didn't compute for Sunny. Her ex had hated any time she did anything he didn't care for — which had seemed like everything by the end. Being a brat wasn't a term of endearment but the first step to something she would dreadfully regret.

Gold undid her hands. "You're not getting fucked, little Fox, not tonight."

The disappointment shocked Sunny. How many times had she turned down men over the past five years when she didn't want anything more, when the men couldn't deliver?

Finally, she *wanted* more, and they were telling her no?

"Why not?"

Silver, still crouched down in front of her, still so close to her cunt that she had no way to ignore it, offered her a smile that could almost be considered sweet.

If not for the proximity to her pussy and the wetness still on his lips...

"You got what you needed."

She swallowed hard, then forced herself to respond. "But what if I don't want to be done?"

Silver smiled wider. "We give you want you need — not always what you want." He rubbed his hands up and down the outside of her thighs. "How're you feeling?"

Sunny wet her lips but didn't answer. She wasn't even sure what the answer was. The wonderful afterglow kept her relaxed, even as Black tossed Silver a rag and he swiped it up her cunt. It irritated her sensitive clit, made her gasp.

"Easy," Gold rumbled in her ear, his deep voice sinful.

Silver slid on her panties, his hands teasing her skin.

Black leaned in and pressed a kiss to her breast, before he pulled her dress over her again, covering her, the fabric rough against her still-aching nipples.

Dressed and in Gold's lap, Sunny started to wake from her post-orgasm coma. The sounds from outside the door, the ones that had been blocked out by her lust before, filtered through.

Moans. Laughter. Music.

Had they heard the sounds *she* had made?

She shifted, all those worries hitting her again, starting to fill her.

She'd come to prove a point to herself, and she was terrified she'd discovered the opposite...

Trent couldn't believe how hard his cock was. The little Fox had made the *best* sounds, the tiny whimpers as he'd toyed with the nipple clamps, and it had brought all his instincts to the forefront.

Sometimes, when playing with a woman, they weren't into everything, they faked it — but he could always tell.

This girl didn't fake *anything*. Her flushed chest, the way she breathed in shuddering little gasps — it had all been so wonderfully honest. Even when she didn't like something, even the fear, had all played across her face without obstruction.

And that sort of honesty was even better when it was hard fought, when the girl didn't give it up right away. This one was exactly like that. She'd wanted to try this, to prove she didn't need it, so she'd held on to her control with all her might until they'd peeled it away.

And what a beautiful submission it had been.

Not fucking her was one of the hardest things he'd ever had to do. Connor was right, of course. It wasn't the night for that, not with where she was mentally, but damn if he didn't wish it were different. He'd love nothing more than to end the night sinking into her sweet cunt and fucking her through another few orgasms.

Don't always get what you want.

So instead, he'd have to settle for wrapping that girl in a blanket, for resting with her sweet body against his. Connor had had his turn, and now Trent wanted her in his lap, to toy with her long hair, to take the minute while she came down until he was sure she could get herself home.

And maybe get her name…

Garrison took out the wipes and cleaned off the toys while Trent removed the cuffs from her wrists.

She didn't speak, but getting a person's brain working after what they'd put her through was a process. Besides, words would probably just wake her up faster, and Trent wanted to enjoy the time afterward, when a woman was unguarded.

She moved again, this time to her feet, letting the blanket fall away. It seemed her legs hadn't gotten on board with the whole 'up and at 'em' thing, because she stumbled. Trent caught her easily, her soft body against his the best feeling. "You need a few to get everything together," he whispered to her.

"I need to use the restroom," she said, that shyness back, as if even after what they'd just done to her, she still wasn't sure.

Trent nodded. "Come on, there's one just across the hallway. I'll walk you there."

"I can make it on my own."

He shook his head. "Not how this works, Fox. Until you've got your feet under you, you're under our care. Just the way it is."

She pressed her lips together, a sign she didn't care for that, but that wasn't all together unusual. Subs, especially ones who were new or had only dealt with shitty Doms, had a tendency to not realize the people who topped them actually wanted the best for them, that they didn't want to throw them away the second it was over.

Please, don't let it be over.

Trent helped her to the restroom—the single-stall one was located at the end of the hallway with the private rooms.

He caught her hand, then tugged her chin until she met his gaze. "Tell me your name, Fox. I want to see you again."

She shook her head, the slightest shake.

"Why not? You enjoyed tonight, didn't you?"

She blew out a long breath, then her voice came out soft. "Yeah, I did."

"So what's the problem?"

"I don't want to be *this*. I can't be, not anymore."

"This? Meaning a shockingly sexy woman who makes the best sounds I've heard in years — one I really would like to fuck to absolute exhaustion sometime?"

And there was another of those sounds, a whine, and it teased him. As soon as it happened, though, she cut it off. "I can't."

Trent couldn't deny the disappointment, but boundaries were boundaries. He nodded. "All right, Fox. Use the restroom, then we'll go back. I won't push."

She nodded, then ducked into the restroom.

After a moment, Garrison walked up to stand beside him. "Any luck?"

Trent shook his head. "Nope. Girl has some ugly wounds, and I don't think she's quite ready to move past them."

Garrison sighed. "I get it. Don't like it, but I get it." He peered at the closed door. "Fuck, that sucks. Didn't think I'd find a girl who reacted so well."

"Yeah," Trent agreed, cursing the situation.

"Maybe she'll come back," Garrison said.

"Maybe."

They waited for another minute until Trent frowned. It had been a while…

He knocked on the door, silence coming back. "Fox?"

Nothing.

He twisted the handle, finding it locked.

The security guard looked their way, and Trent waved him over. The man, Lucas, was a sweetheart who had worked there for years, and who knew Trent well.

"A girl went in there a few minutes ago, but she isn't answering now," Trent explained.

Lucas knocked. "Miss? You okay?"

Nothing.

Lucas took keys from his belt and slid them into the lock.

Trent cursed himself for letting her out of his sight. It felt like a rookie mistake. What if she'd fallen? What if she'd hit her head because she wasn't steady on her feet? What if she'd gotten hurt because he hadn't taken care of her like he was supposed to?

Lucas opened the door, and the bathroom was empty. The door on the other side, the one used for people wanted to leave when they felt uncomfortable, an emergency exit, was open.

His fox had run off.

Chapter Three

Sunny handed over the card to the poor woman, who had a black eye marring the left side of her face and the same sort of fearful cowering Sunny had seen over the years.

The same sort she had *done* over the years.

Still, she could read the people who came into a women's shelter, and this was one of her many no-shows.

People who walked through her door fit into three groups. The ones who wanted help, the ones who weren't ready but were close, and the ones who might never be ready.

This woman was group three, and despite that black eye, she'd go right back to the monster who had done it. It killed Sunny, but the one thing she'd learned was that she couldn't save people who didn't want to be saved yet.

The woman—she'd given the name Kelly, but no doubt that was fake—had spent a night at the shelter.

Whether it was fear or love or not wanting her life to change, she'd chosen to sign out come morning.

Sunny couldn't force her to stay, so she did what little she could, which was ensure the women who left knew where to get help if they decided to.

"Call that number." Sunny tapped on the back of the card. "They'll come and help."

"Who is it?"

"It's a group that's known for helping out in cases like this. They have some branches all over the country, but this is the local one. We've worked with them a lot, and they're safe to call."

The woman held the card carefully, as if just as afraid of it as she were of whatever was back home. "I don't think I should bring this home."

"It's safe. The card reads for a landscaping service, and if you call it, that's how they'll answer. All you have to do is say 'I need a quote on sunflowers,' and they'll know what that means."

"Laurance, he's scary…"

"So are they, trust me. I've never seen a case they couldn't handle. They'll make sure you have safe transport back here if you need it, day or night, no matter what else is going on."

Her words took her back to a few of the men from that group who had come by the shelter, always with plenty of notice so she could make the more skittish residents scarce. The group was large, from what she'd seen, and well organized. They'd set up security for the shelter, helped with dangerous transports, and often arrived before police in the event of a problem. The woman who had run the place before, Beth, had been the one to make contact, and while Sunny would have women call them, she'd never reached out to any of them personally.

They might be nice, but she wanted nothing to do with them. Sunny knew men weren't worth it, especially not the ones who came around, the ones who walked with that sort of confidence. Any man was a threat, but *these* ones seemed like far too high a risk.

Kelly nodded and tucked the card into her pocket. "Thanks."

Sunny wanted to say so much more. She wanted to take the woman's hand and promise her there *was* a light at the end of the very dark tunnel she was trapped in. She wanted to tell her that other women had gotten through it and that she could too, that she didn't need whatever man had beaten her down and told her she was worthless. She wanted to tell her she was strong, that she *could* do this.

But people didn't hear things until they were ready, so Sunny let her go. This woman had to walk her own path, decide when she'd had enough.

Sunny just hoped she'd see her again.

The shelter was quiet, which was fine by Sunny. She'd worked there for four years, ever since she'd spent her first six months post-ex hiding out there. It had made her realize how important a place like that was, that it saved lives, that she had to be a part of it.

She couldn't do anything about the man who had abused her — he was rich and well-connected in her little town back home — but she could damn well help women *here*. It felt like her own little rebellion, a way she could strike back at the man who had hurt her, even if it wasn't direct.

She tried to push that aside, to focus on the small administrative tasks that filled her day.

A flash of darkness came to her, the wonderful press of hot, demanding lips, the exquisite bite of pain, the deep masculine groans.

It had happened all damn morning. Each time she thought she was focused, she'd get another memory, as if the night with those men at the club refused to be forgotten.

I found out what I needed to.

It wasn't what she'd gone there to learn, but things didn't always work out the way she wanted. She'd gone so she could walk away knowing that it was *always* what it had been before, like some scientific method where she tried to recreate her old disaster. She'd wanted to wake the next morning able to forget it, to move forward, to know that all Doms were like her ex and that it wasn't for her.

Instead, she'd left more conflicted than ever.

The night had been beyond her wildest fantasies. All those dreams she'd had, the ones where she'd woken sweaty and drenched between her thighs, had paled in comparison to reality. She felt herself in a way she hadn't in years. It was as though they'd helped her find some part of herself that had gone missing.

Or a part that was stolen.

That made them even more dangerous than she'd realized. She'd known they could hurt her physically, but they'd done so much worse. They'd *destroyed* her resolve.

Which meant that club, and those men especially, were off limits. All the stories had taught her not to play with wolves, not to let them into her home, and they'd reminded her of why.

The ringing of a phone caught her attention, dragging her back from her musing, so Sunny jogged into her office where her cell sat on the desk.

She lifted it to her ear, not recognizing the number. "Hello?"

"Hello, Ms. Kaylor."

The feminine voice was one Sunny wouldn't forget, one of complete confidence and steel. It took her back to when she'd met the woman, Toya Banks, who ran Sanctuary. She'd met her in the office of Sanctuary during the week, when it was closed. Sunny had sat through the interview process that allowed her to attend the club as a guest.

Sunny swallowed hard, the same fear making it hard to talk to the woman. She was a Domme, and the sort of woman Sunny had always secretly wished she were. Sunny would have loved to have that sort of power, to walk around as if unafraid of everything. Not to mention life would have been so much easier if she were the one in charge in every relationship. She'd never have fallen prey to a man like Tanner.

It made her recall how Toya had walked, when Sunny had followed her through the empty club, to the office. Her heels had clicked against the floor, her shoulder back, chin high. It had been a level of confidence that had enthralled Sunny.

"What can I do for you?" Sunny forced out.

"I was made aware that at the end of your time in the club last night, you left through one of our quick exits. I always follow up on such cases to ensure no one hurt you or crossed your limits."

Sunny was glad she wasn't at the other end of the threat in Toya's voice. She imagined a woman who didn't mind playing roughly with a man's goods for fun wasn't the sort of woman she wanted to piss off.

"It wasn't anything like that," Sunny assured the other woman.

"I understand you went into a private room with three of our members. I won't disclose their names, in case you don't want that, but I am able to handle this privately if they did anything that caused you to flee. I pride myself on Sanctuary being a safe environment, and if there is a problem, I need to be made aware to keep our members safe."

Sunny traced the desk with her thumb, guilt biting at her. The men hadn't done anything to her that she hadn't wanted. They'd been unfailingly careful with her, in fact. It wasn't fair to risk their standing or reputation all because of her own hang-ups. "Really, Toya, it wasn't like that. They were fine. They didn't do anything wrong."

"So why did you leave like that? Were they pressuring you into staying?"

Sunny walked around the desk so she could sit, letting out a long sigh. "I just didn't want to face them. I guess I lost my nerve."

Silence came through the line, and the disapproval in it made Sunny want to cower. There was nothing like the disappointment of a Dominant—it seemed it didn't matter if they were male or female. Finally, Toya spoke, her voice gentler than it had been but no less sure. "I see. Well, I am reassured that no one broke any rules. Are you planning to return?"

"No. I don't think so."

"So you found what you were looking for?"

Not hardly. "Sort of," she answered instead, drawn to be honest, since Toya had been nice. Or as nice as any Domme could be. "I just don't think it's the right place for me."

"Very well," Toya said. "Can I offer you a piece of advice?"

Sunny wanted to say no. In her experience, people who had to ask that knew the person wouldn't like the advice. Still, she couldn't be rude like that, not to someone who had done nothing to deserve it. "Sure."

"I have seen many submissives walk through our doors. I've run Sanctuary for fifteen years, and during that time, I've seen everything you can imagine. I've seen good Doms and bad ones, good subs and bad ones, but there is one thing I've learned—no one gets what they want if they run from it."

Sunny pressed her lips together, because she'd been right—Sunny didn't want to hear that.

Thankfully, Toya didn't expect Sunny to respond, because she continued. "I will keep your file open for Sanctuary, should you choose to return. If you need anything else, please don't hesitate to reach out."

Sunny thanked Toya before hanging up, feeling far too exposed. How was it that after so short an interview, the other woman seemed able to read Sunny so well? She preferred her privacy, where people couldn't see the cracks she had. Then again, that was why it was never a good idea to play games with Dominants. They were far too observant.

Her phone rang again, and she sighed, figuring Toya hadn't quite called her out enough. She answered it without looking.

Silence met her, one that made her pause. She'd gotten these calls for years, no matter her number, and they *always* made her heart race.

"Hello?" she asked again, a quiver in her voice.

Breathing.

"Just leave me alone," she whispered, no idea if it was *him*, the man who had tormented her, but unable to stop her fear that it was.

Sometimes it was hard to separate real fear from paranoia. After surviving as she had, after fighting so hard to escape, Sunny's sense of danger was all messed up. She had to stop herself, to think through the instinct to run, to panic, and figure out if there was actually something worth fearing. Every little sound, every wrong number, everything she couldn't immediately identify was always him in her mind, waiting to grab her, to drag her back to her nightmare.

It was a call. She wasn't even sure if it was breathing, or if she was just freaking herself out. Tanner, her ex, had no idea where she was, had never reached out or found her in all the years since her escape. If he hadn't come for her in five years, she had no reason to think he had now.

Relax. The rumbled voice from Gold the night before came back to her, and even if she hated herself a little for it, she used his voice to calm her. She held on to that voice, to the demand there, sinking into the safety of it.

She hung up, chastising herself for taking it so to heart. Prank calls and wrong calls happened to everyone. It must have been the night before that had set her off, like something that aggravated a wound already there, made her more sensitive, more on alert.

She would *not* let Tanner steal the peace she'd worked so hard to create for herself. He was five hundred miles away, out in Utah, while she had taken refuge in the California desert.

The shrill ringing of the shelter phone forced the thoughts away. If there was one thing that helped her when she started to slip, when the past became too real, it was work. It let her focus on something good, let her see there *was* good in the world, helped her to add more good to it.

"Marla's Bakery," she answered, the fake name they used to help protect the shelter and any woman whose spouse might have gotten the number.

Silence.

Her chest constricted as if something had wrapped around it so tight, her lungs couldn't fill anymore.

A laugh, dark and sinister and *familiar*. Breathy, cold.

The room spun, and Sunny grasped for the desk, for something to keep her upright. This made her other panic attacks look like a party.

Everything shook, the walls moving as if they breathed, and still that laugh came through, so quiet she almost had to strain to hear it.

It had to be Tanner, right? And if he'd called the main phone, he'd found her.

Everything went black as she collapsed.

Chapter Four

Sunny woke to fingers running through her hair and no idea what had happened. She yanked away, nothing working quite right.

"It's me," shouted a voice she recognized even through the blind panic.

She paused, blinking as the room came into view, as she found herself in the familiarity of her office.

In front of her was Gracey, another worker at the shelter, her blue eyes wide.

"I found you on the ground," Gracey said, her voice full of unshed tears. "What happened? Are you okay?"

The call came back to Sunny.

Despite the fear, though, the immediate crisis being over let her breathe. "Sorry," she said. "I didn't mean to scare you. I got a call." It sounded so *stupid* when she said it out loud. "I just panicked, I guess."

Gracey let out a long breath, as if that was an answer she understood and could accept. Then again, panic attacks were a normal occurrence around here.

"I didn't know what to do," Gracey said, that hesitation saying she'd done *something*.

"Okay..."

"I called the landscaping number..."

Sunny held in a curse, not wanting the poor girl to feel worse. "You didn't need to do that."

"I didn't know what else to do. You're the one who always tells me how to handle this stuff!"

Sunny used the desk to get herself to her feet, glad to find they held her. "It's okay. I'm not mad. What did they say?"

"They're sending someone over to check. I didn't know if someone had broken in here or poisoned you or..." Gracey's bottom lip trembled.

Sunny sighed, tugging Gracey to her feet and into a tight hug. The girl was a sweetheart, too fragile for what she'd been through. She didn't withstand the blows of her past but molded from them, changed into something new and dented. "I'm okay — I promise."

"We can't do this without you," Gracey said.

"That's not true. This place was here before me — it'll be here after me, too."

Gracey went to argue, but Sunny stood straight, trying to show her how to pull oneself back together. Everyone lost it sometimes, and the past became too much.

But after that?

The only choice was to lift her chin and keep going. It was a lesson Gracey needed, the girl still too fragile, too willing to crumble and freeze.

"This place is more than me. It's every woman who comes through those doors, and we all leave a mark. Eventually, I'll be gone, but this place?" Sunny held her hand out. "This place will stay. Now, will you go check on everyone? Make sure no one else saw what happened, and if they did, make sure they're okay?"

"You're going to wait here?"

Sunny nodded. The *landscapers* would arrive soon. Since she'd been the reason they were coming out, they'd demand to see her, to know she was okay, which left her holding the ball.

She took a seat at her desk, busying herself with paperwork, scolding herself for letting her paranoia get the best of her.

A few minutes later, a buzz from the doorbell filled her office.

She rose, left her office, then went to the intercom by the entryway. "Hello?"

"It's us," came a rough, masculine voice. "We got a call?"

Sunny hit the button to open the outer door, and on the camera, in walked a man who she'd seen from a distance a time or two. Huge, with his blond hair back in a bun behind his head. He wore a pair of faded jeans and an old shirt with a band name on it that had seen better days.

The camera that showed the entry way didn't give her many details, but when the door shut behind him, when she was sure it was only him, she hit the button to open the interior door.

They took security seriously. It only took facing off against the abusive ex of one of the women at their shelter once before a person realized how important it was to have a secure building. The very group who had sent this man were the ones who had set up the double entry door system and the cameras.

The man entered, and for the first time, she realized he was *far* taller than the camera had made him seem.

He had a beard and the gait of a someone on alert but not all that worried.

His gaze landed on her, and she took a step backward.

His eyes were a dark green, and some familiarity tugged at her, but she wasn't sure why.

She wrote it off as the aftereffects of her little morning panic. Everything seemed more dangerous in the wake of it. Her mind was trying to make sense of random bits of information, to find a pattern—nothing else.

"Ms. Kaylor?" He didn't come closer, didn't try to shake hands. The men who came here knew better, since the women in such a place didn't usually want to feel crowded, especially by men who were strong, large and more than a little terrifying.

Sunny nodded, letting him know that was her.

"I got a call saying you were unconscious."

A woman walked into the hallway farther down and paused, pure fear running across her features at the appearance of the huge, unknown man.

Right. Sunny gestured for the man to follow. "Come on, let's go into the office."

He nodded, following without complaint, as if he understood. Best to keep men—especially ones *that* size—out of general view. They tended to cause a stir.

"My friends are on their way, too," he said once Sunny had closed the door. "They wanted to take a walk around the perimeter, then check the cameras and fences."

"Of course." She grabbed the phone on her desk and dialed for the other end of the house, waiting for Gracey to pick up. She relayed the information, asking the other woman to let them in when they finished and show them to the office.

Sunny took a seat behind her desk, then gestured at the chair for the man. "I'm sorry you had to come all this way, Mr...."

"Connor's fine. Don't worry about us coming—it's what we're here for. What happened?"

Sunny waved her hand as if it weren't important. "Nothing."

"The director falling unconscious to the floor is something." His voice held an edge of command that made Sunny shift beneath his stern gaze.

"I'm embarrassed to say it, but I let my imagination run away with me. I received a call, and I jumped to conclusions. I'm fine now."

"A call?"

Sunny nodded and folded her hands in her lap, beneath the desk, where she could wring them without him seeing. "Yes. No one was there. It wasn't worth panicking, but knowing that doesn't change how you feel in the moment, you know?"

She tried to downplay it, to pretend it had been a stupid mistake.

It had been.

Still, some unease refused to go away, a fear that told her to be cautious.

Connor lifted his eyebrow. "If you had a woman here, and she got a hang-up like this, what would you do?"

Sunny fidgeted beneath his firm stare. "I'd tell her to relax, but I would also see if I could find out where the call came from."

"So what are you going to let me do?"

Sunny *really* wanted him to leave. She wanted Connor to accept her apology for causing the issue, to walk out of her office and right out of her life.

But she also couldn't argue with what he'd said...

He tilted his head, as if pointing out that she hadn't answered him yet.

She picked up her phone from the desk, then held it out to him. "I'm going to let you take a look."

He snorted, a sound that felt...familiar? He took the phone and moved through the screens with ease, his attention focused.

A buzz told her his friends had arrived, and when the door opened, when they walked in, Sunny realized she should have taken the meeting outside.

Her office wasn't small, but she'd never crammed three men this large into it before.

The two new ones were, thankfully, not quite as large as Connor. They were taller, but leaner. One wore a suit, his hair a dark brown, almost black, and trimmed short. He had blue eyes and dark stubble over his jaw. The other had slacks and a button up shirt on, but no jacket. His hair was shaggier — a light brown — and his eyes were so light amber, they were almost yellow.

And again, that nagging bothered Sunny, one she couldn't place.

They're familiar.

Which was insane, because there was no way she would ever forget these three if she'd met them before. She'd seen glimpses of them, but she'd seen all the men who came to the shelter to help from a safe distance. So why couldn't she shake the feeling she knew them?

Connor didn't look up from the phone or toward the other men. "She got a call where no one talked — I'm checking for the number." He didn't mention the panic, the passing out or her stupidity.

Which she was grateful for...

Even so, she felt the need to be honest. "It really was nothing, I'm sure."

The man in the suit smiled as he took a seat beside Connor. "Sure it is. I know you feel like because you're the director here, you have to put on a brave front, but you don't need to, not with us. Any potential threat is worth looking into. I'm Garrison, and that's Trent. I don't think we've met."

Sunny went to say no, they hadn't, when Trent interrupted. "You've worked pretty hard to make sure we've never met."

Sunny sat up straighter. "That isn't true. I'm just very busy."

Connor snorted, his attention still on her phone, though he'd pulled his out as well, as if checking something.

That sound…

"I appreciate your help, really," Sunny said, trying for her best consolation prize voice. "But I think this really has been overblown." She rose, wanting to subtly tell them it was time to go.

Connor set her phone on her desk. "I can't trace the number here. It seems like it was pretty well hidden, because the number that shows up is a dead end. I've taken down the info, and I'll see if I can't get someone to look a little more closely into it later."

Sunny took the phone and tucked it into her pocket. "Thank you. I'm sure it was nothing, though. It was just when they called the shelter, too—"

Garrison stopped her short. "You got a call *here* as well?"

Sunny bit her lip as she realized she hadn't said that part of the story earlier. "Yes. I get lots of hang-ups on my personal number, but right after the first call, someone called the shelter. I thought they laughed, but now I think I was overreacting. It was just a prank call, I'm sure—"

Garrison exchanged a loaded, unhappy look with Connor before he glanced back at her. "That's a very different thing, Ms. Kaylor. That implies someone might not only know where you are, but about the shelter, too."

"It's not like that," Sunny tried to assure them. "It's been years since I've had contact with…" She couldn't get his name out, even after so long. "He doesn't even know where I live, has never tried to find me or contact me. I'm sure it was just a coincidence."

Garrison answered her, lowering his voice as if not wanting it to carry. "I respect your desire to be tough, Ms. Kaylor, but you've worked here long enough to know how dangerous this could be. If it was anyone else, what would you do?"

Sunny wanted to lie. She wanted to say whatever it took to get them out of her office and to get back on with her life, to push this fear to the back of her mind like she always did.

Still, his question compelled an answer. "I'd have them call you guys and ask for help, then make sure we had police drive-bys for the next few nights. I'd also ensure all employees had escorts to and from work."

Garrison nodded, as if she'd answered correctly.

Which, to be fair, she'd had plenty of time to learn.

"So, you need an escort home, don't you?"

She sighed. "Apparently so."

* * * *

Garrison couldn't help but chuckle at the feisty little brunette who ran the shelter. He'd never had the pleasure of actually meeting her before, but he'd heard stories.

She was tenacious at protecting the women at the shelter, but apparently far laxer when it came to her own well-being. The fact that she hadn't called them herself chafed, and he'd had to keep his desire to lecture her to himself. She wasn't his. It wasn't his place to tell her what she needed to do, even if she was making poor choices.

She also really did *not* want to be around him. It was written in the way she walked, the space between them, in how, as she drove, she leaned against the door to get as far away from him as she could.

It didn't bother him—he'd grown used to that reaction when dealing with women who had bad histories with men. He couldn't exactly take it personally, not when he was well aware that *someone* had put that fear into her.

Still, she'd admitted that getting their help was the right choice, so the girl was smart enough to think past her initial fears.

She drove a white SUV with four-wheel drive, something tall enough that she had to grab the roll bar to hoist her short frame into. It surprised him, because he'd expected her to be more of a compact sedan sort of woman.

She maneuvered the large vehicle down the roads like it was nothing.

Garrison didn't try to tempt her into talking. What was the point?

Connor and Trent would meet them at her house after they'd finished checking out the shelter. They'd make sure all the security systems were working properly, contact a few others they worked with to handle escorts for the other employees and volunteers, and ensure that Gracey, the woman who had called them, had all their information.

While they did similar things for a lot of women at the shelter, keeping the director safe was even more important. She single-handedly ran that place, along with overseeing a few others in adjacent towns. She'd taken one tiny, run-down building and grown it into a real haven for women who needed it.

Garrison had seen other directors come and go, most trying their best but without the head for business that Sunny seemed to possess. While he'd never personally met her — Trent wasn't wrong, she'd always seemed to be gone or busy when they arrived — he'd been impressed by her work ethic for a long time.

The last director had been an older woman named Beth who had been sweet but absent-minded. She'd constantly missed details, had reached out many times when something had fallen by the wayside because she'd forgotten something important. Since Sunny Kaylor had taken over, they hadn't been called for anything but escorts.

Women from the shelter would call on their own sometimes, but other than basic security, the shelter rarely needed anything. He'd gotten involved years before, back when Beth had needed new security cameras and other Doms he knew from Sanctuary had called him in. As it turned out, the Doms at Sanctuary tended to like chipping in. It must have been that protective streak they had.

He wanted to pick Sunny's brain, to find out how she'd turned the dog and pony show into the well-oiled machine she'd created. Still, Garrison gave her the quiet he was pretty sure she wanted as he looked out the window and let out a big yawn.

The night before had been *amazing*.

Well, all except the little fox running out on them. He couldn't help an unease at that, a desire to find out if she was okay.

Sure, part of it was wanting to see her again, but another part was needing to know she'd made it home safely. He chalked that up to his damn Dom tendencies.

Well, that and the memory of how sweet she'd been.

The sighs on her soft lips, the way she'd arched her back, her taste, how she'd given *everything*. It wouldn't go away, no matter how many times he'd told himself to forget it.

He'd had plenty of nights of meaningless, anonymous sex before. He was hardly a fifteen-year-old with his first girlfriend.

So why couldn't he put this one out of his mind?

Because it isn't meaningless.

The vehicle bounced as it went over an aggressive bump and down a tricky, washed-out road. In fact, Garrison thought for a moment the woman would need to put it into four low to make it.

"I know the number of someone who can drag this," Garrison said as he placed his hand against the roof to steady himself.

"No, thank you." Her curt words caught him off guard.

Then he thought about it and let out a soft laugh. "You keep it this way on purpose, right? Not many cars can sneak up on you through this."

She nodded, before pulling the vehicle in front of a cute little house, the desert plants around it all cleared away for lines of sight.

The girl might have been a long way from whoever had hurt her, but she still lived as if waiting for them to come back at any moment.

Which made Garrison all the more certain the threat needed to be properly explored. No one did this if the asshole who had hurt them was really gone, if they were sure they'd never come back.

The girl might not show it, but she was still terrified.

When she got out of the car, Garrison shook his head. "You should stay here while I check to make sure it's safe."

"Trust me, no one is in my house."

Garrison held out his hand. "Then you won't mind me checking, will you?"

She pressed her lips into a thin line, the color blanching, and he had to admit...he sort of liked that.

Stop it, you idiot. She isn't interested.

Especially in what he was interested in. He again recalled the way the cuffs had looked on the woman's wrists last night, how hard he'd gotten watching her touch the toys.

Yeah, this woman wouldn't be into that, which meant it would never work. Garrison had long before accepted that he'd never be happy with a vanilla relationship. He needed that other part to a relationship, needed a woman who would want to play those games, who would melt at his dominance, who craved it. That woman wasn't Sunny.

Still, she handed over the keys, then lifted her eyebrow as if letting him hang himself.

Which seemed odd, but Garrison let it go. People in moments of stress did lots of strange things.

She walked with him, and while he'd have preferred she stayed in the car until he knew the house was clear, he also understood that allowing a man she didn't know into her home wasn't easy, so he compromised.

He slid the key into the lock, then opened the heavy, black security door. Different keys went to each of her locks inside — there were two deadbolts plus the one on the handle — and he couldn't fault her security. It was easy to figure out, since the locks were a different metallic shade which matched the key that went with it.

Once he'd made it through all the locks and pushed the door open, an odd, deep sound came from inside.

He frowned, listening carefully, until his eyes adjusted to the interior dimness and made out where the noise came from — a black Neapolitan Mastiff, his lips curled up and his teeth bared.

Garrison jumped backward, because the damn thing hadn't even barked in warning. It could take his arm with one bite if it wanted to.

Sunny let out a chuckle that was far too amused before she knelt in front of it. "It's okay, Spike."

The huge dog chuffed in Garrison's direction before knocking Sunny backward, onto her ass, when it butted her with its head for attention.

She laughed — a real one this time — as she snuggled the gigantic black beast. And wow, that laugh was something.

"Spike?"

She dug her fingers into the loose skin behind the dog's ears, lavishing it with attention. "From an old cartoon. It was a dog who chased a cat."

Garrison thought back, recalling how the cat in it had chased a mouse. It seemed fitting, in a way. Clearly, she saw herself as the mouse, and she'd gotten the dog to keep the big bad cat away...

"So this is how you knew no one would be in your house?"

She nodded before pushing Spike off her.

Garrison extended his hand to her, so used to the motion it didn't strike him as a bad idea until she stared at his outstretched hand.

Right. Probably doesn't want to touch you.

Still, Sunny did, as if she had something to prove. *Brave girl.* She stood with his help. "Yeah. Spike here keeps an eye on my place. I started out with just locks, but there isn't anything that feels quite as safe as having someone living to watch your back. I found him at the animal shelter when I went there to volunteer, and big black dogs are rarely adopted. So, I ended up bringing Spike home with me." Loneliness sat in her voice, and it made Garrison want to do...something.

What, he didn't know. In reality, all he had to offer was a bit of help at the moment. He doubted she'd let him give anything more.

"Well, can I check the place out anyway?"

Sunny gestured to the open door. "Go ahead, if it'll make you feel better."

Garrison entered, the house cozy and quaint. It was small — only one bedroom, two bath — which told him she had no intention of bringing anyone else into her life.

Then again, he'd seen that plenty of times. Women often cut themselves off from the world, from any sort of future with anyone, after an abusive relationship.

Not that he could blame her.

If he'd cozied up to a tiger who then bit the hell out of him, he'd be reluctant to invite another into his home, no matter how much it swore it was different.

He walked through the small space, peeked into the main bathroom and the kitchen. He checked the back yard, which had a large patio and one hell of a view.

Voices from outside told him that Connor and Trent had arrived.

Inside her bedroom, he checked the connected bathroom. The décor was much like the rest of the house—understated and comfortable. She had a large black comforter thrown on her bed, a sign that she made it in the morning but wasn't fussy about it being perfect. Lastly, a door that had to lead to a closet and the last place he hadn't checked.

Sure, with Spike around, there was little chance anyone could have snuck in, but Garrison preferred caution to regret.

He pulled open the door, finding a closet full of down to earth and functional clothing. Ballet flats, sneakers, jeans, tank tops, fuzzy sweaters and sundresses.

And there, hanging on the inside of the door, something that made him freeze.

It can't be…

The fact that Spike didn't bite any of the men put Sunny out a bit. Sure, she wasn't afraid of them, but she would have preferred he at least show a *little* more distrust.

Instead, the second Connor had come inside, Spike had walked over, plopped his butt on the man's shoe and waited for pets.

Traitor.

Trent chuckled at the display before Sunny waved them both inside.

"As you can see, everything is fine here. I appreciate your help, and I agree that caution is warranted, but I don't need a babysitter."

"It isn't babysitting," Trent responded, his gaze moving around the room as if surveying for danger. "It's called being smart and careful."

"I know, which is why I allowed you here."

Which isn't something I ever do.

Having men in her home was odd. Having anyone in her home felt strange, but even more so with men.

The times she'd dated, when she'd tried to see if she still had any lust in her left, she'd always gone to the men's homes. The thought of allowing one into her private space had chafed. It felt like tainting her own haven. This was *hers*, and if the relationship went bad — which was a real risk — she didn't want the memories of this place ruined.

Yet...while she was uneasy with Connor and Trent there, she wasn't afraid.

"Tea?"

Both men answered with a yes, so she went to the small, open kitchen and grabbed four glasses — no doubt Garrison would want one as well. The pitcher of tea sat in the fridge door, and after adding ice, she filled all the glasses, then moved them to the small, four-seat kitchen table. "What do you do for a living?"

"When not saving damsels in distress, you mean?" Trent asked, a playful grin on his lips.

"Something like that."

Connor rolled his eyes at his friend. "I'm a livestock vet, Trent works in construction and Garrison owns a security store in town."

Sunny stole a glance at Connor before taking a sip of her tea to hide the reaction. Yeah, livestock vet made sense. It explained the muscles, the way he moved. He dealt with huge animals all day long — a man like that had to be steady. It also might have been why Spike liked him.

"How did you meet?" she asked.

Trent answered her this time. "We have a few hobbies in common. Met a good twelve years ago, back when we were young, and we've stuck together since then."

Sunny narrowed her eyes, but not at them. Instead, she stared at the floor, feeling safter doing that. "And you just help us out for fun?"

"Fun? No." Connor took his glass from the table. "I can tell you, not a lot that we've seen from that shelter has been fun." Shadows played in his green eyes, ones that reminded her that they'd probably seen the same things she had, sometimes worse. Still, Connor kept going. "But it's important, so we do it."

"And how did you get into that?"

Trent answered, which was fine by her, because he seemed friendlier — less intense. "I said Garrison owns a security store. Some other folks who work with the same group reached out to him about outfitting the shelter with new cameras about ten years ago."

"Other people you know?"

He shrugged. "Call it friends."

Sunny thought about the men she'd seen, always from a distance. They were all large, confident and clearly used to being in control. They were the kind of men she worked hard to avoid, which was exactly the reason she had always ignored them. "Some friends you have."

Connor let out a snort but didn't say a thing.

Garrison walked in, something in his hand, but he stood too far away from her to identify it.

"Is everything okay?" Fear prickled at her, as she worried he'd found some sign of her ex, that maybe she wasn't as safe as she'd thought she was.

"Yeah," Garrison said, an odd tone to his voice. He approached and set the thing he held onto the table. Her mask stared back at her. "I think we need to have a talk, Fox."

This was *so* much worse.

Chapter Five

Sunny swallowed hard as she stared at the fox mask. She didn't even have the hope to pretend it wasn't exactly what it looked like.

The way Garrison had said "*Fox*" brought it all back, made her realize why everything with the men had seemed so familiar. She knew their voices, knew what they sounded like when they rumbled out demands, how their lips felt—

Focus!

"That was you?" The question came from her, soft and quiet.

Connor turned his gaze from the mask to her, and it was then she realized, yeah, Connor was Gold. It was the long hair and the green eyes.

Which made Trent, Black—his smirk and humor should have clued her in—and Garrison, Silver.

They were the three—her wolves—who had brought her so much pleasure and confusion the night before.

And now they were in her house, where no man had ever stepped foot.

Then again, no men have ever done what I let them to do to me either. Seems like they're unique.

Garrison nodded and crossed his arms. Where he'd seemed intense but harmless before, the memory of what had occurred, of the way he'd used that commanding voice, of how he'd licked her until she'd almost cried with pleasure, came back to her, making her take another step away.

It was overwhelming. It was *too* much.

"Easy, darlin'," Connor said, just as he had the night before, further mixing up then and now. She struggled to keep them separate.

"This was a mistake."

"You ran out on us last night," Trent said. "We were worried about you."

"So you show up at my job?" If she'd had a moment to think, she'd have realized that made no sense. There was no chance this could have been planned. She'd passed out, and her employee had called them.

Still, she didn't know what else to say.

"We didn't track you down," Garrison said. "You made it clear you wanted it to be the one night, and we respected that. We had no idea *you* were our Fox."

"I'm not yours," Sunny snapped, then cringed at her own words, at the sharpness of her voice.

Trent lifted his hands as if to prove he weren't coming toward her. "I'm glad to know you're okay. You shouldn't have left, not until we were sure you were okay."

"I was fine, obviously." Sunny wrapped her arms around herself, feeling trapped and surrounded and helpless and entirely *not* fine.

"So why'd you leave?"

"Because it was a stupid one-night stand. You've had those before, I'm sure."

"We have," Connor agreed. "But I think you know that it was more. And you don't strike me as the one-night-stand type."

"I needed to be."

Garrison leaned his hip against the kitchen. "You were there to prove you didn't want that, but that's not what you learned, was it?"

Sunny shook her head, then cursed at herself for falling into his trap. These damned men had that asking thing down, the tone of their voices making her want to answer before she realized she shouldn't. It was worse now, when she recalled how they'd been at the club, how *she'd* been.

"You realized you liked it, and that scared the hell out of you, so you bolted."

"Yes," Sunny admitted, voice soft.

No one spoke for a moment, the silence thick and choking.

Connor broke it. "If you like it, what's the problem?"

"I don't have to answer that. We had sex, but that doesn't make you my Doms." Using that word crashed down Sunny's bravery.

The word, out loud, was the key that unlocked everything it had meant to her before.

She remembered the times Tanner had hit her, the times he'd grabbed her by her hair and gotten in her face, when he'd told her she belonged to him, that he was her Dom.

And here comes the panic attack.

She grabbed for the table, trying to keep upright. She'd passed out once today—she didn't need to make it twice.

Still, none of her tricks worked. Not the counting, not the breathing, not the finding things to see and smell and hear. The attack came over her so fast, she could find nothing to ground her, to focus on. Nothing seemed able to get in the way of the train, to stop how the world spun, how her throat closed, how the memories overwhelmed her.

Spike whined as he always did when these attacks happened, coming to her side.

Voices moved around her, deep and masculine, but she couldn't make out what they said. They only added to the horror inside her head, to the way her brain forced her to relive it all, dragged her back to that hell and refused to let her move forward. It was like even now, Tanner had his claws in her, that he could yank her to her own nightmares whenever he wanted.

I'm never going to be free, I'm never going to —

A hand closed on the back of her neck, then pushed her down, to her knees. She was so far gone, she didn't fight it, especially because she'd almost collapsed on her own.

Her cheek pressed against something warm and rough, and a hand grasped her hair. It didn't hurt, the tug against her scalp.

"Sunny!" Her name was snapped out in a voice that wouldn't take no for an answer, and it reached through the haze of her mind. "Look at me."

She obeyed, lifting her gaze to find blue eyes and a stern face. The person crouched there, blocking out the rest of the world, so that between him and whoever was behind her, they shielded her from everything.

It wasn't his hand in her hair, though, but the tight grip didn't let her look around. Instead, she shuddered, locking on to that deep blue that was *nothing* like Tanner's dark brown, until the panic drained from her.

She rested her cheek against the thigh beside her and closed her eyes, exhaustion replacing panic.

Connor stared down at the girl, her eyes closed, her cheek against his thigh.

Boy, hadn't she taken herself straight into that panic attack?

And all over what?

The word 'Dom'?

He tried to think back, to recall if she'd uttered it the night before. Once, at the start, but she hadn't reacted like this.

Then again, she'd had a harder day today.

And she lacked her costume, which he suspected had felt like armor to her. Her anonymity had probably given her extra courage, as if it wasn't really her there but some fox creature who lacked her baggage.

So Connor kept the grasp on her hair but loosened it a bit. After another moment, he moved to massaging her scalp, letting her rest against him, trying to take away what she'd seemed to hold inside, trying to carry it for her. Her hair was incredibly soft, and the strands were curled at the end. It had looked brown at Sanctuary, but now? Now he could tell there was a reddish hue to it.

Garrison was across from Connor, sitting back since she'd settled and calmed.

This girl was their Fox? The woman who had turned them inside out the night before, the one who had easily given Connor the best night of his life despite his cock never even making an appearance?

He sure recognized her. Her hair was down, loose around her shoulders and wavy. He wondered how he'd missed it when he'd spoken to her in her office. The sweet, hazel eyes, the narrow waist, her pink lips.

Yeah, it was her.

And she was *far* more damaged than they'd realized at first. Wasn't this a perfect example?

He blew out a breath as her body relaxed further, as she fell asleep there, resting against him.

The girl really didn't realize how much she needed this all — the ability to submit, to relax, to have someone there to protect her, to trust that someone had her back — did she? She might not want to need it — she might have shown up the night before to prove something to herself — but her reaction said it all. She'd relaxed there because she craved that submission. Clearly, she'd been holding herself so tight, unable to let go, at least until right then.

"What are the odds?" Trent asked, voice soft to not wake her up.

"A million to one," Garrison responded. "That means something, right? How could we run into her *again*?"

Connor shook his head, not one to believe in fate. "It's a crapshoot, and we're too old to be romantics. It's not cute anymore."

Garrison narrowed his eyes. "So what do you suggest?"

Connor peered down, finding her thin shoulders, the strap of her tank top reminding him of how they'd slid her dress down the night before, of how perfectly her breast fit into his palm, of how sweet her lips were.

"I don't know," he admitted. "But damaged women who are reluctant subs isn't a game you really want to get into, is it? We've always said we shouldn't play games we're liable to lose."

"She isn't all that reluctant," Trent said. "She's just…confused."

Connor sighed, knowing it didn't mean a thing what he said about it being a bad idea. Even if he knew with absolute certainty that she'd stomp all over them, it wouldn't really change how he felt.

The reality was that after the night before, after tasting the girl's passion, after seeing her in her element at the shelter, after realizing she might just be in danger, every instinct Connor possessed demanded he take care of her.

So it seemed, for the short term, whether she liked it or not, she'd just gotten a few Doms of her own…

* * * *

Sunny woke with a headache that put her teenage drinking days to shame. She groaned as she rolled over, blinking her eyes open to find a glass of water and her bottle of ibuprofen on the nightstand.

She frowned, then her open closet door, complete with the white dress, brought it all back.

The men who had come to help at the shelter were the men from the club, the ones she'd had sex with, who had done things to her she'd never experienced before.

Her complete meltdown *also* came back to her, how she'd nearly passed out for the second time that day and had ended up kneeling at Connor's feet like a well-trained pet.

Worse? Not that she'd done it, but that it had *helped*. That somehow, she'd pulled in enough breath to regain her center, that it had relaxed her enough to fall asleep.

Which made her pat down her front, fear creeping in. She didn't really know these men, and they had evidently put her to bed. What if they'd done something to her? What if...?

Her clothing was still in place, the same things she'd had on before her panic attack. She wasn't sore anywhere, didn't find any signs that anything had been done to her.

It let her sit up and take a deep breath. The pills were a nice forethought, so she downed two of them with the water.

The sun outside was below the mountains, with the tops lit up. Even without looking at a clock, she knew the desert sky well enough to guess the time to be about five-thirty in the morning.

She'd slept through the entire night? How was that even possible? She *never* slept well.

She pulled herself from the bed, then hit the lock on the door handle just in case. She changed out of the clothes from yesterday, and into some jeans and a T-shirt. She had the next two days off from work, so she wouldn't need to go into the shelter.

Which sounded good to her. She needed a day or two to recuperate.

Or maybe a year...

She put her hair into a bun, though the tug at her scalp reminded her of how Connor had gripped it, how it had instantly lowered her stress level.

What is wrong with me?

She washed her face and brushed her teeth in the master bathroom — there was no way she'd be getting naked for a shower, not until she was sure they were gone.

It took nearly thirty minutes before she dared venturing out, to risk running into the men.

Though they couldn't still be there, right? It was the next day. She had evidently slept through dinner, the evening and into the next morning. No sane men would hang around that long.

In the living room, she found her answer.

Garrison was stretched out on the couch, his hands folded on his stomach. On an air mattress was Connor — they had to have brought it with them, since she didn't own one — with a blanket tossed over him.

She remained silent, staring at them, trying to figure out how to proceed. It would probably be rude to wake them up, right?

She took her lip between her teeth, a sharp pain telling her she'd chewed on that lip enough to leave a wound.

Just great.

A door opening made her frown, and she twisted to find Trent coming out of the bathroom, a pair of sweats hanging low on his hips, his hair going in every direction and wet from a shower.

And it was one heck of a sight. She wasn't the sort to ogle men usually, but damn…

He might not be nearly as large as Connor, not as immediately impressive, but the sight of his chiseled form stole every coherent thought from her brain.

Well, all of them except for those about just how that body could be put to use. She recalled how he'd put the clips on her, how his warm breath had felt against her nipples, how he'd tortured her after removing them.

And just like that, her body heated. Any of the worries she'd had went away as she watched a drop of water slide down his throat, over his chest and each defined ab. When it hit the waist of his sweats, she whined, wishing she could follow the path with her tongue. It reminded her of how badly she'd wanted more, and how they'd all denied her.

A clearing throat forced her gaze up to find him openly smirking, as if he'd caught her and damn well enjoyed it.

If it was physically possible, she was pretty sure her cheeks would have caught fire at that moment.

He nodded toward the back door, then looked at her, the question obvious. Did she want to go out there?

Maybe, if he takes those pants off...

She tried to give her brain a shake, as if she could wake it up and make it behave.

To try and hide the reaction and give her time to get herself under control, she pointed at the coffee maker, then lifted her eyebrow.

Trent nodded, his smirk still in place, before he went outside.

Sunny took her time making the coffee — an entire pot so whoever wanted some later could have it — but the moment she followed him, she knew days of time wouldn't have been enough to prepare herself.

Trent sat on one of her outdoor couches, and the desert sunrise suited him. It had risen enough to cast breathtaking purples and reds across the sky that lit up his tan skin.

"Thanks," he said, which made her realize she'd once again been staring, two cups of coffee in her hands and zero appropriate thoughts in her head.

Sunny tried to play it off by offering a smile as she handed over the coffee and took a seat in the chair. She avoided the couch, wanting there to be no room for anyone to sit beside her.

"Sleep well?"

She breathed in the steam that escaped the top of her cup, letting the bitter scent of the coffee into her lungs like a ritual. "Yes, though I don't normally sleep so long. You didn't have to stay, you know."

"I tried to explain this to you the other night—once you're under a Dom's care, they like to make sure you're okay."

Dom. The word drew up a moment of panic as it always did, like the filthiest thing a person could say. After the night of sleep, though, she kept it together this time.

"You don't like that word, do you?" Trent spoke casually, though his gaze was sharp. He might play dumb, like the funny one who didn't know what was going on, but his eyes gave him away.

"No, I don't."

"Why?"

"My ex used it."

Trent nodded, then put his feet up on the table. It made him appear relaxed and drove home the point that they were just talking, that he wasn't going to press or come any closer. "And, judging from what I can guess, he was a shitty person, right? And now you think what he did is what all Doms do?"

"All? No. I'm sure there are good ones out there. I just don't think the odds are worth the risk."

He huffed a soft sound before sipping the coffee, not complaining about it being black. Sunny never added anything to hers, and since she didn't have guests, she didn't have a reason to keep sugar or cream on hand.

"Yeah, I've seen that enough times. Assholes try to justify abuse by calling it BDSM. You're not the first little sub some fucker has twisted up."

"I am *not* a sub." Sunny rushed out the words, realizing 'Dom' wasn't the dirtiest word. *Sub* was. A Dom might be a jerk, but a sub was a doormat who accepted that behavior.

"You sure? Because I remember the other night, how you just about purred when we got our hands on you."

"Sex is sex. Maybe you're just good at it."

"Oh, I am good at it, but I also remember that the only thing to pull you out of that panic attack was you kneeling, and Connor's hand in your hair. You may not *want* to be a sub, but that doesn't change that you are."

Sunny folded her legs, holding the cup between her palms, reminding her of the hot chocolate Garrison had had the other Devil-Dom get for her. "What are you even doing here? I've taken care of myself for a long time now. I am perfectly capable of continuing to do it."

"Would it be so bad if I was interested?"

She gave him a look she hoped screamed that it was a stupid question. Of course it would be a bad thing — she had no room in her life for that measure of disaster.

He chuckled and set his coffee cup on the table beside the couch. "What? Come on, after the other night, you can't blame me."

"There are a lot of other women who would be a better fit with whatever you all want, I'm sure."

"I'm not so sure, and trust me, I've had quite a few of them. You are special, Fox."

The name warmed her, like something special between them, but as soon as it happened, she tried to push it away. Sunny didn't need them to have any connection to bind them together. "You've said it yourself — you can make some guesses about my past. That should clue you in that I'm not a good bet. You and your friends have..." She paused, not sure how to phrase it. "Specific tastes. I'm not judging you, but I can't fill that place for you."

"Why not? You did fine the first night."

"That doesn't count. It was just a one-time thing."

"Why does it have to be? Why are you so convinced that you can't like that, that you have to be something or someone else?"

"Because I've done that, I've seen where it leads. I'm not—" Sunny stopped speaking, tried to calm herself down before she blurted something out she didn't mean to say. "I just can't."

"But you want to?"

"Maybe," she admitted, her voice soft. "Maybe I went there because I wanted to be able to walk away from it all, to stop dreaming about things that are bad for me."

"That's not what you learned, though, was it?"

She shook her head. "I learned that I'm screwed up, that I want something that almost destroyed me once. So, I appreciate your help, I really do, but I *can't* do this. I can't just give up my power again, because I can't put myself back together if it bites me in the ass a second time."

Trent stared at the girl, at all the fear on her face, at how afraid she was of him and herself and what she wanted.

And all that shame.

Boy, he understood that. Hadn't he gone through the same thing? Hadn't almost every person who discovered their kinks struggled against that sense of shame? People had that epiphany followed by a shitload of guilt created by a world that was quick to label them perverts and deviants. It wasn't an easy path to come to terms with it all.

He wanted to reach out, to grasp her thin wrist and tug her into his lap. He wanted to wrap his arms around her and reassure her that she wasn't twisted or broken or wrong.

Fuck, he wanted to prove it to her, but that was too far.

It wasn't his place, and he knew it wouldn't be welcome. Doms might give their subs what they needed, but there were limits, and those limits were set by the subs.

So he stayed put, no matter how little he wanted to. "You aren't broken. You might be wired a bit different from the majority, but that isn't a bad thing."

"That's easy for you to say. You don't risk anything."

"You think I don't? Because I've had my heart shattered more than a few times."

That made her pause, as if she hadn't expected such an answer.

"Last woman to really get under my skin, Renee, she was just mine. Shared her sometimes with Connor and Garrison for fun, but she was only with me. Girl took every penny I had after cheating on me, repeatedly. I remember getting over it, when after two weeks not leaving the house, Connor dragged me out of bed and tossed me into the shower like some unruly foal he was dealing with. Yeah, Fox, I know the risks involved."

Sunny didn't respond right away, staring, as if trying to determine if his words were true. She curled her shoulders in, then dropped her gaze to her cup. "Even if I wanted to, even if I thought I could..."

"Then what?" He prompted her, letting some of the sharpness of his voice compel her to answer.

"I wouldn't even know where to start."

He recalled her at the club, remembered how she'd cringed, how she'd not told off Jordan when she hadn't been interested. Funny to think that this woman was her, that the one who stood up for so many women at the shelter hadn't been able to just say, "no thanks," to a Dom.

Then it hit him. Why hadn't he put it together before? Spend long enough with an asshole who doesn't like being told no, and a person would learn that keeping their opinions to themselves was safer.

"You were a sitting duck at the club," he admitted. "But you aren't like that normally. Are you like that on dates? With men?"

She shook her head. "I tried to date after, well, you know."

"And?" He knew the conversation would take ten times longer than it needed to, because he had to prompt her to continue, but luckily, he had no issue sitting there just as long as it took. He enjoyed this — not the topic, not digging at her wounds, but the slow uncovering of her truth, of what she hid.

"And they were nice, but something was always missing. No matter what, it was like soup without any salt. It wasn't bad, but it wasn't good."

"Because you aren't vanilla, honey, even if you wish you were."

"So I can't date regular men, and I can't date..." She stumbled over the word 'Dom', but this time didn't manage to even try.

"You could date Dominants." He tried the full term to see if it helped. Her shoulders didn't bunch, and her breathing didn't change, so it seemed to have helped. "You just need to understand how it works a little better and know how to find a good one."

She took another drink of her coffee, and Trent cringed. Black coffee was like eating straight flour to him — pointless and gross. Coffee was supposed to be a part of a drink, not the whole recipe. Still, he got the sense she rarely had people over, so he wasn't going to make her feel bad about it.

After she swallowed, she nodded, as if conceding to his point. "I could do some research, I guess..."

"Research isn't always great because there's too much bad information out there. That's the negative of the internet — any idiot can put his opinion up and claim it's fact."

"So I go back to the club? The owner said I could, if I wanted..."

"What if you let us help?" Garrison asked from the doorway, a cup of coffee in his hands as well, having obviously caught the gist of their conversation.

Which was fine by Trent, because he'd discovered the best way to get a sub to behave was by having more than one Dom on her ass.

And he *really* wanted to be on Sunny's ass...

She jerked her gaze around, eyes wide but no real panic there. That was something — that she seemed to accept their presence, that panic didn't set in quite so fast. "What do you mean?"

"You know exactly what I mean," Garrison said as he walked out, Connor on his heels, no coffee for him since he didn't care for it. "You want to understand BDSM better, right? But you need someone to guide you. You already know us. We've been cleared and background-checked by Sanctuary and we've got more than enough experience for you."

She hesitated, doing that damn chewing-on-her-lip thing that drove Trent crazy. "I'm not interested in dating you."

The words disappointed Trent, no way around that, but he understood them, too. The girl was terrified of what she wanted, of herself, of everything. She didn't want to risk any entanglements that could end up tying her down.

And that was something Trent understood.

"Maybe that's your first lesson," Connor said as he took a seat beside Trent. "BDSM doesn't have to lead to people dating. It doesn't mean they're a couple. We could top you, but that doesn't mean anything long term. Plenty of people enjoy casual dynamics."

She gulped, no coffee in her mouth this time. "And you'd teach me what it really is?"

Garrison nodded from his spot, still standing. "Yeah, we would. By the end, you'd know what it was all about, whether you liked it or not, how to find an appropriate partner, and how to communicate your limits."

She ran her finger along the rim of her cup, clearly deep in thought, considering their offer.

Trent kept his mouth shut, because nothing he said would help. Begging her to say yes would be stupid and entirely unethical. If she wanted to try this, it had to be one hundred percent her choice.

So he held his breath as he waited, trying to look at ease while feeling anything but.

"Okay," she said in that sweet voice he wanted to hear as she sighed his name later, once he'd gotten her naked. "But I don't want to have sex with you."

Connor made that snorting sound he liked to do to call people on their bullshit, and at her sharp look, Trent answered. "Sure, Fox. That's the thing, you'll call the shots and set the limits. You say no sex, then that's how it is."

She narrowed her hazel eyes, suspicion in them. "So why are you smirking?"

"Because I have no doubt that you'll be *begging* us to fuck you before long."

Chapter Six

Sunny fidgeted, sitting in her car, anxiety like a passenger for her.

What the *hell* was she doing here?

She sat outside the club, but whereas last time she'd had no idea what she'd encounter inside, this time she damn well knew.

Connor, Garrison and Trent were inside. They'd already send her a message letting her know, so any hope she'd have that they'd not show had left.

She'd spent the rest of the week without seeing them, though each man had sent her messages. It had been strange, to get texts so casually, but before long, she'd caught herself smiling as she'd looked at her phone.

The silent call she had received had been a dead end, with the person Connor knew not able to turn up anything about who had placed it. Nothing else had happened — no new calls — so Sunny chalked it all up to one big mistake. Just a wrong number, and her anxiety.

Her phone beeped, and she peered down to find Trent's name.

You're going to get old if you don't get out of that car.

She glared at her phone, as if it might transfer to him — and her not being in the same building made her rebellion safe.

Still, she couldn't move.

Maybe her legs had more sense than the rest of her.

It was *far* safer to be outside, to drive away and never look back, to tell them it had been a huge mistake and she was out.

Except…her body refused to do that, either.

When her phone rang, she jumped. She lifted the cell to her ear and answered with a sullen, "Hello?"

"Are you ever going to get the courage to come on in?" Garrison's voice, smooth and sweet, let her pull in a breath as she rested her forehead on the steering wheel.

"What if this is a mistake?"

"Then you make a mistake. At least you'll know it is one, though. If you drive away right now, you'll always wonder."

He was right, of course. If she left, she'd never get this out of her head. She'd forever think, 'what if?'

"I'm surprised you haven't come out to get me."

"That isn't how this works," Garrison said, the background noise quieting as if he'd stepped away from the crowd. "I told you before — we won't force you. We won't press the issue. It has to be your choice to come in, your choice to play with us, your choice to do any of it."

And *that* was part of the problem. If they'd been rude or overbearing, she could have dismissed the whole thing. "This would be a lot easier if you weren't so nice," she said.

"You know, calling Dominants nice is a sure way for us to prove to you we aren't." His playful words didn't strike fear in her, probably because he hadn't used *Dom*, because he'd made it clear that it was still entirely her choice.

That gave her the courage. "Okay. Give me a minute."

"Sure thing, Sunny."

Sunny. The name on his lips sounded…good. Sweet and endearing and far more appealing than it should have been. When she hung up and slid the phone into her purse, she tipped the rear-view mirror so she could see herself.

She swiped her thumbs beneath each eye for any mascara that had smeared during her mini freak-out.

Her clothing had been sent to her house from the men, something that had made her uneasy and yet somehow also happy. She didn't like that they'd taken the liberty but was also flattered that they cared, as though the forethought showed she mattered to them. She wore a skirt that fell to her knees but had enough volume to twirl, and the crinoline beneath was pink to match her eyeliner and lipstick. The top was a corset that tied up the back, giving her some actual cleavage, which was rare for her.

The outfit was *far* sexier than the last time she'd come, but that time she'd been terrified of calling attention to herself. She'd been all alone in a sea that she hadn't understood, without backup or help.

This time she'd be there with three men who were…

She wasn't sure how to finish that thought.

She pulled in a shaky breath before exiting the car, wrapping her arms around herself. It didn't get all that cold, but October was the month the temperature dropped. It made her recall where she'd come from, where the snow would pile high on the sidewalks and coat the trees.

Out here, snow only fell once a year — maybe — and it all melted by noon. Still, something about the browns in the landscape had called to her, and after meeting up with Beth, the woman who had run the shelter, the one who had offered to help her, she'd fallen in love with the town.

Sunny realized she hadn't moved a foot. She'd reminisced as a way to buy time, to stand there, shivering, not having to go closer.

Stop being a coward.

The words didn't get her moving, but her own courage did. She put one foot in front of the other, making it halfway through the parking lot before another bout of crippling anxiety hit her. It was like those shows where a person goes up to pet an alligator. The closer she got to the beast, the less her body wanted to move.

"You'll catch a cold out here." Connor's deep, dark voice didn't frighten her the way she expected it to. It felt like sipping whiskey, and she would have sworn it stole her senses just as well.

"I thought you guys said you wouldn't come out."

"Garrison said that," he pointed out. "Besides, I'm not here to talk you into coming in."

"Then why?"

A jacket came to rest over her shoulders, the interior warm, telling her he'd had it on a moment before. "It's too cold out here, even for foxes."

"I'm not dressed as a fox."

"You're always a fox," he said, affection in his tone.

Sunny pulled the jacket around her tighter, her legs still freezing, but grateful her arms were warm. "Any chance you could just order me in?"

He shook his head, his black shirt less faded than his others had been, as if he'd dressed up for the night. "Not how it works, darlin'." He caught her chin, tipping her face up toward his. "But if you come in, I can promise I'll have a lot of orders for you."

She thought he'd lean in, that he'd brush his lips to hers, but he didn't. He ran his thumb across her bottom lip then pulled back. "It's up to you. That's at the root of what you've got to learn. You make the choice if you want to play or not, if you want someone or not."

Sunny's past sat at the edges of her mind, like something prowling behind bars, waiting for her to venture too close. So many horrific memories, and so much of what was inside that club that reminded her of it.

But she'd *grown*, damn it. When she'd gotten to this little town, she'd been a mess. She hadn't been able to go outside by herself, let alone to stores, to meet people, to be around anyone. Now she was stronger, better.

She lived her life, other people be damned, and it hadn't ever been easy.

There was a time when the space outside her front door had been as scary to her as this club was now.

But she'd lifted her chin and she'd faced it all until it no longer frightened her.

Sunny drew her hands into fists before she straightened her back, lifted her chin, and walked toward the front door.

"Brave girl," Connor rumbled from behind her, and even if she didn't feel like it at the moment, she agreed.

Garrison offered Connor a glare when he walked in on Sunny's heels. It had been hell for Garrison to wait inside, to give Sunny the time to make the choice, but he'd done it.

Still, judging from the jacket around the girl, Garrison couldn't entirely blame Connor.

Sunny and Connor stopped in the entry way to check in. The receptionist held up a club cuff, but Connor shook his head. The corners of Sunny's lips tipped down, showing that spark of fear she had, but she overcame it quickly enough.

That was the thing about her...

If she'd been a few years closer to her ordeal, Garrison would have never considered such a thing. He'd worked with the shelter long enough to know the women needed time to start healing, to find their own feet again. Rushing in too early was a recipe for heartache for all involved.

Sunny might slip up sometimes — and really, who could blame her? — but she'd clearly put in the work. He could *see* her using the techniques to calm down, to take control of her emotions, to think through her fears — at least most of the time. The memory of the call, of when she'd said 'Dom' that time, all said her control wasn't quite perfect.

She moved through the crowds with Connor just behind her.

The lights weren't turned down too low — people needed see what the hell they were doing, and this wasn't a rave — which let him get a look at what she was wearing.

They'd picked the perfect outfit. The corset was pulled tight enough to show off her small waist and give him a hell of a view of her cleavage. Even though it was sexier than her previous one, she somehow managed to still look sweet and innocent and like the best kind of bait.

That appealed to his Dom side, since nothing was better than a sub who looked ready to be devoured.

Sunny approached the sitting area that Garrison was already at, while Trent was getting bottles of water for them.

She peered back and forth between the two men. "It's not a costume night, so why are you dressed alike?"

"We're wearing black," Connor said with a frown.

She glanced toward the crowd of people and the multitude of black outfits, especially on the Doms. "Original."

Garrison held his hand out, waiting for her to place hers in his grasp — it took only a second, her reaction likely more instinct than thought — before he pulled her into his lap. "That wasn't very nice, was it?"

A moment of fear skittered across her features, but it didn't stay long. She dropped her gaze. "I'm sorry. That was rude."

He smiled at her sullen apology. "It's fine. What can we say, though? We're traditionalists and prefer dressing in a way that shows off that we come as a group."

"Like couples costumes?" There was a rare, playful edge to her words that he liked.

Garrison pinched her ass for the joke, and was rewarded with a tiny, surprised squeak from the sexy little sub in his lap. "You're lucky you're adorable," he warned.

He got the feeling that she wanted to glare at him but didn't quite trust him enough for that. Instead, she sat up straight and glanced around, probably realizing for the first time Trent wasn't there.

Before she could ask, the man himself appeared, four water bottles tucked between his arm and his body. His gaze traced down Sunny's body, taking in her outfit and pausing on her chest.

Trent had always been a man who loved a good set of tits, and there was little doubt Sunny offered him that.

Trent curled his lips into a smirk before handing over her water bottle. "Well, don't you look scrumptious?"

Sunny beamed, even though her gaze darted away. It made Garrison pretty sure she hadn't received much in the way of praise.

Good thing he didn't mind offering that up. He had a feeling that if they tied her down and told her exactly how sexy she was as they took their sweet time fucking her, she'd come apart. Then again, with how wound up she was, they could probably do anything, and she'd react beautifully.

"Why didn't they put on the cuff at the door?" she asked as she fiddled with the label on her water bottle.

Trent handed out the other waters before leaning down to pull out their bag from beside the couch.

And didn't that get Sunny going? She tensed at first, an automatic reaction, before she squirmed. It was subtle, but Garrison caught it. She was probably thinking about the things they'd used on her from that bag before.

Trent didn't pull anything too fun out, though. Instead, he took out a pair of cuffs — brown leather on the outside and padded on the inside. A small padlock on the silver buckle of each would keep them secure. They were also monogrammed with the initials of all three of them. "You're here with us for the night, not a free agent, so the club cuff isn't needed."

"I thought all guests needed it? That's what the owner said."

Garrison nodded, thinking about Toya, the woman who ran the club. She was a bit like a mother bear, quick to defend anyone not treated right. He still recalled the dressing-down she'd given a Dom who had ignored a sub's safe word.

She was a ballbuster in every sense of the word, which was why Garrison had never let her near *his* balls.

"That's for guests. As long as you're here with us, you're not a club guest, you're *our* guest. These cuffs show just that. It means other Dominants won't try to play with you, that they can't touch you."

She swallowed, as if 'play with' and 'touch' were terrifying ideas to her. "But you can?"

Ah, so it isn't others — it's the idea that we could do what we want with her.

"Within reason," Trent said. "Just like before, you set the limits. Cuffs don't change that. So, are you ready?"

She nibbled her bottom lip, the poor thing red from the abuse. The girl had no poker face — all her worries showed in her expression. She did that thing where she lifted her chin, as if the little action gave her courage, then held out her hands.

Trent carefully fastened each cuff around her thin wrists, checking them for tightness by sliding his finger inside, between the padded cuff and her skin.

She shivered at the click of the padlock.

"We've each got a key," Trent said, holding one up before sliding it into his pocket. "Also, if there is ever a problem, the security guards have cutters on them at all times, so they can take off the padlocks in a second."

She blew out a slow, controlled breath, as if committing those facts to memory, as if reassuring herself that because of them, it was safe.

Which, Garrison had to admit, he wasn't sure he could do. If the shoe were on the other foot, if it were him who had suffered like she had, he doubted he could hand over his safety to three people he barely knew.

It reminded him that despite the fact that he seemed to be in control, subs were tougher than they were given credit for. No matter what happened to them, they rallied.

The thought made him slide his arm around her waist and pull Sunny tighter against him, enjoying how well she fit in his lap. "How was your week?" he asked.

She did that slow look-over thing he'd seen from her before, something that said it wasn't the question she'd been expecting.

"What?" he asked.

She furrowed her eyebrows. "I just thought…"

"Thought what?"

"That we'd do something else. Not talk."

"You have a problem with talking?" Connor took a seat beside Garrison, where her knees where, while Trent went to the other side, behind her back.

She didn't need to answer.

Yes, talking was a problem for her. She might have gotten used to the idea of them playing with her, but somehow a conversation made it too personal.

It made Garrison chuckle again at how little she really understood. "Believe it or not, this club isn't all public sex and whips."

Just then, the crack of a flogger made him wince.

"Well, I mean, there is some of that."

Sunny stared at him before a smile appeared on her full, sexy lips, as if she couldn't help it.

That was what he liked, those moments where she didn't want to like them but did anyway.

"My week was fine," she answered, words short.

"No more calls or anything, right?" Connor asked.

She tensed, but Garrison couldn't blame Connor for asking. They needed to know, and she seemed the type to weasel out of giving information she didn't want to give by omitting it. She wasn't a 'lie to a man's face' sort of girl, but she'd get away with what she could.

"No," she answered, telling him that it still bothered her, that she still hadn't fully moved past it.

Which prickled. He'd wanted to find an answer for her, to be able to tell her it was some kid having fun or a scammer who wanted her social security number. It was still probably one of those things, but he wouldn't lie just to make her feel better.

Instead, he ran his hand up her back, playing over the laces of the corset. "How's everything at work?"

That eased her. "Good. Uneventful, but that's always the best. I'll take an uneventful day over an exciting one anytime." She shifted, as if unused to the closeness, the personal conversations. Still, she didn't pull away. "And you?"

Garrison grinned, enjoying the hesitant way she asked. "Fine. Sales were good, nothing important."

Trent set his feet on the table, his water bottle in his lap. "Hit my quotas, so I can't complain."

Connor took one drink before grabbing her legs and resting them over his lap. "I had a mare who was having trouble in delivery. No, don't worry, mama and baby are both doing fine."

The moment of worry on Sunny's face reminded Garrison what a softie she really was.

Connor danced his fingers over her bare legs, teasing her calves, her shins, the sensitive area behind her knees. They weren't outright sensual, but after a moment, she started to relax.

"Why don't I have any ribbons on my cuffs?"

Garrison followed her gaze to someone else, to a man with cuffs that had a multitude of ribbons tied to them.

"Because you aren't going to be playing with random Dominants. No need to advertise what you're looking for or your limits. These" — he grasped her cuffs, rewarded with a quick inhalation from her — "mean no one else needs to know what you're into."

She nodded, fidgeting when Garrison didn't release her. He rather liked having her restrained…

And judging from the way she shifted around, she liked it too. Of course, all that squirming had had an effect on him, and his cock pressed against her ass, eager as hell.

"Speaking of limits." Trent grasped her shoulder and leaned her back, a pillow to his side so she rested over his lap too. This stretched her across their laps like some curvy little toy for their amusement.

And Garrison's cock throbbed at the desire to play.

Trent ran his fingers along the top edge of her corset, where the garment created cleavage. "What are yours?"

"Limits?"

"Things you won't do."

She hesitated again, and Garrison recalled what she'd said before. Limits were a way for her ex to know what he should do to her.

He didn't speak, letting her work through it, letting her remember that the last time she'd set limits, they'd respected them. She had to understand that herself.

She darted her tongue out, wetting her bottom lip, leaving a spot that glistened in the dimmed lights of the seating area. "I don't like pain."

"You liked the clips," Trent pointed out, running his finger over the corset, right where her nipples would be, as if to prove the point.

"That's not pain."

"Yeah, it is," he countered. "I'm going to guess you mean you don't like severe pain. There's a difference between some clamps or spanking and using a whip."

She shivered when Trent dipped his finger just beneath the edge of the corset.

"So, we can play with some light pain, slowly, and see where your limit is. What about anal?"

That got her trying to sit up, as if the word alone was scary.

When her hands went up, Trent caught them, then, in a quick motion, lifted them above her head and hooked them to a strap on the edge of the couch. It stretched her out more, immobilized her, and the way she twisted was a thing of wonder.

"Easy," Garrison assured her, his hand on her stomach. "We're just having a conversation."

Her chest rose and fell in panicky little motions before she seemed to realize she wasn't going anywhere and that they weren't forcing her to do anything.

She inhaled deeply, the action making her cleavage even more noticeable, before shaking her head. "I don't like that."

That. Again, her shyness was fucking adorable.

"So you've tried?"

Her pale color said it hadn't gone well. Then again, it could *really* hurt if a bastard was the one trying it.

"Okay," Connor said as he continued to stoke over her legs. "We'll put that in the limits for now. Later, you should think about it, though. You might be surprised about how you feel with the right person."

She swallowed, her throat moving, before she nodded.

Trent went through a list, piece by piece. The longer they talked, the more relaxed she became, the less she seemed to notice the rest of the club and the less the questions seemed to bother her. They teased her as they asked each question, stroking over her bared skin.

Yes to bondage, no to suspension, yes to gags, yes to giving and receiving oral, no to watersports, yes to swallowing, a big no to humiliation, a maybe to exhibition.

She *was* stretched out in view of others, but the darkened seating areas offered a bit of privacy. They weren't entirely on display, not doing a scene where others could watch.

Not that Garrison was all that into having an audience. He liked to focus on his partner, but if his partner liked it, he usually gave in. He didn't mind others seeing what was his, enjoyed when they saw how beautiful a sub was, but he didn't care for sex in public.

Trent released a hook on the front of her corset, then another. He worked down the front until he reached halfway. It kept it closed enough to hide her nipples but parted to show the delicious skin between her breasts.

And despite Sunny seeming zoned out, she noticed *that*.

She rubbed her thighs together, her skirt having ridden up so it barely hid anything.

"How are you feeling, my little Fox?" Trent asked as if having a normal conversation.

And she gave him a look that said he was an idiot.

He traced the inside curve of her breast with his thumb. "Just checking in. Have to know how you're feeling."

"I'm fine," she said, a quick answer that made Garrison suspect she was used to giving it no matter the truth.

"Do better." Garrison ran his fingers along the waist of her skirt, then slipped them to the inside to repeat the motion. "It's an important question. If you can't tell your top how you feel, how do you think they're going to know? Believe it or not, we aren't mind readers."

She arched up at the touch, like an offer, but Garrison kept the stroke innocent.

Well, as innocent as it could be, given she was bound across their laps and no doubt drenched.

"Come on, use your words," Trent said.

Her lips parted, but no words came out. She tried, but frowned.

"You're not used to talking about how you feel, are you?"

"It never mattered before," she snapped. Had the lust inside her helped her to voice her frustration?

"It's always mattered, even if some asshole ignored it, and it sure as hell matters to us. Can't possibly expect us to do this right if you won't tell us what you like and what you don't like, what bothers you and what doesn't. So the rule for tonight? When we ask, you give us a number. One to ten. One means you hate it—it means stop it now or that you're afraid. Ten means you love it. Ten is the equivalent of getting on your pretty knees and begging us for more."

Another shiver ran through her, her body so responsive even if she wasn't entirely sure, even if she was nervous. So, it seemed she liked the idea of being on her knees.

So do I.

"So, that first night—give me a number on the cuffs."

She licked her lip. "Eight."

"Good girl. What about the clamps?"

"Nine."

Garrison undid the bottom clasps of her corset until only one tiny hook held it closed. "My tongue on you?"

"Ten." The number came out breathless, strained.

And boy, did it help Garrison's ego. Trent might like a bit of pain, and Connor was all about restraint, but Garrison never got off to anything as much as having a woman mindless over what he did to her. His perfect night was wringing orgasm after orgasm out of a pretty body, watching her succumb to all that pleasure.

"This?" Connor slipped his fingers up the seam where her legs were pressed together, a clear request to part them.

"Ten," she whispered again, her body quaking, probably unable to regulate itself anymore.

"You made a clear limit," Garrison said. "You said no sex, and we said we'd follow it until you asked. We can keep going like this, discussing things in public, without crossing any boundaries."

Sunny opened her eyes, the pretty hazel clouded by desire. She blinked slowly, as though figuring out just *what* he was trying to say. Finally, it seemed to come together for her.

She wasn't getting anything more unless she wanted it. They could tease her, could keep her clothes mostly in place, could dominate and teach her without ever getting intimate again.

Sunny's next deep breath tested that one hook that held her top closed, before shaking her head. "I need you to touch me."

"So you changed your mind? You want us to fuck you?" Garrison could have used less blunt phrasing, but when it came to limits, he wanted it clear.

Sunny met his gaze, then dragged her tongue across her lips. She nodded. "Please?"

And that was something he could do…

Chapter Seven

Sunny would have gone to her knees if she could have. She'd have pleaded in her sweetest voice for them to not stop, to keep going, to give her more.

They teased the exposed skin of her stomach, her chest, her thighs, but never went where she really needed them to. They tortured her by avoiding anything *good*.

Connor would stop at the hem of her skirt, Garrison wouldn't dip lower than her waistband and Trent refused to stroke across her hard and aching nipples.

A click, then Trent helped lower her arms and sit her up. He had unhooked them from the strap and from each other.

She frowned. She'd wanted more, so what were they doing? She'd expected Trent to spread her thighs and press his fingers into her wet and desperate cunt. Even if they were in public, even if she wasn't sure about that, she'd thought the moment she gave them her permission, they'd pounce.

"Don't look so worried," Garrison said as he stood her up. "You said you didn't like too much public play, which is fine by me. When you come, Fox, that's for our eyes only." His voice was lower than usual, and the words ratcheted her need up another level.

Trent undid the last hook of her corset, then caught it before it fell to the ground.

The sudden cold against her nipples was shocking, but so was the fact that she was topless in a club, in full view of other people.

A thin whine left her as she tried to cover herself, but Garrison was quick to grab her wrists and gently bring them behind her, locking them together again.

"Nervous?" Trent asked, amusement in his tone.

"There are *people* around," she whispered.

"Yes, there are, and they can see that you have the prettiest tits in this entire club." Trent cupped her breast, the sensation all the more erotic with the fact that he was doing it in full view of others.

"I don't like public."

Trent leaned down, past her lips, so he could drag his tongue around the edge of her areola, a slow tease while avoiding her actual tip, then pulled back. "You said you didn't want to be fucked in public. Do you even remember your answers?"

No, she really didn't... It suddenly came back to her, though, how Trent had asked about being on display, and she hadn't said no. Her body had heated at the idea of others looking at her. She didn't want an audience when she was going to come, when she was entirely vulnerable, but as it turned out, some exhibitionism turned her on...

Tanner had never done this sort of thing, had never taken her into public, had never shown her off. He'd hidden her like a thing he owned, always seeming disappointed with her. The fact that these three seemed *proud* of her felt odd but welcome.

Trent ran his thumb over her nipple, pulling a soft cry from her, before he took her lips in a kiss. He was demanding, rough, and he refused to leave her poor, sensitive breasts alone even then. Instead, he closed his fingers on the points, squeezing, making her cunt pulse with need.

When he broke the kiss, he squeezed her breasts once more. "Oh, I'm going to have fun with these," he whispered before moving back.

And Sunny was sure she'd die. There was no way a person's heart could pound this fast, that she could feel *this* out of control and survive, right?

There have to be limits to what a body can endure!

Connor walked first, with Garrison behind him and Trent beside her. Trent draped his arm over her shoulders, his hand hanging so he could fondle her breast at will while they walked.

Sunny kept her gaze down, afraid to see anyone, but when they moved through one area, she looked up.

No one laughed at her. No one stared with mockery in their expression, as if she were some freak. A few smiled, kind ones that said they were happy she was enjoying herself. A few others had lust darkening their gaze, and while that would have set her off before, something about Trent's possessive hand on her breast, the way the cuffs pressed against her wrists, all said the same thing.

I'm safe.

It let her enjoy it, even as it made her uneasy. Maybe that was the truth, though. She'd needed that unease, that edge, to really enjoy something.

They passed the security guard—it was the same man from the previous day—and went to a different private room, this one a few doors farther down than the last.

When Trent pulled away to close the door, she frowned.

Connor let out one of his snorts before setting their bag on a table to the side. "What's wrong, darlin'?"

"There's no bed."

"Don't need one."

"I thought…" She paused as she couldn't get out the words. *I thought we were going to have sex.*

Garrison tapped on something that looked a bit like a sawhorse, something meant for construction work, not sex. He crooked his fingers for her to come over. "This works well."

Sunny refused to touch it, as if it were a monster she feared might take her hand. Now closer, she realized it wasn't at all like the construction type, beyond the basic shape. The top was padded, as were two lower pieces. Straps were on both pieces with hooks drilled into other places. The wood was smooth and stained a dark color. It was well-crafted and someone took good care of it.

"What do you think?"

She didn't answer.

"Give me a number," Garrison pressed.

Number? She had to think, to slow down her brain. "Um, five?"

He nodded, then patted the top. "See, you get on all fours on it. Your stomach goes here, your knees here. The straps keep you still."

"But why?" Her ex hadn't had things like this. He'd never have spent the money on such a thing, would have wondered what the point was.

Her breath came quickly as she thought back, as the reality of the situation hit her for a moment.

Fingers went into her hair, and a quick tug broke her free.

"You can say no," Garrison said as he pulled his hand away.

Did she want to? Sunny stared at the equipment again, and this time it didn't look quite as scary...

Besides, her ex had managed to hurt her plenty of times without needing something like this, so there was no reason to fear it.

She grasped the top, trying to figure out the best way to...mount it?

She chuckled at the stupid word.

"Well, I like that sound," Garrison said before moving around to help her. He placed her knee on the pad, then had her shift over the center and place her other shin on the other side. The center was narrower than she'd realized, a point made clear when Trent walked to the front and reached beneath her. He took her breasts in each of his warm palms, shifting her so they fell to each side of the center.

It made her feel even more exposed, especially when he didn't bother to pull away at first. No, he teased her nipples, the sadistic jerk, pulling on them as if to drive home the point of just how much access he had.

And she could do nothing but whimper softly, a pathetic little sound she could scarcely believe came from her.

Garrison bent down and clipped her wrists to the bench, then strapped her legs down, over the calf, and one more over her back.

She shifted to see what range of motion she had.

Which turned out to be next to none. She had an inch, perhaps, and despite the moving, Trent continued to tease her nipples the entire time. He crouched, taking one between his lips.

Her hands were slightly in front of her instead of directly below her shoulders, and the top of the bench extended out enough that she could rest her cheek on it. It meant she didn't have to strain to be comfortable.

Well, as comfortable as a person could be when bound and at the mercy of these three men...

Finally, Trent released her with a noisy pop and, after one last hard nip, he pulled back.

And she was panting, already sweating and completely desperate for more.

A hand was set on her bare back, making her jump before she twisted to find Garrison there. It would take time to get used to so many hands. Before, she'd made sure to know where Tanner's were, because it had been a matter of her safety.

This time, though, she couldn't keep track of everything. It was impossible, especially with how they twisted her until she could hardly count her *own* hands.

The fabric of her skirt shifted, and a breeze stroked across the back of her thighs then her ass.

Connor let out a deep groan, the sort she knew she'd feel if she were pressed against him. "So, maybe you showed up expecting to ask us?" He ran his finger along her bare cunt, as if reminding her she'd chosen to wear no panties.

And it *had* been a choice. She'd had the pair they'd sent, but after a good five minutes of staring at them she'd gone without.

She might have said 'no sex' at first, an easy thing to say when standing there in front of them — the reality was that she wanted to feel like she had again that first night. She wanted to be overwhelmed and out of control and at their mercy. How else could she possibly understand this need inside her until she really sank into it?

Connor didn't seem to want an answer from her — *the answer is obvious, isn't it?* — and he pressed two thick fingers deep into her.

She shifted forward, not out of fear but surprise. Again, the way they touched her excited her, as if they had every right, as if she were just a plaything for them to enjoy at their whim.

Yet each thing they did excited her, too. Each confident touch, each eager stroke all made her need more.

She couldn't close her thighs, not with them bound and spread on the sawhorse. It left her exposed to Connor, to whatever he wanted to do. She was lower than them, so had to peer up to see their faces.

The power imbalance was clear...

Garrison left her for a moment, going back to the bag, before bringing something black and round. That fear started to creep in, but she refused to let it take hold.

Or maybe the way Connor fingered her did that...

Garrison crouched so he was eye level. He lifted the thing he'd grabbed — a ball, it turned out. He squeezed it, and it squeaked, then he tucked it into her hand. "If you need to take a break, if you need us to stop, you squeeze that. It's loud enough we'll hear it."

"Am I not allowed to speak?" The idea of them stealing her voice terrified her.

Garrison stroked his fingers over her cheek. "I'm not going to gag you, and you're always allowed to speak, at least unless we discuss it first."

"So why do I need this?"

He moved two fingers from her cheek to her lips, sliding across them as if applying lipstick, then pressed past them. "I'm planning on putting your pretty little mouth to use. You drove me crazy with it that first night, especially when you bite your lips, when you lick them. I've been wanting to slide my cock between them ever since."

He didn't ask her if it was okay. Instead, he pulled back his fingers and pressed them in again, a mimic of thrusting, and Sunny did what he asked without needing to ask. She sucked, teasing her tongue across the joints, at the seam between his two fingers.

He withdrew them. "Give me a number, sweet."

For tasting him? For feeling his cock with her tongue? "Nine," she offered without hesitation.

"That's a good answer."

He rose, then undid the belt of his slacks. Another moment of fear skirted through her, but when he left the belt through the loops and removed his pants entirely, it faded away. He murmured, "Good girl," so quietly, she wondered if she'd heard it at all.

He removed his boxers next, then set it all on the dresser. His shirt was last, leaving him finally naked.

He is absolutely mouth-watering. If she'd seen this the first night, no doubt she'd have begged them to take her. His body was flawless, with a sexy *V* that led to a trail of dark hair from his navel to a neatly trimmed patch at his groin. His cock was curved up slightly, hard enough that it rested against his lower stomach rather than hanging forward. He was long but not too thick, with the head wider than the base and a vein she wanted nothing more than to trace with her tongue.

From her peripheral vision, she caught the other men disrobing, but didn't get to ogle them the way she did Garrison.

He wrapped a hand around his shaft, stroking himself once from tip to base, letting out a deep, masculine moan. "I have to admit, I've been looking forward to taking your cunt, especially after the taste of it I got before, but there is something about your lips. I knew you'd make the perfect picture with them stretched out around me."

His words were *so* graphic, so filthy. He spoke as if he weren't talking about her giving him a blow job, as though it were any old conversation. Yet she didn't feel ashamed. They didn't make her want to cover herself — they made her want to show him more, to prove he was right, that she was good.

Garrison came forward, grasping her chin with his free hand, then rubbing the head of his cock against her lips. He left wetness behind, like a gloss, and she used her tongue to taste it. Salty, masculine and absolutely addictive.

He pressed against her closed lips, and she let him in, opening her mouth to give him access. She moved her hands, trying to reach, to grasp the base of his cock.

The rattle of the hooks and her lack of progress reminded her that they'd taken all her freedom. She couldn't control the speed, the depth, couldn't demand more or less. All she could do was accept what they gave her.

And they gave her plenty.

Connor plunged his fingers into her, rough and quick. He twisted his hand so his knuckles rubbed against different areas inside her, sparking each to life. He still hadn't touched her clit.

Like that matters... She dangled on that edge of release even without it.

Garrison didn't choke her, didn't deepthroat her. She wasn't sure if she would mind if he did. She'd hated it before, with Tanner, because she'd never trusted him, because she'd always feared he'd not pull back in time.

These men made her crazy, made her want things she'd never had before. Things that would have terrified her suddenly intrigued her. Garrison might have known her hesitancy, though, because he shifted his hips forward, thrusting into her with small motions, using her tongue to rub against the head of his cock.

She'd nearly forgotten about Trent—she was a little distracted—but when strong fingers tightened on her nipples, she *remembered*.

She cried out, the sound muffled around Garrison's cock, making it dirty and so much hotter.

There was something about her voice, about knowing that Garrison's cock kept her from speaking, that had her tightening around Connor's agile fingers.

Trent leaned down, but she couldn't turn toward him. Instead, he whispered into her ear, his breath hot and rough. "I know you like your breasts tortured, and in case you haven't noticed, I'm a bit of a sadist." He curled his fingers so his nails pressed into her and bit into her pebbled nipples, and even if she'd have denied being a masochist, her reaction called her a liar.

She would have come, *hard*, but as if they knew it, they all stopped. Connor's fingers froze inside her, her cunt tightening uselessly around them. She shifted her hips to try and get what she needed, but he gave her nothing.

She whined, lifting her eyes to Garrison, *begging* him with her gaze.

He curled his lips into a smile, but her heart sank because that wasn't the look of a man willing to give in.

"Not yet, sweet," Garrison said. "You don't get everything you want, not right away."

Bastards. She cursed them in her head, using words she'd *never* consider uttering out loud.

Trent released her nipple, but because he hadn't held it long, the pain afterward wasn't nearly as intense. It made her realize...she wanted more. She craved it.

What does that mean?

She figured she could analyze it later, when she wasn't out of her mind with need.

"I have different clamps this time. I think you'll like them." Trent's chuckle was warm and terrifying in the best way. "Well, eventually."

The not-so-subtle threat hit all the right marks, and she struggled slightly. The band over her back kept her still.

Not that any of them seemed to notice or care. They wouldn't move, wouldn't release her, wouldn't give her more or less or anything other than what they damn well pleased.

And while Sunny had thought she'd hate this, while she'd come to prove it to herself, she couldn't deny how close to release she was from it.

A metallic sound echoed, but Sunny couldn't turn her head far enough to see what it was. It reminded her of a necklace chain. Trent's strong fingers captured her nipple again, teasing the same one he'd focused on before. "Deep breath," he said a second before that familiar sharp pain shot through her.

He didn't take time to linger, though, walking around the bench to the other side. Knowing what was coming and having to wait for it was the worst.

No, Connor's fingers are still worse. Move them already!

Trent leaned down and dragged his tongue across her other nipple, then blew a stream of cold air over the damp tip. "One more," he warned before that same pain struck again.

She yelped, shivering as her body tried to make sense of all the sensations, of the denied orgasm, of Connor's unmoving fingers stretching her cunt, of the pain in her breasts.

She whimpered, her lips tightening again around Garrison and sucking, as if his hard cock were her only solace. He stroked his fingers through her hair, his fist against her lips as he held the base of his dick. "There you are, sweet. You're fine."

No, she wasn't. She was better than fine. She felt free, which was an odd thing to feel when bound up like a present for three men.

It didn't change the fact that it was true, though. Everything else she'd experienced, her preconceived notions, none of it could reach her there, as if they blocked it all out.

Something scratched against the floor, and from her peripheral vision she spotted Trent pulling a chair over. Metal groaned, then he did.

She tried to twist, but she could only catch a glimpse of him, his cock in his hand as if her trussed up was all he needed.

Or, maybe not, she thought as he reached forward. "You know what I like about *these* clamps?"

No, she didn't. They seemed like the same sort from the other night. She enjoyed them and all, but they didn't strike her as different.

He reached beneath the bench and fiddled with her other clamp. The movement made the teeth of it shift.

The ball was there, in her hand, but she didn't even consider squeaking it. This was everything she wanted.

Trent repeated whatever he did to the other clamp, brushing against the curve of her breast afterward as if he couldn't help it. "You see, these work well in this position — ass up. Gravity is something fun to play with. Your breasts hang like this, like some sort of gift, and what can I say? I'm a fan of decorating gifts."

Sunny had no time to wonder what that meant before Trent shifted, and something *pulled* on the clamps. It made it impossible to forget they were there, made it so her body couldn't adjust to their presence and deem it unimportant. It tugged constantly on her, something she couldn't get away from, and the more she shifted, the more whatever it was moved.

Trent leaned in, his lips to her ear again. "Shh, you can take it. I didn't put a heavy weight on them, just enough for you to stay *interested*. But, fuck, you look good. Your poor nipples are *so* hard — I bet one good stroke on your clit would get you off, wouldn't it?"

"She's close," Connor acknowledged. "Keeps squeezing down on my fingers like the best sort of begging."

Wetness tracked down her cheeks, and she stopped trying to hide it, trying to keep the tears in. It was all just *too* much.

She cracked, splitting wide open to whatever they wanted, to whatever *she* wanted, without reservation.

It was as if they'd reached into her and yanked out the slivers of her past that she'd had stuck there, as if they'd broken her free from whatever held her trapped and unable to move forward.

So she gave in, completely, entirely. She cast her gaze up to Garrison, finally understanding just what submission meant. Not what her ex had tried to teach her, tried to force from her, but what it meant when a person really gave in because they wanted to, because they needed to.

Garrison ran his fingers over her cheek, his voice soft and sweet despite the fact that his cock was buried deep in her mouth. "You see, this is what we wanted, for you to give in before you got anything. So proud of you, my brave little girl."

She wanted to ask if that meant they'd let her come, but she couldn't. Besides, the part of her that craved this *enjoyed* being at their mercy, of her body being used against her. She felt safe and wild and able to relax for the first time in years. She let them hold everything, let them carry the weight of her fears so she didn't need to.

Connor withdrew his fingers, and the emptiness shocked her at first. She shifted her hips, but when she did, it made the weight connected to her clamps sway, increasing the pressure.

A gasp escaped her, around Garrison's cock.

Trent chuckled. "Oh, I like that sound. I'm not going to take them off until Garrison finishes, until you swallow his cum, because I want to *hear* all those pained little noises you make when I do clearly. Until then, I'll just enjoy the way they're going to move when Connor fucks you."

She'd thought having to guess what was going to happen was the worst thing, that having to sit there and wonder made her anxious. It turned out it was *way* worse to know exactly what would happen and have to wait for it. It was like feeling a roller coaster going up, seeing the top, knowing how fast it would go down and knowing she couldn't do a damn thing to get out of it.

Connor pressed his cock against her, the smoothness telling her he'd put on a condom. His grasp was solid against her hip, and he plunged his thick shaft into her with a quick, hard thrust.

And he was *huge*. She recalled how he'd felt when she'd been in his lap, and she'd been nervous then. That feel was nothing compared to this, to having him spreading her cunt. Despite her being drenched, it was a stretch.

He let out a low sound, too feral to be a groan, before pressing another inch into her. "Fuck, you are tight. I stretched you with my fingers, but you're a damned snug fit."

She tried to shift, to make room, but there was nothing she could do. She breathed through her nose and closed her eyes, trying to focus on relaxing, on accepting every last inch of Connor's hard cock.

Not that he seemed to be giving her a choice. He withdrew a hair's width, then pressed in deeper. Over and over, he repeated that until she would have sworn he was as deep as possible.

She was wrong, though. He had both hands on her hips and, with one last hard jerk, his body pressed against hers, telling her he'd filled her entirely.

She shuddered out a breath, exhausted, some of the lust having abated from the struggle.

He massaged her hips, his large hand reassuring, as if telling her she'd done well.

Jayce Carter

The idea that she'd pleased him reached into her, a swelling of pride, something she'd never cared about before.

Pleasing her ex had only had the purpose of keeping him in a good mood, but the idea that Connor was happy, that he was proud of her, that he *enjoyed* her, made her want to try harder.

Not that she could do much of anything.

Connor pulled back until he was barely inside her, then plunged in *hard*. It made her rock forward, and just like Trent had warned, the weight connected to the clamps swayed forward, tugging at her nipples.

Garrison also took the chance to press in deeper into her waiting mouth, almost far enough to trigger her gag reflex.

The message was clear.

They'd teased her, they'd toyed with her, and that was over.

They were serious now.

Chapter Eight

Connor couldn't believe just how tight Sunny's cunt was. He'd had trouble with some girls in the past, especially when their nerves got the better of them. They'd tense and tighten up, and he was only interested if everyone was having fun.

Sunny had let out the softest little whines, but even if she didn't realize it, she'd pressed back toward him, too.

Funny to think that such a small girl — such a soft one — could take him so well, even when he was rough.

And he *was* rough. He wasn't like Trent, didn't enjoy giving out pain for the sake of it, but he also wasn't a gentle man. Maybe it came from his size, from his work with livestock, but he'd just never been the sort to go easy in life.

So he didn't do that with Sunny, either. He grasped her hips, enjoying the way they fit into his hands, and fucked her just the way he wanted. Her little gasps and broken moans said she didn't mind it a bit.

It was perfect—more than he could have ever imagined. That first night had been great, even without getting inside her, but *this* was better. Not just because he filled her up, but because he *knew* her, because there weren't any games between them, any of that 'no names' bullshit. Instead, they'd pushed her until she'd melted for them, until she was clearly in that marvelous space where she wasn't thinking about a thing except what they did to her, except how her body reacted, and that was exactly where he wanted her.

The bullshit of her past, that fucker who had hurt her, was all so far gone in that moment.

Sure, those things would come back, but they'd deal with that later.

He leaned forward slightly, not pulling out as much so he could sink deeper and take her harder. He didn't want a moment outside of her sweet little body.

Trent stroked his cock, his gaze moving over Sunny from his place on the chair, the heat in his eyes saying he liked the sight.

Then again, who wouldn't?

Garrison had his fist against her lips and his eyes pinned to where his cock disappeared into the heat of her mouth.

Fuck, Connor had never felt this before.

It was downright magical, which was a stupid thing to think, yet he couldn't come up with a better word. They'd run into the woman a second time, against all odds, and he had to admit…maybe it was fate. Maybe she was something they were supposed to find, a piece they'd been seeking for years without any luck.

Connor threw the thought away, because there wasn't room for what-ifs right then. He wanted to savor each second, to drown in the way her cunt wrapped around him, to gorge himself on the broken little sounds she made.

His balls tightened, that nagging release coming far too fast.

Then again, he wasn't sure she'd had much sex recently. While a little soreness was a good reminder, too much?

He didn't want her really hurting.

"Fuck," he groaned, slamming into her, timing with Garrison's thrust so when Connor pulled back, Garrison pushed forward, never leaving the girl empty for even a second.

Trent reached beneath her and flicked the weight, making it tug at her abused nipples, and the way she reacted?

Like a bucking mare, but he wasn't a man to be thrown. Her cunt squeezed down, tightening around his dick, making resisting any longer impossible.

The woman came hard, like she'd done every time, as if each release was her breaking apart and fitting back together. The muscles in her back tensed, but the bindings kept her from moving, let him keep fucking her right through it until it set off his own release.

He gripped her tighter, some primal instinct inside him wanting to make sure she didn't get away, that he spilled every last drop inside her hot cunt.

He thrust again, slower, his breath heavy as her pussy did that marvelous squeezing thing around him and the aftershocks milked him dry.

Finally, he pulled back, rewarded with the sight of her cunt, flushed and swollen and wet from her own pleasure.

Yeah, fucking magical.

Trent was about to explode. He enjoyed a good show, and Sunny had put on one hell of one. The weight attached to the clamps swung forward and back, driven by just how hard Connor had fucked the sweet girl. Each time it happened, when the weight hit the top of its arc, when the pull against her nipples was at its highest, she whimpered out that soft sound that made him slow his hand so he didn't come just yet.

Garrison slid his fingers into her hair, moving the strands from her eyes, forcing her to look up at him. His cock spread her lips out, her cheeks red and her mascara running.

What is it about running mascara that is so dammed sexy?

"You ready to swallow?" He didn't ask her if she wanted to.

This was what she'd come for, to feel the way they took control, to realize she'd been able to tell them no already, that she could stop it, but that they'd enjoy her as they pleased up to that point.

And right then, that meant for Garrison to spill into her mouth, to watch her throat work as she swallowed him, as she took him into her.

Garrison pressed in deep enough that she gagged for a second — probably just testing, though Trent would bet her tight throat would feel amazing — before he pulled back so only the head of his cock remained in her mouth.

Garrison didn't look away or close his eyes. He stared right at her, as if he wanted to *see* the moment the girl swallowed, as if he needed that sensation.

A groan left him, the muscles at his hips twitching, a slight rock as he came. After a long, tense moment, he withdrew, dragging his cock along her lips once more and leaving a spot of white behind. "Swallow," he said, his voice so deep it came out like a growl.

Sunny did so, then went so far as to lick her lips.

Trent squeezed his cock, hard, right on the brink. So many ideas came to him, all the things he'd love to do with her, to her. The bad thing about a night like this, the ones where he never knew if it would happen again, was having to choose. There was just never enough time.

There were so many things he wanted to do. He wanted to paint her pretty tits in cum, to pull her into his lap and force orgasm after orgasm from her until all that squeezing got him off. He wanted to lie her on her back and fuck between her breasts, pulling the clamps off as he did it to push them both over the marvelous edge.

In short?

He wanted *everything*.

But since that wasn't possible, he knew exactly what he needed.

Sunny panted, appearing worn out. Not that he was done with her. In fact, he liked it, the way she rested, the way she breathed heavily, the sweat on her back. She looked well used, and that appealed to him.

"Such a good girl," he said as he walked behind her, Connor having taken Trent's seat, and Garrison pulling over another to sit on the other side. "You did so well, little Fox."

She swallowed, her lips curling into a sated, exhausted smile, as if she enjoyed that praise.

Clearly, she'd reached that point where she stopped putting up fronts.

Trent could have warned her, could have slid his hands up her thighs, but he was a man who enjoyed some surprises in life.

He pressed his middle finger into her cunt.

She gasped, the sound all his this time, since Garrison's cock didn't muffle it.

She twisted, but the straps kept her from seeing him.

Trent thrust his finger into her messy, swollen cunt. "So, a number? For what just happened?"

"Ten."

No surprise there.

"You tired?"

She nodded.

"See, I haven't come yet. That means I'm not quite done with you. I don't mind waiting until last, though. I mean, I would have probably fucked your ass, but since that's off the table, I guess I'll have to enjoy your other holes."

Her eyebrows furrowed, but she didn't seem overly concerned. At least until he shifted his hand back and sank two fingers into her.

Ah, that one got her. It helped wind up her tired body, bring back to life the fire she'd probably thought her orgasm had quenched.

Worse? He brought his other hand down and pressed his thumb to her neglected clit.

And just like that, she came. She tried to arch, even her toes curling, her feet flexing and a thin sound leaving her full, pink lips.

Not enough.

Trent didn't stop there. He pulled back, then pressed three fingers into her. When she whined, he let out a harsh laugh. "Come on — you took Connor. He's thicker than this." He caught eyes with Garrison. "Maybe she needs more?"

Garrison muttered, "*Sadist*," before reaching down and flicking the weight that connected to the clamps.

And off she went again. Each orgasm was weaker than the last, as if her muscles had run to exhaustion, as though she lacked the energy to even react, but he still felt her pussy crank down, the waves as it pulled her under.

He pulled back and folded four fingers together, pressing them in, wanting to own her with a power that made him nearly come. Resistance met him, her body not quite ready to take him this way. "Pity," he sighed, pulling back. "Guess I'll have to try that another night, one where I can spread those thighs of yours wide, when I can see your pretty eyes as I press my whole fist into you. What do you think about that?"

"Four," she whimpered, a catch in her breath that said she wasn't sure about her answer.

He chuckled. "You'll see, sweet. Amazing exactly what a pussy can take, and I bet you you'll love it. You'll squirm and you'll whimper, but you'll come so hard around my fist." He leaned in and pressed a kiss to her ass cheek, then a hard bite. "Guess we'll do this the old-fashioned way, then."

He reached for a condom on the table behind him, sliding it over his length before wrapping her hair around his hand. He pressed the tip of his cock to her, felt the way she twitched like the best welcome. "I'm a little busy," he said. "Any chance you two could help?"

Garrison rolled his eyes, but Connor? Oh, Connor had a streak of darkness in him, too. His eyes lit up as he reached down, grasping the clip on his side.

Garrison and Conner pulled the clips off at the same time, and Trent plunged his cock into her, sinking fully into her all at once.

Sunny exploded. She shook, she cried, she said things that made no sense, but how couldn't she? Her breasts were on fire, the clamps so much worse than the last time, and Trent had just filled her in a single rough thrust.

Fingers rubbed at her nipples — not as hard as Trent had been, but since they were far more sensitive, it was at least as bad. Even as she twisted, the straps trapped her, kept her still and impaled on Trent's insistent cock, caught by the demanding fingers of the other two Doms that drew out the agony of her nipples.

She came again, or had it ever stopped? It seemed each movement, each touch, each stroke by the men over any part of her body set her off again, like a cascading wave of pleasure that pulled her so far under, she didn't know if she'd surface again.

Or if she cared.

"Fuck, yes," Trent said, voice broken. "This was worth it. You have the perfect cunt, sweet, you know that? If you were mine, I'd fuck you every goddamned day, never let you be empty long, take you everywhere. You'd be my favorite plaything."

As he spoke, the words washed over her, adding to everything else, intensifying it all. He fucked her at least as hard as Connor had, but his grip in her hair, the way he pulled her head back, made her more aware of it. She wasn't distracted by a blow job, could only feel each time he bottomed out, each time he took her pussy with the confidence of a man who thought he owned it.

But...she was starting to fear he did. That they all did.

Trent let go of her hair, then reached around her, beneath her, to between her slick thighs. He rubbed his fingers against her clit, setting off another rush of pleasure. When he spoke, his words had less control, less thought. "You know, your pretty tits aren't the only thing I can clamp." He pinched her swollen clit, taking it between his fingers in a tight grip, sending streaks of something too intense to be pleasure or pain through her. Even over the sounds she made, he spoke. "You undo me, sweet. I want to put a clamp tight on that sexy little clit of yours, fuck your perfect ass, spank you until you're a crying mess. You look amazing when you cry, when your mascara runs down your face, when you're not just a disaster but when I know *we* turned you into that. Fuck, you've got *no* clue how filthy the things I want from you are." He stilled, his cock deep inside her, his fingers tight around her clit, before he shuddered, clearly pushed over the edge by his own words and the idea of doing all the things he talked about.

Sunny was nothing but adrenaline and endorphins, but she wasn't *quite* done. Or, at least she realized that when he released her clit, then rubbed it between his fingers in a way she *never* thought would have been pleasant.

And it wasn't? Or it was? She couldn't tell, but she knew she came again, that her body responded even if she wasn't sure about it.

It left her panting hard, unable to move, sticky and exhausted to her very core.

And so very confused.

After this...she wasn't sure how she'd ever go back to her regular life again...

Chapter Nine

Connor cursed to himself, pacing their living room. "Three days."

"Give her time." Garrison sat at the kitchen counter, his papers spread across it as he often did. The man hated to work in a closed room, choosing instead to set up in the middle of the living room.

Garrison claiming their central living space didn't normally bother Connor—they'd lived together for years, so he was used to his friend's oddities—but Connor's mood was beyond foul. He could pretend it was just a random hissy fit, but he damn well knew the cause. "How can she ignore us for three days?"

"Because she's nervous," Garrison answered without looking up. "We got under her skin and she's trying to shore up her defenses."

Connor shook his head. Garrison was right, of course, but that hardly soothed him. After taking her apart that night, after tucking her against his chest for over an hour as she'd come down from her high, Sunny had retreated. It wasn't uncommon, even with people who were perfectly well adjusted, so it wasn't a shock that she'd done it.

Sex was…complicated. So fucking easy to do in the moment and so hard to understand or come to terms with later.

Or so he'd come to learn after spending years dealing with subs.

So not hearing from her the next day wasn't a surprise. She'd responded with one-word answers to any text about her health, about how she felt, as if she knew ignoring *those* would bring one of them running. She gave *just* enough to keep them away but not enough to constitute a conversation.

Stubborn woman.

He suddenly thought she should have dressed up as an ass that first night, to go along with her hard head.

"You're going to wear yourself out," Garrison said from his spot, as if scolding a child but not really caring what they did.

"How are you not annoyed by this?"

Garrison sighed and set his arms on the papers before giving his full attention to Connor. "Because I expected it. You should have, too. She needed to get her head on straight, to come to terms with what happened."

"She shouldn't do that alone," Connor griped. "She'll just twist herself into knots that she doesn't know how to untangle, and then she'll end up worse off than she started."

"But *we* will only make it worse. We swore we wouldn't press her, and don't you think showing up when she's pretty clear about not wanting us there would be pressing her?"

Connor tightened his lips into a thin line, silenced by the fact that Garrison was absolutely correct again.

Not that it eased Connor's frustration. If anything, knowing he could do nothing made it worse. He pictured Sunny, chewing her bottom lip to hell, all alone in her house, pacing and talking to her dog because she had no one else. She'd think and think and worry and think some more until she had no idea what direction was up any longer. He hated her doing that on her own, without someone else at least keeping an eye on her, making sure she was sleeping and eating and taking care of herself.

Which had him blowing out a long breath. "What if we ask someone else to go check on her?"

"Like who?"

"Toya?"

Garrison made a mocking sound. "I have a feeling if *we* scare her, that Domme would send her running."

"She was talking to Kat that first night. What about her?"

Garrison leaned back. "That might work. Kat wouldn't push her, wouldn't try to make her pick us, but she'd be able to talk to Sunny and make sure she's okay. Maybe talking to another sub would help her work through some of the bull in her head as well."

Connor had his phone out before Garrison had even stopped talking. Sure, he wanted Sunny—he wanted nothing more than for her to call him up and ask him to come over.

Since that wasn't happening, however, he'd at least be able to sleep if he knew for sure she was okay. It was about doing what was right for her, not about what *he* wanted.

Sometimes being a Dom sucked.

* * * *

Sunny jumped at the knock on her door, her heart speeding.

The men would never show up without texting her, and no one else ever came to her house. The fear threatened to overwhelm her, but she shoved it backward. Even with her nerves on edge, she refused to fall to pieces over nothing.

Spike stood by the door, his lips already back to bare his teeth, but he didn't bark. He was the sort of dog to wait until someone got close before he bit—no warnings.

Another knock, then a familiar voice called out, "Sunny? You home?"

Kat? The woman from the club that first night?

Sunny undid the multitude of locks before cracking the door open. For some reason, she expected to find Kat standing there in fetish gear.

It was a stupid expectation—she knew the woman wouldn't walk around town like that—but somehow seeing Kat in brown slacks and a professional-looking button-up shirt felt weird.

"Yes?" Sunny knew her voice came out rude, but she couldn't quite put together how the woman had gotten there or why she'd come.

Kat lifted two cups of coffee. "I come bearing gifts. Can I come in?"

Sunny wanted to say no. Not because she didn't like the woman—she actually did—but more because it felt like another line she hadn't intended to cross. She'd never planned on allowing people into her home, yet

Connor, Garrison and Trent had been there. She hadn't planned on falling for anyone yet—

She cut off that thought before it could fully form, chastising herself for even starting it. *I'm not falling for anyone, and certainly not them.*

Sunny ended up stepping back and opening the door to let Kat in. The woman had been nice, and she really hadn't had a friend who wasn't connected to the shelter in...

The math became too hard, so Sunny left it at '*a long time*'.

Kat handed over one of the cups, and when Sunny smelled it, she got a good whiff of brown sugar and cinnamon. Kat was a woman not afraid of calories. A quick laugh, and Kat switched the cups, taking the sugary drink herself and giving Sunny one with black coffee.

How does she know?

Kat peered around the small living room, and Sunny couldn't help but feel as if she should apologize. She'd spent years creating the haven, and she knew it wasn't much. It was small, and most of her furniture had been purchased used. Sunny recalled her ex, remembered how nice everything had been, how large their home had been, and the same old fears came back.

"It's just me," Sunny said like some sort of middle ground, where she made it clear it wasn't great but didn't put it down.

Kat turned, an honest smile on her lips. "Are you kidding me? I love it. You probably have an amazing view, and without many neighbors? We should do parties here!"

Sunny shook her head, the thought of random people traipsing in and out of her home an absolute no-go. Still, a warmth in her chest said she liked that Kat thought her home was good enough for Kat to want to have get-togethers there.

"So why are you here?" Sunny frowned. "Also, how did you get my address?"

Kat leaned down to pet Spike—he had stopped growling, because her tough guard dog was evidently just a big softie with everyone. "Connor called me."

The idea that Connor would have given Sunny's address out made her chest tight. It felt like a betrayal, especially when he knew how nervous she was about that very thing.

Kat kept talking, as though oblivious to Sunny's distress. "He gave me your number, told me to call you and check in, to make sure you were okay. Phone calls are for telemarketers and family members you don't like, though. I rifled through the paperwork at the club to find your address."

"That's invasive," Sunny said, grateful at least that Connor hadn't breached her trust.

Kat nodded. "Yeah, I hate to tell you, but that's a good word for me in general. Think of me like Sanctuary's little sister. I am in everyone's business— no one particularly likes me, but they also can't seem to get rid of me." She smiled as if all those unflattering descriptions warmed her.

What an odd woman.

"Well, I don't know what Connor told you, but I'm fine."

"Uh-huh. Look, when the Doms are away, we get to play. So sit down and talk to me—none of it goes past here."

"But don't you *have* to tell them what I said? Like, if they asked you, don't you need to answer?" Sunny followed Kat into the living room, taking a spot on the couch even though Kat sat on the floor, like a kid. Worse, a fear crept in.

I don't want to put Kat in any danger.

Kat snorted. "Please. They're not *my* Doms. I don't have to tell them anything." She set the coffee between her crossed legs. "Come on, Sunny, talk to me. You've been ignoring them after from what I heard was a pretty damn good night. What's up?"

Sunny blew out a slow breath as she traced the bottom of her cup, trying to put into words what she still hadn't figured out in the days since she'd seen them. "I just don't think it's a good idea to get any more involved with this lifestyle."

"Why not? Did you not like it?" Kat didn't have the same *'gotcha'* voice that Garrison had when he asked questions—that leading voice that said he already knew the answer. It was more like Kat was really wondering, that she needed Sunny to tell her.

It made it easier to tell Kat the truth. "No, that's not it. I did enjoy it—too much, probably."

"Ohhh," Kat said, dragging out the sound as if it had all come together. "So you're at that stage of 'I like it but I shouldn't like it, so I'm going to pretend like I don't because it's easier'?"

It sounded so stupid when Kat said it out loud, didn't it? "You don't understand," Sunny pressed. "It isn't just them—it isn't just this. I've *done* this before, and it almost destroyed me. It's not smart for me to get involved, to risk that all again."

Kat paused, tilting her head. "Look, I'm not going to tell you what to do. I'm not going to tell you that Connor, Trent and Garrison are perfect or that they're worth taking that risk for or anything like it. If there's one thing I've worked out through all of this, it's that we've got to decide that on our own. What I can tell you is that I get it—I've been there. I've had this same struggle and had to figure out if things are worth it, if men are ever worth it long term. But..." She paused, then let out a slow sigh. "Going to bed alone sucks. Leaving the club week after week on my own hurts. If I had a chance at something real, at something deep, boy, I'd grab that with my greedy little hands and I wouldn't ever let it go."

Sunny watched the other woman, at how Kat's jovial attitude slipped and the frayed edged of her pride and resolve crumbled. Suddenly it wasn't the bubbly troublemaker, the vixen from Sanctuary, the sub who seemed in control of everything—it was a woman who didn't have the life she really wanted.

Before she had to say something, though, Kat peered up with another smile, one that was tired but still seemed real, as if she didn't pretend her pain didn't exist but just let other things bury it. "Enough about men. I saw the SUV outside. Can you drive that thing or is it just for looks?"

"Of course I can drive it."

"Then who needs boys? Let's go off-roading."

And Sunny realized a little fun with a girlfriend was *exactly* what she needed.

* * * *

The sun had dipped below the mountains by the time Sunny pulled the vehicle back into her driveway. She'd spent hours on the back roads with Kat, enjoying the scenery, the chance to just have a friend.

It was then that she'd realized that while she spent a lot of time with other women, both employees and people who needed to use the shelter, it was always in a working relationship. It was friendly enough, but it wasn't personal.

Kat was the first *real* friend she'd made since Tanner.

And she'd had no idea she'd needed it so badly. Just one afternoon with Kat had made her feel lighter, freer. They'd laughed, they'd talked, they'd just relaxed and had fun.

For the first time in years, Sunny felt like a real, full person instead of someone just trying to get by. Even better, Kat's stories were wonderful. She was more than willing to spill every detail about the men, and it seemed they had enough history for there to be plenty to share.

They were in the middle of one such story, and Sunny couldn't help smiling at it.

"Then Connor actually stuttered. Full on, flustered stuttering!" Kat slapped her hand on her knee, barely able to get out the words between her laughter.

"I can't imagine him ever doing that," Sunny admitted as she put the car into park in front of the house.

"Well, to be fair, I *had* just told him his scary Dom voice sounded like one of those voice modulators kids play with. I don't think he was used to brats at that time. It was back when he first started going, and he didn't have the other two for backup."

Sunny grinned as she filed away that story, as she had so many others, like little pieces of the men's past that they'd never shared themselves. Hearing it from Kat made them real. They were people, not just scary Doms with scarier costumes.

They walked toward the front door, Kat already saying she'd need to use the restroom then head on home. It made Sunny admit the house would be a bit lonelier without the boisterous woman.

"Maybe we can get together again soon? I really had a good time," Kat said, and whether it was because she'd noticed Sunny's disappointment or because she really wanted to hang out again, Sunny didn't care.

The locks clicked as Sunny turned her keys, undoing each one until she could push open the door.

But…Spike didn't rush up.

A moment of dread hit her, a fear that made her throat tighten and threaten to close. Spike was *always* at the door when she got home, always waiting for her.

"Spike?" Sunny called into the darkness, fumbling blindly for the switches.

Light bathed the room, and Kat gasped first, when the sight was too horrific for Sunny to process right away.

The back slider was open, frame bent, glass broken, and Spike lay in front of it, not moving, in a puddle of blood.

Chapter Ten

Garrison yanked the door open, his chest pounding. The receptionist took one look at him, and he could *see* her reaching for a phone to call the police.

Then again, he was sure he looked a mess. He hadn't brushed his hair, had pulled on the first thing he could find, and he had to have the crazy gaze of a man who had no problem causing trouble.

Then again, the call he'd gotten from Kat would do that to anyone.

Sure enough, Sunny sat in a chair in the lobby of the veterinary hospital, her arms wrapped around herself, her body hunched forward.

Broken. There was no other way to describe her stance.

Kat looked up, meeting his gaze, her eyes red as if she'd been crying, too.

"It's okay," Connor assured the receptionist, and went that way to smooth things over after coming in behind Garrison. They didn't need the police calling just because Garrison looked ready to kill someone.

Let Connor deal with that — I need to talk to Sunny.

Garrison sat down beside Sunny and draped his arm around her shoulders. "Any word?"

She didn't pull away, didn't seem to even react to his touch.

Not a great sign.

He peered past her to get an answer from Kat.

"Spike had a broken leg and a busted rib. They think he was hit with something. They have him in surgery, but they aren't sure if he'll pull through right now," Kat said.

Fuck. Garrison's chest hurt, for the dog and for the woman whose heart had to be breaking.

"He got a hold of whoever it was," Sunny said, her voice pained and hollow. "He had blood all over his muzzle, and there was some on the back porch, like the person was bleeding. I think someone broke in, and Spike grabbed him. He put up a good fight, but whoever broke in must have had something to hit him with — maybe a bat?"

Trent leaned down in front of Sunny, placing his hands on her knees. "Look at me, sweet."

She did, lifting her gaze as if drawn by his order.

"Did you call the police already?" he asked.

She frowned, as if she hadn't considered it.

Kat broke in to answer. "I called Marcus — he's already at her place. I also called a glazer to fix the slider and a locksmith to rekey all the locks, just in case."

Garrison mouthed "*thank you*" to Kat. The woman was a brat to her core, but she kept her head on straight when everything went sideways. Furthermore, she'd called Marcus, a detective who went to Sanctuary, a man who would understand how important it was to do this right. It let Garrison relax, let him know someone qualified was looking at it.

She nodded, as if it were a given. Then again, even if Sunny didn't want to accept her place in the community, it seemed the community didn't have any such hang-ups about claiming her.

"Why would someone break in?" Sunny asked. "I don't have anything worth stealing, and I'm too far out for it to be someone casing places. This shouldn't have happened."

Could it have been the man she's so afraid of?

"You need to tell me about your ex." Pushing her was the last thing Garrison wanted to do right then, but it was another example of when what she needed was more important than what they wanted. "We need to make sure he is wherever the hell he was before — make sure this wasn't him."

Connor came over, but he didn't crouch, didn't try to touch Sunny. He'd moved into veterinarian mode, probably because it was easier to deal with, gave him a clear path to take. "I talked to the doctor, and Spike came out of surgery okay. Until he comes to, we can't be sure of his condition. They had to amputate the leg, Sunny. There wasn't any way to save it."

Sunny crumbled at that, dissolving into broken sobs that tore at Garrison. He wanted to take that pain away, to fix it, but there wasn't anything he could do.

That was the hardest thing about being a Dom, the desire to protect someone and the knowledge that no matter how hard he tried, he couldn't always do it.

He pulled her into a tight hug and pressed a kiss to her head, while he tried to ignore the fear that the worst wasn't over yet.

* * * *

Sunny leaned her forehead against the window of the car and closed her eyes. She was exhausted — there was no other way to put it. She felt it down to her marrow, a tiredness that no amount of sleep could fix.

Garrison, Trent and Connor had stayed with her at the veterinary hospital the entire time, even after Kat had left. They'd helped coordinate the people who'd repaired the door, stayed close when the police took her statement and helped to explain the details about Spike.

While she had wanted distance from them, she couldn't deny how much she leaned on them, how much of the stress and details they'd taken for her. When it came time to leave, though, Garrison had made it perfectly clear that she couldn't go home. Without knowing for sure who had broken in or whether they could come back, her safe haven wasn't so safe anymore. So, instead, he'd offered to drive her to his house.

Or *their* house, as it turned out, since she hadn't realized the men lived together. She should have, in hindsight, since they were so close.

She might have argued — being in such close quarters with three dominant men hadn't been in her plans — but between the shock of the incident and how many unknowns there still were, she acquiesced.

She'd seen Spike before they'd left, but the hospital had needed to keep him for at least a few days. He hadn't been awake, but the sight of his leg — or what was left of it — bandaged had said it was for the best he hadn't woken yet.

She thought about how he'd loved to run and play fetch, how his life would change when he did wake, when he couldn't do the things he'd cherished before. In an odd way, she understood that. She remembered after leaving Tanner, how all the things she'd loved, she hadn't been able to do anymore, the things that had made life worth living that he'd stolen. He had tainted everything.

Sunny pushed off that thought. She couldn't think about it, because each time she did, she found herself stuck in a spiral — guilt, fear, all of it. Instead, she let out a slow breath.

If she hadn't been so numb, she might have worried about being in their space, at being in their home, at being so alone with them. It would have set off her anxiety any other time, but after tonight?

What more could they possibly do?

The sedan shook as Garrison took it up a steep driveway, about fifteen minutes from the veterinarian. She wasn't tracking too well, but she'd guess they were about thirty from her house. Garrison pulled the car up in front of a large but unassuming home. "Go on in, sweet. I'll pull the car into the garage and check in that everything is handled."

The thought of forcing her feet to even move felt insurmountable. Just when she felt trapped in some hole, when she couldn't imagine getting up, someone reached a hand out to her.

It was a lifeline, something tossed out to her just as she started to drown and pull her back above the water.

She took the hand, and Connor pulled her out of the car, then tucked her against his side. He led her, not asking her questions, not demanding she do anything but follow him. He gave her a quick tour of the house, showed her the kitchen, where to get water, the bathroom. She didn't take in any of it, as if her brain were too full to accept any additional information.

After making their way through the house, Connor pulled her into a room that she was sure was his. It was in the slight smell of hay, in the masculine, faded furniture and the old leather jacket hanging from a hook on the back of the door.

"You need to sleep," he said, his rough voice something for her to hold on to. "You'll feel better tomorrow."

Will I?

It didn't seem possible right then.

He grasped the bottom of her shirt and pulled it up and over her head. Her bra came next, him unhooking it with ease. He placed the items in a hamper, then crouched to slide her pants off, leaving her underwear in place.

Despite the fact that he was stripping her naked, she didn't feel ogled. It didn't make her anxiety rise, but whether that was because she trusted him or she was too tired to manage it, she wasn't sure. He did the motions efficiently, as if they had nothing to do with sex.

Which made no sense to her. In her experience with Dominants, *everything* had to do with sex.

He turned and plucked a T-shirt from his closet, and when he slid it on her, it hung to her mid-thigh.

"You should be more comfortable in that," he said, then used a hand on the small of her back to push her toward the bed.

The covers were warm, and when Connor pulled them over her, she had to admit...there was an odd sense of safety there. Everything smelled like him, and already it felt familiar and let her relax.

Connor went to leave, but Sunny caught his wrist, looking up at him, not sure what she wanted. She wanted him to fix things, to make her world make sense again, to let her wake up and go back to when she'd been happy.

None of that was possible, though, so all she wanted was to not be alone.

Connor stared down at her and, after a moment, he nodded. He extracted his wrist, turned the light off then crawled into the bed behind her.

She closed her eyes as he rubbed his large hand over her side. It had been years since she'd fallen asleep beside anyone, and even longer since it had been anyone she trusted. Still, her panic slumbered, and she could only relax into the rhythmic motion of his hand.

Tomorrow would come no matter what she did. She couldn't avoid it, couldn't go backward, couldn't make the whole damned day unhappen.

If she couldn't stop it, she might as well let sleep take the reality away for a while.

How can life go wrong so quickly?

* * * *

Trent stayed put, even when Sunny walked into the large open kitchen. Her brown hair was damp, and she wore another long shirt since she'd only had the one set of clothing, and those had had Spike's blood on them.

She looked better than she had the night before, but sleep could do that. It got people out of the horrible moment and into the next, into the place where they had to do things, had to keep going.

Garrison brought over a bowl of oatmeal and fruit and, without asking, set it in front of a spot at the table.

His meaning was clear — *eat*.

Sunny took the indicated chair.

Connor had already left his bedroom, probably wanting to rise before she woke up. Sleeping beside a man was no doubt new for her, and the last thing they needed was for her to freak out when she found him still there. He worked early anyway, doing the rounds on a few patients he needed to check in with daily, and he'd planned to stop by the hospital to check in on Spike.

It left Trent and Garrison to the hard conversation.

"You look better," Garrison said, as if trying to broach a topic slowly, to gauge a reaction.

Neither Trent nor Garrison had eaten breakfast — they weren't morning eaters — but Sunny would do well with the calories. It also felt incredibly right to have someone to take care of...

She nodded as she swallowed a spoonful of the oatmeal. Afterward, she responded. "I think I'm feeling better. I'm sorry Kat got you involved," she said, voice soft.

She was *sorry*? The girl clearly had no idea just how involved they already felt...

"You should be sorry," Garrison said. At her startled look, he softened his voice. "You should have called us yourself."

She shook her head. "It's my problem. I can deal with it."

Trent blew out a breath, again reminded of how little she understood. "We agreed to help you, and whether you like that fact or not right now, that makes you ours. Even if you weren't, I'd like to think we're at least friends. If we'd had something so horrible happen, wouldn't you want us to call you?"

She paused, spoon hanging in the air as though she hadn't ever considered that, as if the idea of Doms needing *anything* were strange to her.

Then again, he doubted her last relationship had been a two-way street.

Which brought him to the core of the conversation, one he really didn't want to have for a million different reasons.

"I need you to tell us about your ex."

"I don't want to talk about him."

"I know you don't, and we let it slide before, but now? You know this could be him."

She shook her head. "I left him five years ago, and he hasn't come looking for me. If he hasn't showed up yet, he won't. He's moved on."

Garrison reached out and set his hand on hers. "I know it's scary, but the only way you're ever going to feel safe is if we make sure he isn't here."

She stared at where Garrison touched her, at the place where his hand covered hers. Would she panic at the closeness? Especially with how tense the conversation was?

She inhaled deeply, then spoke, words so soft they were hard to hear. "His name is Tanner Hoult. He's from Utah."

"Is that where you're from?" Trent asked.

She nodded. "I met him in a club when I was eighteen and used a fake ID to get in. He was older and dangerous and amazing. Everything was okay at first."

Trent nodded, having heard the same story countless times before. "It usually is. That's how abusers get you, by drawing you in, by acting like the perfect catch until it's too late to get away."

She shivered. "Pretty much. I spent eight years with him."

"What was the last straw?"

She leaned forward, setting her spoon down and pulling away from the men. "He was jealous — insanely so. He hated if I had friends or saw my family. I ended up losing every person I cared about because he'd twist things and manipulate them and ruin all my relationships. It ended up just he and me, and my dog, Sparkle. She was tiny, maybe ten pounds at most, but she was all I had. She stayed by my side day and night, made me not feel quite so alone. Well, Tanner came home one day in a bad mood, looking for a reason to get angry at me. He ended up screaming that I loved the dog more than I did him."

Trent drew his hands into fists, the story like watching a car crash, knowing it was going to happen and not being able to stop it. Given that Sunny didn't have Sparkle anymore, he had a feeling where it was headed.

"I told him that wasn't true, but he wouldn't listen. He got quiet, just stared at me and said he didn't appreciate lying whores. He got mad like that a lot, blew up and afterward things would be okay again, so I tried to put it out of my head. The next day, I had to go to the store, but there was this pit in my stomach. The thing was, I always felt like that, so I chalked it up to nerves. I told myself I was being stupid, but when I got home, I called for Sparkle — she didn't come. Tanner walked in from the back yard with a shovel, not even trying to hide it, and said he'd handled the problem." She didn't cry, speaking the words as if they haunted her but she had no more tears to shed over them. "I left the next day after he went to work."

Trent grasped her wrist and pulled softly until she settled in his lap, until he could wrap his arms around her. She had such a soft heart—he couldn't imagine how she felt, how she blamed herself for it. "I'm sorry, sweet. That had to have been hard."

"If I'd left sooner..."

"You know better than to play those games. How many women have you talked to? What would you tell any one of them in your place?"

She leaned against him, as if finally accepting his help as something useful. "That she left when she was able to. That anything that happened was his fault, not hers."

"That's right," Trent said. "So tell yourself that, and I'll make you repeat it each time you start questioning yourself."

She twisted to offer him a slight glare. "You know, I can sit in my own chair."

"You could, but I like having you here." He reached out and caught her bowl with a finger, then pulled it closer. "Eat. I'll put a call in tomorrow to Mitch, a private investigator I know. He'll get a for-sure that Tanner is still in Utah, and that he hasn't left."

Sunny nodded and picked up her spoon again. "Okay, but I'm telling you, I'm sure he isn't a part of this. This has to be some random break-in. I mean, it's been five years. Why would he decide to come back *now*?"

Trent didn't answer, because nothing he said would reassure her. The reality was that the sort of man she'd described, the sort who would kill a dog out of some crazy jealousy, wasn't the sort who would just let someone go. Even after five years and seeming to be gone, he was the type who would show back to up ruin everything.

Which meant they needed to work fast and figure out if he was behind this, because Trent wasn't ready to give Sunny up without a fight.

Chapter Eleven

Having time off felt as surreal as the rest of Sunny's current situation. She'd called the shelter after breakfast to take a few more days off. She needed it, especially because the idea of going back to the shelter and taking care of others seemed too difficult. She just didn't have anything inside her to give to others right then.

Connor had gone by the vet in the morning, and she'd been grateful for the update when he'd called. Spike was doing better. He was still on a lot of pain meds and asleep most of the time, but it seemed he'd pull through. Connor had said they'd go that evening to visit him.

Trent had needed to head into work, leaving her at the house with Garrison.

It was surreal to walk around their house because the men were *everywhere*.

Connor was in the painting of horses that hung above the fireplace, Garrison was in the simple black couches and Trent had to be responsible for the 'wash your hands, you filthy animals' sign in the bathroom.

Garrison had let her be to explore the house to her heart's content. She'd gotten a tour the previous night, but she didn't recall much of it. They had four bedrooms, but one had been converted into a small home gym. It had a treadmill and a weight bench, along with a suspension workout set that hung from a hook over the window.

Of course, knowing the men as she did, she wondered if that was *all* it got used for. She had a feeling the straps would be useful in other ways.

Still, after washing her leggings by hand that morning and throwing them in their dyer—her shirt had been a loss because of Spike's blood—she'd decided a walk on the treadmill would do her some good.

Stretching her legs would help clear her mind.

The story she'd told them that morning, regurgitating her history with Tanner, hadn't made her feel better.

People who claimed that getting secrets out made a person feel better were liars.

Maybe, eventually, it would help, but at first it only felt like scraping her skin raw, as if she were bleeding from a million little places that had been healed. Each word had been a new wound, each memory another strike.

The only positive had been that the men hadn't treated her like she was broken. They hadn't coddled her, hadn't acted as though she was suddenly diseased or weak.

Trent had pulled her into his lap as she'd finished breakfast, and they'd moved on.

Still, she couldn't quite shake the feeling that Tanner had managed to get his claws into her life again. Even if this wasn't him, even if it was all a random occurrence, he was *there*. He was in her head, tearing apart her life even from states away.

"Hey there." Garrison's voice made her jump and lose her footing.

Luckily, Garrison was quicker — or he expected it — because before she sailed backward and hit the wall behind her, he caught her and pulled her off the treadmill.

"Jumpy, aren't you?"

She smacked his shoulder. "You *know* better than to sneak up on me."

He smirked, telling her yeah, he'd probably planned it.

Then again, she was pressed up against him, his strong arm around her, her breasts melded against his chest. He'd clearly gotten what he wanted.

Or maybe not quite yet, because he lowered his lips to hers, not asking but taking a kiss that was all heat.

Of course, as quickly as he started it, he ended it, much to her disappointment. "Pity," he muttered.

"Pity?"

He nodded, then gestured toward the kitchen. "Yeah, a damn shame. As much as I'd love to keep going, we need to talk."

We need to talk was a bad thing for a person to say. Fear gripped her as her brain went back to times when Tanner had said that before, when it had meant she'd displeased him, that she'd failed in some way and those words existed in the silence before she paid the price for it.

Fingers grasped her chin, and it was Garrison's blue eyes that pulled her back, that reminded her it wasn't Tanner who had spoken.

It was Garrison, and this man hadn't given her a reason to fear him.

He nodded after a moment, as if he could see her work through it. He pulled his hand away from her chin, then held it out and waited for her.

Sunny took a deep breath, her chest aching from her earlier panic, but still gave him her hand. He wrapped his strong fingers around her wrist, then tugged her closer before setting his hand on her lower back and leading her to the kitchen.

She sat in one chair, and he took the other.

"You really hate talking," he pointed out. "Why's that?"

She wanted to explain to him how screwed up the question was. He was asking her to explain why she hated to explain. It was almost enough to make her laugh.

He didn't speak again, waiting, that amazing patience of his unnerving.

And it did what he'd planned, no doubt, drawing her to answer to end the tense silence. "Tanner didn't much care what I had to say, so the more I said, the more he used it against me. It never helped me to explain, never changed anything. It was safer to just stay quiet."

"I can understand that, and it makes a lot of sense in that environment. Is this house that same environment?"

"No," she admitted softly.

"That's right. Look, you need to hold your breath when you're underwater, right? But, if you tried that on land, it would kill you. That's because what worked when you were in that situation can be harmful when you're out of it. It kept you safe before but will bite you in the ass now."

It made sense but letting go of those old fears was hard. "Was this all you wanted to talk about?"

"Not exactly, no. You've made some of your limits clear, but it occurred to me...you don't tend to say much in the moment." At Sunny's look of confusion, Garrison went on. "Like when Jordan tried to talk to you that first night. When we're actually playing, you don't usually tell us no or that you don't like something."

"So? If you know what I don't want beforehand, speaking up doesn't matter, unless you're planning on ignoring my limits."

"It does matter. See, what's fine one day might not be another. Maybe you didn't sleep well, maybe you're on your period and hurting, maybe there's something you never figured would bother you but suddenly does. I need to know you'll speak up."

Sunny wanted to say she would speak up, that she'd tell them to stop, but the desire to tell the truth kept her from uttering it.

"That's what I thought," Garrison added. "See, that's dangerous. This is a two-way street. It's give and take. I *need* to know that you will use your safe word when you need to."

She glanced down in her lap, trying to get a break from his intense gaze. "I understand what you're saying."

"Understanding and doing it are two very different things."

163

"Well, I don't know what else you want me to say." An edge to her words showed her frustration.

"You think I planned to say something and just expect you to fix it? How would that be fair? No, sweet, I'm a fan of teaching. I'm looking forward to teaching you this particular lesson."

Unease crept in at that, but quicker than the last time, she reminded herself that Garrison hadn't hurt her. So far, she'd enjoyed every lesson he'd given her. It gave her the courage to nod. She didn't want to do this, would prefer to not have to face her own deficits, but that wasn't how this all worked. It was like wanting to be healthy, knowing she'd feel better after working out, but facing the moment of 'I don't want to' that happened when she had to drive to the gym.

Garrison stood and took her hand, then tugged her to her feet. He stripped her quickly, making short work of the oversized shirt and leggings until she stood naked before him. He grasped her hips and set her up on the table.

Garrison captured her wrists, then pulled something from his pocket.

The jerk actually carries cuffs around with him?

She wanted to call him a pervert, but it turned out she wasn't *that* comfortable with him even still.

He hooked them around her wrists, then used the short lead on them and hooked it to something on the table.

"Does your table have bondage tie downs?"

"Of course," Garrison said. "Who would buy a table without them?"

She glanced up at the ceiling instead of responding.

"Let me try, since you don't seem talkative." He traced the small valley at the center of her stomach.

"You don't like talking about this here because it makes it real. If you're in a silly costume or in a club, that's all a game. But if you admit to wanting anything *here*, when it's just us, that's different. That isn't some fun little thing but who you *are*."

She twisted her hands until she could curl her fingers around the strap, as if that gave her any sort of control. Still, she let his assumption—no matter how right it was—go unchallenged.

"The thing is, you are who you are. Whether it's at the club, whether you're dressed in some costume, whether it's at your house or ours, you're still who you are."

"So you're a pervert all the time?" The question jumped out so fast, she jerked, as if she could catch the words and shove them back in.

He paused, his fingers at her hipbone.

Would he get angry? Had she pushed too far?

His chuckle let her breathe again. "Yeah, I really am. I don't think you mind it as much as you say, though."

Garrison slipped his fingers up her legs, but she snapped them closed. "You know, I do have straps for your thighs if you want to be difficult."

She shivered at that, at the idea of being entirely powerless before him.

"You like that idea, do you? Well, lucky for you, we can make that happen, then." Garrison disappeared for only a moment—but *boy* was it strange to lie there, naked and bound, waiting—before returning with more cuffs and a longer leash. He wrapped the fabric around her thighs, just above her knees, then hooked the lead to one. He tossed it to the other side of the table, beneath it, and hooked it to her other thigh. A few quick adjustments tightened the leash and spread her thighs out.

Air chilled her cunt and made it so she couldn't even pretend to not be incredibly turned on.

"Beautiful," Garrison mused, then grabbed a pillow from the couch to place behind her head, lifting it up so she could easily see down her front. He moved to the end of the table so he could stare over her, so he had a perfect view of her pussy. "I think you like this because you don't have to think, you don't have to worry. You don't question anything because if I want something from you, I'll damn well tell you."

She trembled, the table that had seemed chilly at first no longer so. In fact, she felt overheated, feverish.

Garrison reached out and dragged his thumb down her soaked cunt, making a soft sound of approval. He grasped both her hips, then pulled to straighten her arms and bring her to the end of the table. A quick shift and he had a chair. "So here is the deal—I like to be upfront, for you to know what's coming. I'm going to lick that pretty little cunt of yours just as long as I want—and trust me, I have great stamina."

"That doesn't sound like much of a deal."

"I'll stop when you use your safe word."

Just the thought of using it made her stomach cramp in a very bad way. It wasn't excitement—it was *fear*.

Memories came back to her, back to the start with Tanner, when she'd dared to use hers. The bite of his flogger had gone far past sexy, fun pain and into real hurt, especially when he'd hit too high, on her lower back. She'd bitten out the word—*Malibu*—but he hadn't stopped. He'd gone *harder*, as if driven forward by the realization that she'd hit her limit. She remembered the next day, the bruising, the pain. She'd learned that using her safe word only made things worse.

Garrison nipped softly at her thigh, bringing her back from that edge. "I'm going to help you learn it by licking you until you come, over and over, and I'm not going to stop until you decide using your safe word is a better choice." He lifted an eyebrow. "You could use it now if you don't want to do this at all."

She opened her mouth, but nothing came out. Besides...a few orgasms weren't so bad, right?

His lip curled into a smirk and made her doubt her answer.

Because she had a feeling she was playing a game with Garrison and she was about to lose...*badly*.

Sunny looked delicious, all spread out and at Garrison's mercy. Even if the point was a lesson—an important one—he couldn't deny that he enjoyed the hell out of the sight.

He'd talked to Connor and Trent the evening before, discussed her inability to say no in the moment, the fact that they doubted she'd use her safe word and how dangerous that could be.

The last thing any of them wanted was for her to end up enduring something that was painful just because she was afraid of telling them to stop. After everything she'd been through, Garrison didn't want to be the cause of more hurt just because he'd missed some cue of hers.

So they'd decided that this was the best option, and that Garrison was the best person to handle the lesson. Connor was intimidating, and with Trent's sadist side, they didn't want her thinking that was the reason for it.

Besides, she'd be less overwhelmed, less resistant to giving in, if it were just him.

And for his part? He had to admit that if he needed to spend hours between her pretty thighs, well, he figured that to be a day well spent.

She trembled, goosebumps on her thighs, on her arms. It was nerves, but also excitement. Her nipples were hard, calling him in, but he had a different goal.

He pulled her toward him, so she was at the end of the table, and he could sit. He might as well get comfortable, since he had a feeling the stubborn woman wouldn't break for a long while.

Which he didn't mind at all...

He ran his hands over her spread legs, then glided his thumb up her drenched sex. She stared down at him, and he brought that thumb to his lips, using his tongue to clean it.

The soft sound she let out went straight to his cock.

How could she be so enticing? She felt like a trap made just for him, like every desire he'd had, even those he couldn't have ever vocalized, all wrapped into one sensual little body.

No reason to drag things out, I guess.

He leaned in and traced her drenched folds with his tongue, enjoying the way she twitched beneath his touch, the way she shifted but couldn't escape.

After teasing her for a moment, he narrowed his focus. He slid his tongue between the hood of her clit and the nub, then brought his hand up to spread her out, to expose her.

She cried out when he blew a stream of cool air over her, but he wasn't done. Not even close. He glanced up her body, meeting her hazel eyes, then leaned down to drag his tongue right over her while their eyes were locked.

It was a power trip that nearly did him in, the way she stared, bound and at his mercy, while he tongued her as he wanted to. *Fuck.* This was what he loved, the way a woman gave in, the way he played them as he wanted to. It wasn't just sex — it was so much more because of the submission they willingly offered up to him. It was a piece of themselves that was far more precious.

Still, Garrison had to force himself back to the point at hand. He used his tongue against her swollen clit, rough and quick because the point wasn't to make this last. He wasn't edging her — she was the sort of good girl who would last as long as she needed to for praise. This was about getting her uncomfortable enough to do what she needed to.

Her first orgasm hit her quick. Her breasts lifted as she arched her back, and he was sorry he was doing this alone. He could only imagine the fun Trent would have with her in that pose.

He didn't stop — if anything, he went harder, drove her farther. She gasped, a choking sound, as he didn't give her sensitive clit a moment of rest. He took it between his lips, sucking hard, before sliding two fingers of his free hand into her tight cunt. She was snug and warm and so damned welcoming that it was damn near impossible not to sink into her.

Keep on track.

He sucked hard, and she shattered again. The metal where her cuffs were hooked to the table jingled as she yanked her hands, a desire no doubt to hold on to something, to find some control in the wash of emotions.

He gave her nothing.

Instead, he angled his fingers up, searching for her G-spot, for that place to make her see stars. It was so much easier to find when a woman was already so mindless with lust, when her cunt was swollen and eager.

Sure enough, when he brushed it, her thighs twitched and she jerked her hips. *Perfect.* Garrison focused there as he raked his teeth over her clit, knowing she was far enough gone that she'd enjoy the roughness all the more.

Her cunt squeezed down, wave after wave, and he stopped being sure when one orgasm ended and another started. He kept her at the edge, at the top of a wave that he never let crash down, that he never let her recover from.

She twisted on the table, wild, like a caught animal. "Please," she gasped out.

He paused, pulling his lips from her but brushing his thumb over her needy little clit instead, not letting up on the torment. "You know the rules, honey. You want me to stop? You use your safe word. You say *red*. Anything else is a suggestion, and I'm not feeling much like taking suggestions."

She had tears down her pinkened cheeks, looking like an absolutely beautiful mess. Her chest rose and fell in erratic motions, her entire body shaking.

Each time his thumb stroked her clit, she let out a tiny whine, but even still, she seemed unwilling to do as he'd asked.

"I know it's hard," he said before blowing another breath over her clit. "It's a scary thing to risk something that's backfired before. Am I Tanner, though?"

She shook her head.

"That's right. Have I hurt you? Have I ever not listened to your limits?" She shook her head again and again, more tears escaping her bright hazel eyes. "Who am I?"

"G-Garrison." She hiccupped at the name, but even getting that out was impressive. The girl was so far past coherent.

"Yeah, I am. And as soon as you say that safe word, I'll stop. I'll wrap you up in a blanket, let you rest. Won't that be nice?"

Everything in her expression said it would be. She wanted it so badly, written in her features, in the way she stared at him like she could make him stop with that look alone.

And she almost could. If it weren't a safety thing, if it weren't *so* important, he might have given in. Fuck knew that he would have rather stroked himself off to the sight of her, that he'd rather give her exactly what she wanted, but that was what he was trying to teach her.

Being a Dom wasn't just about what he wanted, what she wanted. It was about what she *needed*, and that was to be able to trust them with her limits.

Which meant, no matter how badly he wished he could give in, that he could be the sweet Dom he wanted to be right then, he'd do what was best for her even if he didn't much like it.

So he moved his thumb and dove back in, plunging the fingers of his other hand into her, fucking her hard with them as he tormented her clit with his tongue, his lips.

The table groaned when she came again, the short break she'd had enough to make this one worse, as if having a moment to collect herself made everything that much more intense.

Still, she was almost there — almost willing to do what terrified her. The battle was there, in every movement of her body, in the sounds she let out, the way she twisted and pulled at the binds that kept her still.

Finally, she said it. The word came out whispered, as though ripped from her. "*Red.*"

Garrison moved back immediately. He pulled open the fastenings on her thighs to free her, then reached over her to unhook where her wrists were bound to the table.

She didn't move, didn't sit up, didn't even try to close her legs.

Which was fine by Garrison. He slid his arms around her, pulling her against his chest, before moving her to the couch, in his lap. He grabbed the throw blanket and tucked it around her, unwilling to dress her or let anything else be between them.

She didn't tense, didn't pull away. He could have furthered the discussion, but given the way she cuddled against him, he had a feeling she'd understood it. Not that she'd hear anything he tried to say at the moment, anyway. She was far too deep into her own head.

So instead, he wrapped his arms around her and pressed a kiss to her head, rewarded with her letting out a tired sigh that warmed a spot on his chest.

Damn, he really didn't want this to end...

Chapter Twelve

Connor stood beside Sunny in the waiting room of the veterinary hospital.

She shifted her weight from foot to foot, ignoring the seats in favor of standing and pacing. Connor had heard from Garrison about her day, which he'd have expected to leave her settled and tired. Instead, she seemed filled with tension she had no idea what to do with.

Then again, it was probably adrenaline from her worry about Spike that gave her the rush of energy.

Connor simply stood, his arms crossed, letting Sunny move as much as she needed to. It was after hours, which meant there weren't patients there. Only the overnight staff remained, but as a professional courtesy, they'd allowed Connor to bring Sunny by.

"Breathe." Connor allowed just a bit of demand into his voice, not wanting to spook Sunny but unable to ignore how shallow her breathing had become.

She turned a sharp glare on him, which was a sure sign she wasn't working on all cylinders. He doubted she'd ever have done something so blatantly confrontational if she were.

"You're not going to make it to see Spike it you keel over here."

Sunny narrowed her eyes, but the spark of anger didn't last long. It fizzled away as quickly as it had shown up, and her shoulders fell. "Sorry."

"No reason to be sorry—being in your position would make anyone crazy."

She blew out a long, slow breath. "I just can't stop thinking about him."

"I know, darlin'. You'll get to see him in just a few, and I've already talked to the doctor a few times. He's going to be okay."

"He lost his *leg*, Connor. How is that okay?" The pain in her voice destroyed him.

Connor wanted to fix it. It was a drive inside him, something that made him want to solve whatever what was causing that sort of anguish, but there was nothing to do here. He had someone looking into Tanner, had her somewhere safe, was keeping as close an eye on Spike as possible. That was as much as he could do, and it wasn't nearly enough.

He opened his arms—an offer, not a demand—and waited for Sunny to decide if she wanted the comfort.

She came over, as if drawn in without having to think about it. It soothed him, the fact that she wasn't afraid in that moment, that she took what little he could offer.

He wrapped his arms around her, pulling her against his chest. She hugged back, grasping the back of his shirt in a tight clutch.

Damn, she fit there perfectly. No matter how many times Connor warned himself off getting attached, how many times he told himself that this was temporary, that she was clearly not sure what she wanted and that it would be stupid to go all in—moments like this undid that good advice.

"Dr. Larson?"

Connor turned at the use of his name to find a young woman standing with a door held open.

Sunny didn't pull back right away, clearly unwilling to let go of the warmth and security of the embrace, and didn't that draw Connor in even more?

"Come on, darlin'," Connor said, and shifted, leaving his arm around her shoulders.

He didn't want to lose the connection entirely, but they needed to go see Spike. He suspected that would help her anyway.

They followed the woman through the back hallways and into a large room full of kennels. A few dogs barked, rushing to the door, the ones who stayed there for boarding. Near the end, the woman stopped.

Inside the kennel, on a raised dog bed, lay Spike. He looked so different from the way he had when Connor had seen him at her house, when he'd come over and sat on his foot, then refused to move until given attention. Funny enough, Connor had loved seeing him there, had felt better about Sunny living alone after seeing the huge mastiff.

The woman gestured to the side, waving for Connor to follow. No doubt she wanted to update him on Spike's status in private, so he could relay it to Sunny on his own. He squeezed Sunny's palm before following the other woman.

A chill settled inside Sunny when she lost Connor's hand, when he followed the doctor to the side and left Sunny standing in front of the kennel with Spike.

She opened the latch on the door of the kennel, then crouched in front of the bed. Spike opened his eyes, and while he didn't move, he wagged his tail, a slow motion that showed how many painkillers he was on.

Still, she didn't touch him. She didn't want to jostle him, to cause him pain. The vet hospital reminded her too much of the times she'd ended up in the hospital and put her on edge. How often had she lied about the cause of the injuries? Had Tanner been right by her side like a doting husband after he'd caused the injuries?

Sunny held back tears, despite a sting in her eyes that told her they were there. The bandage at the end of the stump, the way he lay on his other side, the slow thud of his tail against the edge of the bed, all felt like too much.

Everything had been so simple just weeks before. She'd turned her life into a wonderful, safe little rut. She worked at the shelter, helped women, went home to Spike and silence and solace. It hadn't been exciting, but it had been good.

And now what? She'd ventured out of that rut, she'd gone to Sanctuary searching for something that had hurt her before, and look what had happened. Now she was playing with men she had no business messing with, she'd had to take time off her job, and Spike was here injured and she had only herself to blame.

If she had just stayed put, would it have happened? She wouldn't have been out with Kat, so maybe she'd have been able to stop it.

A touch to her shoulder made her jump, but Connor's rough, deep voice calmed her. "Just me, darlin'."

"What did she say?" Sunny nodded toward the woman.

"He's doing well."

"He doesn't look good."

Connor crouched beside her. "He's on a lot of medication to keep his pain levels under control. They're going to make him tired."

Sunny wanted to reach out, but something stopped her.

Connor grasped her wrist, then made her reach out and set her hand on Spike's head. The dog's tail sped, a soft whine leaving him as if that was exactly what he'd wanted.

And there went her ability to keep the tears in. Sunny leaned in and pressed her face to Spike's, digging her fingers into his fur. He didn't smell like him, but like a hospital — like antiseptic and cleaning agents.

After a moment, she shifted, the ground hard and uncomfortable.

Connor moved, sitting himself on the ground, then set his hand on her hips and guided her to his lap. It *was* more comfortable, she had to admit, and she was close enough in the small kennel to still reach Spike.

"He'll be okay," Connor said.

"What kind of life will he have now? I never should have gone anywhere."

Connor ran his hand up and down her back in a steady motion. "If you had been there, it wouldn't have stopped this. It would just mean you might be in a hospital or worse along with him. Do you really think that would have made things better?"

But she *did* think that.

He sighed and shifted his hand to the back of her neck, using his thumb to rub at the tense muscles there. "Since you don't seem to understand that, let me make it clear. It wouldn't have changed a thing, other than you might not be here to take care of Spike afterward. And if he could talk, he would have said that he did exactly what he was meant to do and doesn't regret it a bit. Look at him, Sunny, he's happy as hell to see you. You think he'd have wanted to wake up and never see you again?"

That hit her hard, the thought of Spike having nowhere to go, of ending up in a shelter alone, waiting for her to come back and not understanding that she wouldn't ever.

She shivered, a small, hiccupped gasp as she struggled to get her tears under control. "I just don't like that he's paying the price for me."

"Because you don't think you're worth it."

And boy did *that* dig deep. It was true. The memory of all the things Tanner had told her, the times when he'd torn her down, all swamped her. The words he'd said, the ones that had over time etched so deeply into her that she couldn't ignore them — they all swirled around inside her.

She'd brought Spike home because he needed a place, because she'd fallen for him instantly upon seeing how scary he looked, how no one else would give him a chance, and now he was suffering, all because of her.

Connor made a soft, unhappy sound in the back of his throat. "You are such a mess, darlin'. You sure let that asshole crawl into your head and haven't quite gotten him out yet, have you?" He pressed his thumb down to her upper back, and despite the frustration and upset inside her, he managed to ease some of it.

She pulled in a deep breath, and when Connor shifted, she frowned. He was sitting on the hard concrete, with her in his lap, in a kennel that was probably not nearly large enough for a dog Spike's size and a man Connor's. "We can go," she said, and went to rise.

He wrapped an arm around her, keeping her still. "I don't think so, darlin'. You're not nearly done here."

"But you're on the ground."

"And I'll sit here until well after my ass falls asleep. I know you ain't done, that you want to visit longer, so we'll stay just as long as we need to."

She twisted to meet his gaze, expecting to find annoyance there. Tanner wouldn't have been willing to just wait here, to let her take as much time as she'd wanted. Hell, Tanner wouldn't have even gone to such a place with her, and if he had to, if it was the sort of thing that was to keep up appearances, he'd have made her pay for it later.

Connor appeared one hundred percent fine with spending hours there, sitting on a hard concrete floor, if it made her happy.

Instead of arguing with him — and part of her sure wanted to do that — she accepted his words at face value. She turned back toward Spike and settled in so she could spend just as much time as she wanted there.

* * * *

Sunny was beyond exhausted the next morning. That seemed her normal state these days. She'd slept in Garrison's bed after getting back from the vet hospital, and while he didn't crawl in when she'd lain down, and he was gone when she'd woken, she recalled his arm wrapped around her in the middle of the night. The memory was fuzzy, but she had a faded memory of curling against him, of snuggling into the warmth of his bare chest.

Something about saying her safe word the day before had ripped open a twisted wound she'd had and let it finally heal right.

She'd managed to tell him no in an absolute way and he'd *listened.* He'd stopped immediately, just as he'd said he would. It helped soothe her fears, helped to quiet the memories of the times she'd used a safe word and had it ignored.

Even with that, though, she'd tried her best to keep her distance from the men once she'd woken. Despite the house not being huge, it wasn't that hard to do so. The men seemed to work in shifts, with two being gone and one remaining there. They'd left her be for the most part, other than ensuring she ate. They seemed to be trying to make sure she had the ability to reach out if she chose but wouldn't feel crowded. It had left her hiding in Garrison's room the majority of the day.

And her company for today? The most confusing of the three men she'd become entangled with — *Trent.*

He was the funniest, the most-easy going in so many ways, but then she remembered the way his eyes had lit up when he'd dug his nails into her nipples — or worse, the way she'd responded — and she felt as though she shouldn't trust him.

A knock on the door made her jump, but after pulling at her shirt again, she called for him to enter.

Sure enough, Trent opened the door, looking just as sinful as he always did. He was dressed casually, with jeans and a T-shirt, his hair pushed back but messy. His smirk alone promised things she *knew* he could deliver.

"Hey there. You done hiding? Because I'm hungry."

The mention of food made her think back to the kitchen table, to how Garrison had made her come over and over again, and her cheeks heated at the memory.

"Oh, and to think I missed it," Trent said as if he could read her mind. "You know, one time I'm going to *love* having guests over and watching you turn that same shade of red when we all sit down at that table."

Okay, so maybe he could guess her line of thought…

"I'm not hiding," she said instead of talking about what he'd said.

"Sure, you are. Unfortunately for you, I'm in charge, so come on — we'll eat in the back yard. We don't have the view you do at your place, but it'll work."

Sunny considered arguing. She wanted to stay in the room, to not go anywhere or see anyone. Garrison's lesson came back to her, the fact that she *could* speak up. She could voice her opinion, even if it wasn't something they'd like.

Her voice broke when she tried, cracking like a prepubescent boy, but she got the words out. "Why do I have to go outside?"

Trent didn't look mad — in fact, his smile widened. "What do you know? Garrison's lesson actually sank in. Well, honey, you've been in here alone for hours, which gave you *more* than enough time to sort out whatever is in your head. If it isn't any better by now, it means you might need some help with it. You like the sky, and you need to eat, so I figured eating outside would relax you."

She furrowed her eyebrows. "But I thought speaking up would mean you'd listen."

"I did listen. Listening doesn't mean you'll automatically get what you want. It means I'll hear you out, I'll explain myself, and sometimes I'll change my mind. This time, though? Nope. Come on."

She walked past him, her bare feet against the tile floors, and he smacked her ass as she passed.

The yelp she released was embarrassing, but not as bad as the way her blood heated. Garrison had turned her inside out the day before, making her come so many times that she'd lost count, yet here she was getting ready again for Trent?

What the hell was wrong with her? She had *never* wanted sex in this way before.

Instead of voicing that, she stopped in the kitchen, ready to help put together a meal. When living with Tanner, he'd never done things for her. He'd expected her to serve him, for her to do all the work.

"Out." Trent pointed to the back slider before picking up two already made plates and balancing them in his arms.

Sunny opened the back door, thankful to find a lovely view and a comfortable seating area. The fence was made of wood, which offered privacy, even though the neighbors were still a good distance away. The house didn't face the sunset, but the mountain ranges in the distance and the Joshua trees that sat just outside the small patio made up for it.

When she sat, Trent took the spot just to the side of her and placed her food in her lap.

She peered down, then couldn't stop her laugh.

It was a peanut butter and jelly sandwich.

And not even a particularly well-made one... Part of the bread was torn as if the peanut butter had been spread aggressively, and jelly dripped over the edge.

"I have skills," Trent said as he picked up his own sandwich, "but cooking isn't one of them."

Sunny didn't bother to hide her laughter, especially when Trent didn't look the least bit ashamed of his poor culinary showing. His reaction was odd for her.

Tanner had exploded at the mere thought that he had any flaws. She still recalled when he'd tried to put together a shelf one time, when he'd skipped steps on it accidently and ended up with the entire thing crooked. Sunny breathed through the memory of his reaction, at how he'd somehow made it her fault and how he'd never been willing to see himself as anything less than perfect.

So the fact Trent could so obviously be terrible at cooking, with the evidence there, with him admitting his failures, while not seeming to care at all, felt strange.

They ate the food in silence, since even badly made, a PB&J sandwich tasted pretty much the same as any other. The evening passed, the day passing to night and the light disappearing.

Once the sun had set and it was darker out, she found it easier to say the things to him that she needed to. "You confuse me."

"Oh? Usually people say I'm simple, and they don't mean it as a compliment."

He took her empty plate and set it on top of his, then placed both on the table.

"You can be so lighthearted sometimes but intense others."

"And by intense, you mean that I'm a sadist, right?"

She shifted, the word like an ugly beast who was so close, snarling and dangerous.

He nodded, not trying to touch her or pull an answer from her. Then again, he could figure it out, couldn't he? "I figured as much."

Sunny closed her eyes, pulling together the little shreds of worry until they made something almost coherent. "Tanner, my ex, he liked to hurt me."

"I know."

"So aren't you basically the same as him?" She asked the question so softly, she wasn't sure he could hear her at first. Even though she'd reached a point where she didn't think he'd haul off and hurt her for it, the question was an ugly one. It was one she *knew* he wouldn't react well to. She'd essentially said he was the same as her abusive ex. No man, even the bad ones, wanted to hear that.

Still, it was one she needed to understand, one she needed an answer to before she could truly trust him, before she could let go of that lingering fear inside her.

"No, I'm not the same as him." Trent's voice was careful, and if he was offended, he didn't show it.

"But you like what he liked. How is that different? It didn't start out bad with Tanner either, so how do I know it won't go that way with you? How do I know it wouldn't keep getting worse until I'm in the same exact place again?"

Trent leaned back, as if that would calm down the conversation. "I like causing pain that my partner *enjoys*. That's the difference, honey. If you didn't like it, not only would I not do it, because I'm not a monster, but I wouldn't enjoy it, either. I like putting the clamps on you because you get wet, and you make these little excited sounds, and it is feeding some need inside you that was starving before. It's taking care of you."

She shook her head. "I don't *need* that."

"You sure? Because you responded beautifully, like you'd been missing it."

"I didn't like what Tanner did," she snapped. Trent's words were like a weapon that hurt.

Trent twisted to look at her. "I never said you did. Just because you like pain, because you crave it, doesn't mean what that asshole did was okay. It doesn't mean you wanted *that*. I'm not blaming you or saying you asked for it. There's a difference."

"I don't understand how it's different," she whispered.

"Sex and rape are different, aren't they? Same basic physical mechanics, but consent changes them from one thing to another. Pain isn't any different. You can need it and love it when it's from someone you trust but hate it when it's a violation, when it's against your will."

She looked away, trying to process what he'd said. It made sense, somehow, but she struggled to really believe it. Years of being broken down, of having someone twist her view of sex and consent, made it difficult to accept his point.

"How about I show you?"

Fear crept along the edges of her desire, waiting to strike, to turn the moment to panic, but she wouldn't let it. She nodded, because even though she didn't understand it, even though she told herself it was stupid, she did trust him.

Trent grasped her wrist to pull her over, and she expected him to bring her into his lap. Instead, he shifted her around so she was on her knees, lengthwise on the couch. A hand to her shoulder blades pressed her down until her chest hit the cushions, and he stretched her arms forward. Those cuffs, still on her from the day before, attached to the metal on the armrest of the couch. It occurred to her that she'd not removed them, and she refused to think about why.

He pulled her leggings down, then pushed up the shirt to expose her ass. It felt far more sinister than it had when Garrison had stripped her the day before.

"Now, you tell me how you're doing — if it's too much or not enough."

"Aren't you supposed to know that?"

"Again, honey, as I keep telling you, I'm not a mind reader."

She shifted, then placed her forehead against the cushion and tried to relax.

Trent rubbed his hand over her ass, his warm palm waking up her senses. It reminded her of how he'd swatted her ass as she'd walked by earlier, but she had a feeling that wasn't *close* to what was about to come.

Tanner hadn't done this to her. He wasn't a spanking sort of man, because his punishments had always been more painful. They hadn't been planned. He hadn't told her what was to come. They'd been explosions of anger and violence, which was entirely different from this.

"Am I supposed to count or something?" she asked, an uncomfortable fear inside her of doing something wrong.

"Nope. Just relax and enjoy."

Enjoy? She snorted.

"You have been spending too much time with Connor, because you sound *exactly* like him," Trent said before his hand left.

The first strike of his palm against her was shocking. It wasn't *that* hard, but left a sting behind, silencing anything she might have said.

She went to rise, an automatic reaction, but Trent shifted and set a hand on her back to keep her still before spanking her again.

He changed spots, switched from one cheek to the other, but his rhythm didn't change. Worse, each time he struck, that burn increased, adding together, building.

And before Sunny knew it, the sensation morphed to something she hadn't expected — *pleasure*.

Sure, it still hurt. She knew it each time his hand connected, she jerked at each hit, but instead of her body registering it as bad, her endorphins made her let out a throaty moan.

"Oh, I like that sound," Trent said, stilling so he could rub across her sore ass.

"It is over?" she asked, her own disappointment at the idea a shock to her.

"Not even close. I want to see more of those pretty tears from your eyes — I want you a crying mess before I fuck you."

That should have terrified her, the fact that he so casually mentioned wanting to make her cry, but the terror didn't come.

She wanted what he said, too.

So when Trent pulled his hand from her, she was ready. He went harder, as if the last had been a warmup. Each hit was rougher, but still careful, still seeming to strike exactly where he'd meant to. Her skin felt on fire, and her cunt was so wet, it made her thighs sticky.

She wanted to feel him inside her, she wanted him to take her, to help her with the lust he'd brought to life.

But she also didn't want this to stop.

He let go of her back and caught her hair in his grip, pulling so her head raised, just like he had the last time he'd taken her, back at the club.

"We'll use a ring gag some time, let me spank your sexy ass while Connor gags you with his cock. I don't trust you not to bite, not when I turn you wild like this."

She parted her lips as though Connor were there, and also because she couldn't seem to draw enough breath. There was no shielding her face against the cushion, no pretending this was nothing.

It was like with each hit, Trent stole her ability to hide. He tore down every defense she'd built, shattered her illusions, making her feel that he actually saw *her* in a way no one else had.

She cried out, so close to release it was infuriating.

"You're lucky you're so sweet," Trent said, voice rough. "Because I would *love* to keep you on this edge. I want to rev you up but not let you come for hours, just toy with you until you're *begging* to get off but not let you. Leave you a trembling mess, your pussy soaked and empty and so damned needy."

She curled her fingers, grasping the edge of the couch, the idea *horrible* yet enticing. She pictured it, thought about how it felt now, so quickly, and how much worse it would be if he did this for hours, if she was unsatisfied and he refused to let her have the relief she needed.

It sounded *amazing*.

"Fortunately for you, I don't have the patience for that, not yet, not when your cunt is so damned tight and warm."

He pressed her chest down more, so she arched her back, then his next hit didn't land on her ass. Instead, he aimed lower, and his fingers struck her clit.

The world exploded around her, the pain sparking through her body and searing every nerve, the hit shocking in its intensity.

"Fuck, I like that sound."

She hadn't realized she'd even made a sound, but before she knew it, she'd spread her knees an inch or two as if to plead for another strike.

"More? Yeah, you are so my sort of girl. Your needy little clit wants more? Of course it does." He repeated the action, and her new stance made him able to strike harder.

She didn't hide how loud she was — she couldn't. The sound was forced from her, an endless stream of moans and cries. Wetness tracking down her cheeks said he'd been right, that he'd pulled tears from her.

No doubt she looked like a disaster, but when he shifted, when she turned to catch sight of his face, his expression held nothing but adoration, as if she'd never been more beautiful.

Not that it stopped from him turning back and landing another hit.

She dangled on that precipice, her release so close that her cunt pulsed.

He grabbed her hips and flipped her, the movement so fast it drew a surprised yelp from her.

When her ass hit the couch and even that made her whimper, she knew she'd struggle to sit later.

Worth it.

He reached into his pocket to withdraw a condom before he undid his pants. The way he pulled his belt free caught her attention.

Trent grinned, folding the belt over in his grip, then smacking it against his other palm. "Oh, sweet, you're *begging* for it, aren't you? You're not ready for this, but you will be — promise."

Disappointment swamped her, a stark change from the last time she'd seen one of them handle a belt, when she'd felt only fear.

Trent shoved his jeans off, then knelt on the couch between her thighs. "Don't worry, I bet I can keep you from missing that too much." He grasped her hips and yanked her forward so her ass was off the couch, almost in his lap. He fit his shaft against her pussy, then sank into her, filling her. The position was strange, making her head lower than her center. He grabbed a pillow from the couch and shoved it beneath her hips to help keep her there, then set one leg on his shoulder. Her other, he pushed out to the side and up.

It spread her obscenely, left her legs wide open and gave him a perfect view of where his cock spread her pussy.

That smirk of his said he liked the view.

"Garrison was right — your cunt is a thing of beauty."

She was ready to say something — what, she wasn't sure — but he brought his hand in and *flicked* her exposed clit before she could.

When he'd spanked her, it had still been hidden a bit by her folds. This position gave him total access, and even though the hit wasn't hard, it was more direct.

She twisted, but he used his other hand to hold her thigh before he thrust into her.

He fucked her hard, moving from flicks — they required more focus — back to slaps against the most sensitive place on her aching body.

The friction from his cock, each shocking strike of his fingers to her clit, blurred everything.

It drove her so far over the edge of sanity that by the time she came, it was like *nothing* she'd ever experienced. It was so much more than just a release, feeling as though he'd dug inside her and yanked out so much repression, so many things she'd hidden and ignored.

Even as she came, as she bucked from the intensity, he didn't stop plunging his hard cock into her. He used her to get off, to please himself, and that made it all even better, kept the waves of pleasure cresting over her, kept her body from recovering.

He came, his fingers digging into her thigh just as he set his thumb against her sore and abused clit and pressed hard, an almost agonizingly intense feeling that made her wonder if a woman could actually pass out from this sort of thing. It seemed lightening arced across her vision, everything around her shorting out, and even the twitch of his cock, the way he pressed against her with short, hard little thrusts, like he wanted to make sure he came as deep as possible inside her, was too much.

When she finally came down, when she pulled in gasping breaths and opened her eyes, Trent was panting above her.

And his smile?

How a man could do *that* to her and still smile so sweetly, well, she'd never understand.

But she wouldn't mind testing it again…

Chapter Thirteen

Kat smiled as she carried in a tray of drinks, all balanced perfectly on her hand.

"Impressive," Garrison said.

Kat beamed at the praise and spun. "I was a waitress to put myself through school. There are some skills that just never quite go away."

Their banter didn't bother Sunny, but maybe that was because Garrison's arm was draped around Sunny, and she didn't feel any sort of sexual tension between Kat and the men. Instead, Kat seemed like the little sister she liked to say she was.

Her house was what Sunny would have expected upon meeting the woman — small, chaotic yet somehow welcoming. It was one side of a duplex in a complex with perfectly manicured lawns, despite how expensive those were to maintain in the desert. Even though it was much smaller than where Sunny lived, she'd bet it cost a bundle more given the location in a tourist area.

"Did you decide on your costume for next month?" Kat asked as she moved the cups from the tray to the table.

Sunny peered at Connor, uneasy with the question. The next costume night was weeks away, and she hadn't discussed anything about a future with the men. She couldn't deny that the last few days had been…interesting.

That's an understatement.

In reality, they'd been amazing. Confusing and scary at times, sure, but also absolutely life-changing. She'd found a contentment and happiness she'd had no idea could exist in her life anymore. She'd relaxed, found solace in leaning against Garrison as he read in the evening, or going on walks with Trent when he often spoke almost nonstop, letting her get a good view into his mind, or when Connor would put on an animal documentary and pull Sunny into his lap.

She'd slid into their home and their lives with so little trouble, and while she enjoyed being there, she wasn't sure what that meant long term.

What would happen when they got word back to discover that Tanner was right where he'd been before?

It was a question that had kept Sunny up at night. Right now, things were simple. She stayed with them out of a concern for her safety. It was like wearing the costume to Sanctuary — it wasn't real.

So when the risk passed, when this wasn't a temporary thing they were doing, could she accept it as real? Could she decide to stay, to continue something with the men if it were just them?

A squeeze to her side brought her attention to Garrison, who looked at her with his eyebrow lifted.

All three of the men were too observant, but Garrison was somehow the worst for it. He caught every stray thought of hers and had claimed the other night that they ran across her features like a movie.

Instead of explaining anything that was in her head — she didn't want to have that conversation at all, but for sure not in front of Kat — she gave him a half-hearted smile.

He pressed his lips together but nodded, as if to tell her he got what she was saying, even if he didn't like it.

Kat sat on the floor in front of the coffee table, her glass between her palms.

Whatever Kat had concocted was overly sweet, yet kicked Sunny in the stomach when she swallowed from all the liquor.

Yep, it was exactly like Kat herself. Sunny coughed for a moment after taking a sip.

"I like to make my drinks strong," Kat said. "We can't have alcohol at Sanctuary, so when people come over, I feel like we need to make up for that."

Connor sniffed at his cup, then shook his head and set it down. "We need a designated driver, and it looks like that's me."

Kat put her finger on the extra drink she'd set on the table and pushed it toward him, the glass having a blue rim unlike the other. "While I'm not anywhere close to one, I can make a virgin. I figured one of you would be the responsible one instead of just crashing here for the night, so I was prepared."

"You don't have nearly enough room for us to crash here," Trent pointed out as he glanced around her tiny living room.

"Sure I do. Think of it like a game where you fit the boxes together. Besides, if you all manage to fit on a bed, I'm sure you could make it work."

And that time it wasn't the alcohol that made Sunny choke.

Yes, she was aware that Kat knew she was sleeping with the men. She'd even played with them in the club in public. However, knowing something and saying it out loud were two very different things.

Garrison thumped his hand against her back to help her cough up the alcohol she'd inhaled at Kat's comment, while Connor gave the other woman a glare.

"You can't be mad," Kat said, a pout to her voice. "That was funny."

"You're pushing your luck," Connor warned.

"I'm not yours, and we aren't at the club, so you can't do anything to me."

"But Dominants hold grudges."

"So do I."

Sunny held her breath, an uncomfortable fear inside her. It was a *bad* idea for subs to stand up to Doms. It had never ended well for her, and even though she knew Connor, even though she knew he wouldn't really hurt Kat, some old part of her screamed at her friend to be quiet.

"It's fine," Sunny rushed out through her fear-narrowed throat. "It's really okay. I'm not upset."

Kat looked over, her smile fading. "You don't have to worry," Kat said. "We were just playing around."

Garrison wrapped his fingers around Sunny's hand, and for the first time, she realized she was shaking.

Which was strange, since she hadn't had such a bad reaction to the men in a while. Then again, she'd always been more protective over others than she was about herself.

Sunny took a deep breath then let it out slowly, trying to let the tension drift away with it. "In my experience, subs and Doms don't joke together."

"Well, no one let Toya know that, because if she implements that rule, I'm going to be in big trouble," Kat said, her smirk returning to her pink lips. "Besides, Connor talks a big game, but he can't really do anything to me. Pity for him, I'm one of the few subs who doesn't fall for his whole rough, scary Dom thing. I know he is really just a big softie."

Garrison spoke up next. "You know, I talk to Bradley on occasion."

The temperature in the room dropped a few degrees, the name alone changing the entire tone.

Who's Bradley? Is he dangerous? Garrison wouldn't really threaten Kat with calling someone who would hurt her, right?

As soon as the thought came to Sunny, she dismissed it. There was no chance of that. Garrison, along with the others, worked hard to keep women safe, worked with the shelter to help them. He wouldn't put one in danger on purpose.

Kat dropped her gaze to her glass. "Yeah, Connor is a softie, but you? You're mean as they come. I'll be good."

Garrison let out a chuckle, as if the woman's sullen compliance were funny. Then again, Kat looked like she'd put herself on a leash, not like she was really upset.

It still made her wonder what had happened to get Kat to respond like that...

Two hours later, the men were cleaning the kitchen after Kat and Sunny had cooked dinner. They'd all eaten in the living room, with Kat again on the floor since there weren't enough seats. They'd had spaghetti, which worked well, because as it turned out Kat wasn't the best cook, and it was hard to ruin spaghetti and premade garlic bread.

"You look good," Kat said as they sat in the small back yard that seemed to be shared between four of the duplexes. "Then again, a week of amazing sex will do that to a girl."

The way Kat so openly said these things drew a heat to Sunny's cheeks, but something about the other woman's openness made it easier to talk to her. "Who's Bradley?"

"Oh, *that*." Kat let out a sigh. "It's old history— nothing more."

"He isn't dangerous, right?"

Kat shook her head. "Heavens no. Do you really think Garrison would call someone who was dangerous? No, it's nothing like that. Bradley is my...well, ex seems too simple. Things didn't work out, but some of the Doms in Sanctuary are worse than teenaged girls with their romantic ideas. Garrison thinks that if I wasn't so hardheaded, I'd get back together with Bradley and end up with this entire happy life."

Sunny frowned. "But when you came over that day, you said if you had a chance at what I had, you wouldn't let it go."

"Yep."

Sunny pressed the topic. "So, if that's what you think, why not take the chance?"

Kat sighed and sat back on the swing, making it move more as she lifted her feet to the edge of it. "Because what you have is simple. It works. Trust me, Bradley is anything but simple." When Sunny went to say more, Kat cut her off. "I really don't want to go any more into it. It's bad enough that everyone else at Sanctuary knows all about it. I really don't want to have to recall it all now. That's the bad thing about the club — everyone is in everyone else's business. I guess that's what happens when people see each other's genitals — we feel entitled to dig into their lives. Just trust me — there are problems between Bradley and me that can't be solved."

Sunny stared at Kat, at the hurt woman beneath the exterior she used, the smiles and the jokes and the sharp eyeliner, and she understood. She'd seen people hide from the things they didn't want to face for long enough to recognize it.

Instead of saying anything else, Sunny pulled Kat into a hug. Sometimes that was what a person really needed.

* * * *

Garrison smiled at Sunny as she stumbled down the hallway after changing into one of his shirts. The girl was tiny, so it wasn't a shock she might not hold her alcohol all that well. He got the sense she was a woman not used to drinking anyway.

He doubted she liked to have her senses dulled at all.

She wasn't incoherent, but rather at the lovely, buzzed stage when the alcohol managed to numb worries and dull the sharp edges people had to live with. It meant she smiled, had leaned against Trent the whole drive home, and had a hint of pink across her cheeks.

She stilled at the end of the hallway, her sexy legs showing from the edge of the shirt. Hesitation showed on her features, a look that said she wasn't sure what he wanted from her.

Lucky for her, he was a man who didn't mind making that clear. Garrison crooked his finger to get her to approach.

Sunny came forward, and she melted against him when he kissed her. He tasted the fruit juice from her lips and the rum on her breath.

It was a combination more intoxicating than even Kat's drinks.

"Did you have fun tonight?" he asked her when he pulled away.

Sunny nodded. "I haven't had a lot of friends, and I really like Kat."

"She's something, all right." He pulled her toward the couch.

"Have you ever...?" Sunny didn't finish the question, but she didn't need to.

Garrison had been around long enough to see this plenty of times. People new to the scene tended to have very strict ideas of what was okay and what wasn't. They also tended to be more possessive, which meant when joining such a community, they struggled to understand or accept that casual sex happened.

"Yes," Garrison admitted. "Years ago. It was never serious."

"Why not?"

Garrison pulled her into his lap on the couch. "Because Kat is trouble." After chuckling at himself, he continued. "Kat is a brat through and through. She enjoys annoying her Doms—pushing them. That isn't my sort of thing, nor is it for Connor or Trent. We don't need doormats, but we also don't want to have to fight every day with a sub."

She shifted, as if she wasn't sure she liked his answer.

"Does that bother you, sweet?"

"No."

He lifted his eyebrow at her obvious lie, an offer for her to rethink her response.

She let out a sigh. "I don't know—maybe a little. She's my friend, and you're my..."

She tripped over a title, and it made Garrison chuckle. It was something she'd made clear she was trying very hard not to think about.

Just what were they to her?

"We're your what?"

She offered him a sharp look, one aided by the alcohol no doubt as she never gave him such glares when sober. Still, she answered him. "I guess I don't know. I just know that I don't like the idea of you with her."

"Well, as I said, it was years ago. We're just friends now."

She snuggled against his chest, her hair smelling of peaches like the shampoo she used, something floral he'd ended up a huge fan of.

The moment was sweet, peaceful, and yet Garrison couldn't stop himself from what he needed to ask, to hear. "What do you want us to be?"

"Hmm?" she asked, her voice clouded in sleep, as if she were already halfway there.

"You don't know what we are, and that's fine, but what do you want us to be? What are you hoping for here? After we know you're safe, after we deal with your intruder and you can go home, what do you want?"

She didn't move or answer for a long moment, and Garrison had to wonder if she'd fallen asleep. *That's a pretty good way to get out of answering his question, isn't it?*

Except she did answer eventually, her voice quiet. "I don't know. I was thinking about that when we were at Kat's."

"And?"

Her breath was soft and warm against his chest. "I've liked being here, with you guys, but I don't know if I can do that for real."

"Why not?"

"Because it isn't who I planned on being. After I left Tanner, when I got my life back on track, I swore I'd never be helpless again, that I'd never let a man control me again. Even though I really have enjoyed being here, being with you, I don't know if I could turn my back on who I set out to be."

Garrison didn't care for her answer. He wanted to argue with her, to explain to her that that was just her past talking, her fears. He wanted to ask her if she would really give up what she wanted because of what someone else had done to her.

He didn't say any of that, though. The reality was that people had to come to their own conclusions. They had to make their own decisions, even when he knew they were the wrong ones.

So instead, he ran his fingers through her hair and hoped he could pick himself back up when she left and tore him apart.

Because she seemed determined to do just that.

* * * *

Connor leaned against the counter as he sipped his cup of tea. He'd managed to get someone else to cover his shifts for the day, since he'd worked nearly all the last two and hadn't gotten much time alone with Sunny.

She seemed to be settling in well.

Too well, probably.

This would all come to an end soon, and when it did?

Connor wasn't sure how he was going to let her go, how he was going to go back to the life he'd had before she'd walked into it.

It felt like spending a few weeks filthy stinkin' rich, then having to go back to poverty, like experiencing something he wanted but knowing he couldn't keep it.

Maybe she'll stay...

Maybe. He couldn't quite trust that, though.

Trent and Garrison had headed to work, leaving Connor alone to keep an eye on Sunny. It also left him with the chance to tell her what they'd learned from their friend, Mitch, who was looking into Tanner.

The water turned off in the hall bathroom, and he groaned as he thought about how the water from her shower would follow the curves of her body, going over her navel, her hip bones.

Lucky droplets...

The door didn't open for another ten minutes or so, and the way her hair was braided back told him why. He'd imagine that would take quite a bit of work, between drying it and forcing the waves into compliance.

She seemed to keep it tied back often, which disappointed him. He rather liked running his fingers through the soft strands.

She had a robe wrapped around her, a fluffy, white one they'd probably stolen from a hotel at some point, and it reminded him of the fox costume she'd worn that first night.

Innocent and sweet and tempting.

She locked eyes with him, then froze.

Connor tried to offer a reassuring smile, then gestured toward the living room.

Because she had to wash her leggings each evening, she had little to wear except the robe or more shirts of theirs during the day. Not that he minded. He fucking loved how she looked in his clothes, the way they hung loose on her, the intense feeling of possessiveness that washed over him when he spotted her like that. They'd have gotten her more clothing, but she hadn't wanted them to. None of them wanted her to go back to her place until they knew more, and the idea of buying anything had seemed too much for Sunny.

Not that Connor would complain about her not having much to wear...

Sunny did as he'd said—or rather, as he'd implied. It was one of the things that had drawn him the most. The girl was so beautifully, naturally submissive. He wanted peace in his life and home, and if there was one thing Sunny brought, that was it. From the moment she'd gotten there, it seemed the entire house had let out one big exhalation, as if they all could relax in a way they hadn't before.

She pulled the edges of the robe together, then sat on the couch.

"I heard back from Mitch, the private investigator in Utah."

She sat up straight, fingers in her robe tightening until her knuckles turned white.

"Easy, darlin'," he rumbled out. "Take a breath." He waited until she did before he went on. "Records don't show Tanner on any flights, and according to his job, he hasn't missed a day of work in years. The break-in happened Sunday night, and there's no way he could have done that and driven back in time for work Monday."

Sunny nodded. "And we're sure he's there, now? That he couldn't be here?"

"Mitch pretended to be delivering something, went right up to his door and knocked. Tanner answered, accepted the package. It looks like this wasn't him."

Sunny took a big breath, almost a gasp, as if her shallow little ones before hadn't done the trick.

And, damn, Connor liked that. He liked being able to give her good news for once, to offer her up a sliver of the peace she'd given him.

"Thank you," she whispered.

"Course. The police also checked in. There have been some other break-ins around town lately, and they think it's the same people. There's no match to the blood at the scene, but they've got it for when they catch a suspect."

"So, it's over?"

"Seems that way." Connor hated saying those words. He wanted her safe, of course, but he didn't much like the idea of letting her walk out, of letting her go back to her own place. Without the fear that it could be Tanner there, Sunny would have no reason to stay at their place any longer.

She dropped her hands to her lap. "I'm really sorry about all this. I know I sort of messed up your lives."

"You didn't mess up anything." He kept the fact that she'd improved their lives to himself.

Sunny was the sort likely to bolt, and he didn't want her feeling trapped, or like there were expectations on her. She'd take that as a chain she didn't want.

"I did. You expected a quick lay with some floozy fox at a dress-up party, then all *this* happened."

Connor reached over and took her hand, then pulled her into his lap. Her thighs spread around his waist without hesitation, and it made her robe gape open, giving him a peek at her sweet cunt since she was naked beneath. "You have been worth every damn inconvenience, darlin'."

The set of her lips said she didn't believe it. "You could do better," she said.

"Better than a sexy, sweet little sub like you? Not so sure about that."

"Better than some broken girl who jumps at her own shadow and makes you all ride in to save the day. Better than a someone who doesn't know much about the lifestyle, who you have to constantly correct and teach."

The way she spoke told Connor one thing for sure.

She wasn't anywhere *close* to being done listing her faults.

Connor grasped the edges of her robe, and she set her hands there to keep it closed. His lifted eyebrow — a moment of 'are you sure you want to stop me?' — gave her a chance to reconsider. He preferred allowing a woman to make her own choices instead of trying to force a point.

She dropped her hands, letting Connor take the robe off her and toss it onto the couch.

It left her bare in his lap — which was a hell of a good look for her. Her perfect little breasts were tipped with nipples that had already responded, telling him again how much she enjoyed being exposed, even if she wanted to hate it. Her ribcage went to a narrow waist and hips made for his hands. The dark hair at her cunt and her toned thighs spread around him.

"There isn't a single thing about you I'd change." He brushed his thumb against her nipple, enjoying the tremble that worked its way through her shoulders and down her back. "I love how responsive you are. You just light up at any touch. You're soft in all the best places" — he cupped her breast — "but I've seen you show how dammed tough you are, too. And, if you think we have any problem teaching you, you ain't been paying attention. I will never get tired of training you, darlin'." That twang to his voice came back stronger, as it always did when he got this turned on, when he saw what he wanted and could only think of how to get it.

She wore a mask of disbelief, of a woman who *wanted* to believe but couldn't. It was borne of the years with her ex, where he'd torn her down for fun.

Those sorts of doubts didn't go away in a few weeks' time. It would take years to replace them with better thoughts.

Years I want to have.

Connor undid his pants and pulled his cock free. It rested against his lower stomach, between them, and she stared at it with a hunger that excited him.

"I love the way you're shy but so damned passionate. I love how you want me, how you're a glutton for what I can give you, but you're still sweet."

She reached for him, but he clicked his tongue.

"Don't think so, girlie. We have a discussion to finish."

She narrowed her eyes and *pouted* at him. "You can't expect a conversation now."

"You tired of hearing me talking?"

She nodded.

"Fine." He gave her a smile when she sat up. *Does the poor girl think she's won?* "Then *you* do the talking."

Ah, there it was, the way her confidence crumbled. She must have just realized she might have bitten off more than she could chew. "What do you mean?"

"If my voice doesn't please you, well, I guess you'll have to do it. You need to tell me all the reasons we like having you around."

Pink colored her cheeks, and Connor didn't bother to hide his chuckle. He could have said he'd whip her, and he'd bet she'd have reacted to it better.

"You're kidding, right?"

"I don't kid. Even if you don't believe it, even if you don't think we're right, I want you to repeat all those things we've said to you. I want you to say all that praise we've given you, so I know you've been listening."

She crossed her arms, and it made her breasts push together in an altogether alluring way.

He could understand Trent's obsession, he supposed.

Connor pulled a condom from the pocket of his jeans.

"Do you three carry those around all the time?" she asked, the edge of attitude in her tone telling him that was as disrespectful as she was willing to get.

"Only when we have pretty little subs in the house. What can I say? I don't want to have to go very far when I want inside you."

The lines etched in her forehead were absolutely charming. She probably wanted to be mad but couldn't quite manage it.

"I still don't know why you think this is going to work," she said.

"I figured you would have learned when playing with Garrison not to doubt us. I am amazingly inventive."

She pressed her lips together. Had she just realized that perhaps challenging a Dominant was a bad idea?

Too late.

Connor reached between her thighs with his free hand after rolling the condom over his hard cock. He found her cunt just the way he liked it—warm and very wet.

She really is something...

He grasped her hip in one hand, his cock in the other, then had her rise to her knees.

She grabbed his shoulders, her little hands clutching as though worried he might let her fall. Not that he ever would.

He fit the head of his dick against her pussy, then sank her down onto his length. It went easier than the first time, telling him she'd already started to relax more, that she'd gotten used to his size.

Not that she wasn't heavenly snug even still. Her cunt was tight enough around him that he hissed a sharp breath at the sensation.

Her nails dug into his shoulders, tiny bites of pain he savored, especially because he knew she'd never do it on purpose. It happened because she was so distracted, so taken by the feeling of his thick cock stretching her that she couldn't focus on anything else.

When her body pressed against his, when he was as deep as possible, he stilled.

She leaned forward, her forehead to his, her sweet breath spilling across his lips. She pressed on his shoulders, going to rise, to get the friction she no doubt wanted.

Instead, Connor wrapped his hands on her hips, keeping her still.

She let out a little huff before pulling back, lust clouding her expression.

"I said you wouldn't get what you wanted unless you told me the reasons that we like you. You tell me, you talk, you get whatever you want, darlin'. The second you stop, though, you stop getting what you want."

She squeezed her cunt around him, the pressure enough to draw a deep groan from him. A mischievous light in her eyes said it was on purpose.

"Dirty trick," he all but growled, voice even rougher than usual. "But I can hold out a lot longer than you can. Think of how good it will feel, getting to ride me, getting to use me just how you want."

Those sharp little nails of hers dug in again. She opened her mouth, but nothing came out, as if the words just refused to leave her.

Connor took pity on her. "Do we think you're pretty?"

She nodded, expression lightening, clearly glad to have the help. When she tried to move again, though, Connor held her still.

"Not so fast. *You* have to say it—that's the point."

She breathed in deep, the action making her lovely tits rise and fall, before she said in a voice so small Connor almost didn't count it, "You think I'm pretty."

He loosened his grip, so his hands remained but she could rise and sink on her own, and the friction did wonders for him, too. Sure enough, though, when he filled her once again, he stopped her.

At her look of pure frustration, he only lifted his eyebrow. She was smart—she'd get it.

She closed her eyes. Did not looking at him while she spoke make it easier? Fine by him—the point was to get *her* to realize that they were fucking crazy about her, that she was a catch, and her saying the words would help drive that point home.

"You think I'm sweet."

He let her rise, but stilled her at the top, when his cock was only the smallest inch inside her. "Leave off 'you think'."

She squirmed, but when she failed to get what she wanted, she whined softly. "I'm pretty."

There we go.

Connor let her move again, and she came down hard, taking him in a rough thrust. Then again, fragile as the girl might look, she was more than capable of taking it hard.

At the bottom, he only had to hold her for a second before she offered up another. "I look good naked."

It went on, and he let her have everything she wanted. *"I'm sensitive. I look great on my knees. I'm warm."*

She panted, her words slower, as though she couldn't think straight or remember, which was the exact time for Connor to push her. "And what about your cunt? Because we sure have said plenty about it."

She dropped her head back, seemingly lost to the moment. Still, her words came out in a sensual rush. "I'm tight, and wet…" She swallowed hard.

"And what?" Connor reached up, trusting her to keep going so he could cup her breasts and tease the nipples that had been taunting him since they'd started.

"And I have a pretty cunt."

That nearly pushed him over the edge, the filthy word on her sweet lips.

"You forgot the part about how great you taste, about the fact that I could lick your pussy for hours and never get enough."

She twisted her hips as she rode him, taking him hard, letting him know that the next time, he didn't need to hold back at all. His size was clearly no problem for her.

He circled her nipples with his thumbs, brushing the desperate peaks. "So what does this all mean? You've said it all, that you're sexy as hell, that your cunt is perfect, that these tits are flawless, that you're sweet and funny and kind, and what does it all mean? Come on, darlin', put it all together for me."

She didn't answer him, and if he were a stronger man, maybe he could have held back. Maybe he could have grabbed her hips and held her still, demanding the answer, but after talking about just how great her cunt felt, well, he was only a man.

Her pussy tightened around him, and she grasped his shoulders tightly as if he might escape before she finished if she let him go. He let himself follow her release, gave into the demands of his cock and let out a tortured groan as he came.

After a moment, she rested against his chest, her forehead on his shoulder, her breath quick and warm.

He might have given in, but he wasn't *quite* done yet. He caught her chin and forced her lust-drunk eyes to his. "What does it all mean?"

She brushed her lips to his like the best tease. "That you like me?"

He smiled, then wrapped his arms around her.

"Yeah, darling, we like you."

Talk about an understatement…

* * * *

Trent could feel bad news coming like a fucking freight train. It had always been a gift of his, he guessed, that he knew when someone was about to drop information on him he wouldn't like.

Which was funny since he seemed so out of touch so much of the time, able to move through life without worrying.

Still, from the moment he'd walked in the door, he'd known damn well that Sunny was getting ready to walk away.

Mitch had given them the all-clear about Tanner, and the police officers had said they had no leads and no reason to think whoever had broken in would do it again. In short? Everything that required Sunny to stay with them was gone.

And while Trent would love to beg her to stay, to convince her that they had a good time together even without the bullshit going on, he knew better. The more he tried to hold on to her, the faster she'd run.

So even as they ate dinner, even as Garrison made small talk about a new contract he'd gotten with a distributor of security cameras, and Connor talked about a foal that had been born that day, so Sunny smiled and listened intently, Trent just waited for the bad news.

It was coming, and when she finally said it, he knew it was going to hurt.

Or at least hurt worse, because fuck knew the waiting was already torture.

"I was thinking…"

Here it came. Trent closed his hand around his fork, ignoring the aching of his palm as he likely bent it.

Sunny took a deep breath. "I think we all know I have to go home at some point."

"Do you?" Garrison asked without inflection, no doubt to hide his feelings about it.

"Yes, I do. I really appreciate everything you have done for me, but eventually I have to go back to my real life."

"This could be your real life," Connor said. "There's no reason why it can't be."

The set of her lips said there was, and Trent knew her reason. She'd decided she couldn't have this — she couldn't be this. She'd gotten away from her asshole ex and had sworn to herself she'd never be this person again, and she still hadn't realized it wasn't the same.

Even with all their work, all their lessons, she just wasn't there.

Maybe she'd never get there…

"I just wanted…"

"What, darlin'?" Connor asked. "What do you want?"

Trent expected her to say she wanted them to drive her home right then, or perhaps that she wanted them to never call her again.

When she didn't answer, Garrison tried to help. "You want us to take you home?"

She shook her head, her teeth chewing at her bottom lip the way she always did when nervous. "I know it isn't fair to ask, but I was hoping for one more night?"

An empty aching void consumed Trent's stomach at that. He hated that she asked that way, as if they'd ever turn her down, but just as much he loathed the idea of touching her, knowing she was leaving.

The first night had been one thing—they hadn't known her. She was making it clear, though. She was done. This was it. Just throwing them one last fuck for the memories?

He tasted bitterness and it sure as hell wasn't from dinner.

Garrison glanced his way, a question there.

It was a stupid question.

It didn't matter how much it hurt, didn't matter the wounds it might leave—if their Fox wanted them, even if it was just for a night, they'd never turn her down.

And boy…would it hurt.

Chapter Fourteen

Garrison couldn't take his eyes off Sunny. What was it about goodbyes that made things so much clearer? Maybe it was because he knew he was losing her, knew she'd be gone, so he memorized all the details.

The exact peach shade of her nipples, the way she had a single mole on her left thigh, on the outside, the soft curve of her stomach just below her navel. He committed each thing to memory, not wanting to lose any of it.

She was there, in Connor's room, naked and beautiful and his, even if just for the night.

Trent tossed condoms onto the nightstand, his attitude poor. Then again, Trent seemed so happy most of the time, but he wore his emotions out in the open. He always had, and this was a rough loss.

Still, a night with Sunny was better than having nothing at all.

Connor pulled his shirt off and tossed it to the side, shucking his pants next. It wasn't a night for slowness, for games, for teasing.

Garrison wanted to drown himself in Sunny, in what could have been, in the taste of happiness he'd found. He wanted to take her roughly, to own her for the night that would end too quickly.

She peered around, probably looking for the toys, for their bags.

Garrison shook his head. "None of that, not tonight."

"Why not?" Worry filled her voice. Was she afraid they were angry, that she'd disappointed them?

She had, but he wouldn't tell her that, wouldn't force her to carry it, especially since it wasn't really her fault.

Garrison caught her by the back of her neck and pulled her closer, then pressed his lips to her forehead. "Because I want to get to touch you more, sweet."

Connor chuckled softly, as he walked up behind her, then caught her wrists and brought them together behind her. "Believe it or not, we can keep you under control without any help."

Sunny parted her lips and the softest, sexiest moan escaped her.

It was all the invitation he needed. He leaned in and took a kiss, his hand still on the back of her neck while his other trailed down her side, taking in the gentle curves, the point of her hip bone, the trembling in her body.

Why did this need to feel like such a goodbye?

Because it is.

Garrison shoved the thought away, trying to not let his annoyance ruin everything. It would be like pouting

Jayce Carter

about the last ice cream before a diet instead of just enjoying it. He planned to savor the evening.

Sunny leaned against him despite the fact that Connor had her wrists trapped together. She moved toward him as she always did, a desperation there that said she wanted nothing more than another touch.

And Garrison was happy to oblige. He broke the kiss to lean down, to trace his lips over her collar bone, to lean down as he followed the curve of her breast before teasing her nipple. It was tight, another sign of what she wanted and how much she wanted it.

Which was just one of the things he liked about her so much. Even when her fear got the best of her, when her courage fled, she was unfailingly honest. She never lied, not with her lips and certainly not with her body. She shivered at each touch of his, leaned into him, begged him without words for more.

He moved to the other breast, lavishing it with the same affection, as Connor slid his free hand in front of her and between her thighs.

Connor let out a deep groan. "Drenched. You really did want this tonight, didn't you?"

"Yes," she breathed out, her voice soft in the dim room, saturated in so much desire he wondered if she knew what she was saying at all.

Trent caught her chin and led her face to the side where his lips waited, where he could take a kiss and have her in his own way as well.

Garrison dropped to his knees before her, continuing his touches from her breasts, down her stomach, over her hips and toward his goal. Connor grasped one of her thighs and lifted it to the side, held her open for Garrison, put her on display for him.

Her cunt was as pretty as the first time he'd seen it, when she'd just been some faceless fox they'd caught. Connor had been right, and even in the dark room, the light that streamed in through the window from the moon made the wetness on her cunt glisten.

And Garrison had never been a man to deny himself much, so he dove in.

She might walk away, but he'd make sure she *never* forgot him.

Connor had to admit, the way Sunny writhed as he held her still revved him up. Her body twisted as Garrison licked her pussy, as he put all his skills to use on her swollen clit, and it made her rub against his cock.

She was perfect. There really wasn't another way to put it, and no matter if she was walking out, it didn't change that fact.

Garrison shoved her toward a release so fast, it was clear what he had in mind. He didn't plan to take things easy, to tease her, to edge her. He intended to break her apart over and over again.

Which, Connor had to admit, had promise. She always looked lovely flushed and overstimulated and tired. There was something endearing about that, about the vulnerability when she could hardly keep her eyes open and just cleaning her up made her whimper.

Connor looked down her body to catch eyes with Garrison, who darted his gaze to the nightstand.

Ah. Not only had Trent grabbed condoms, but lube as well. It seemed that since it was the last night, they wanted to try something new. When Sunny pressed against him again, when he thought about how much he wanted to take her at the same time as the other two, well, it sounded like a good idea to him.

Her orgasm crashed into her, as powerful as they usually were for her. Despite how sweet she was, how quiet so much of the time, when she came she always came hard. She arched, and he held her up by his grip on her thigh, by wrapping his other arm around her to keep her still.

When she finished, when she sagged in his grip and Garrison gave one last lick, Connor released her thigh and turned her toward him. He took his own kiss, wanting to get lost in her heat and her desire.

He tugged her forward, keeping her against him even as he moved onto the bed, bringing her into his lap. She spread her thighs around him, much like she had earlier, when he'd taken her on the couch.

Fuck knew he wouldn't be taking her ass, not that night.

And there won't be another…

While he'd have loved to feel her so tight around him, it was a better idea for someone less thick to try it first, and he had no doubt who exactly would.

After taking a condom from the nightstand and rolling it over his shaft, he used a hand on Sunny's waist to position her. Not that it took any coaxing — she moved into place, her hands on his shoulders, hunger in her expression.

He didn't bother to keep in the deep rumble when she lowered herself onto him, when that sweet cunt of hers took each thick inch of his cock. It reminded him of earlier, of when she'd ridden him on the couch, when she'd fought past her own demons to have what she'd wanted — him.

This time she wouldn't just get what she wanted, though.

Trent and Garrison moved around in Connor's peripheral vision, but he ignored them for the moment. He brushed his lips against Sunny's full ones, tasting the mint on her breath from her toothpaste, and set a languid pace, as if that would keep the night from ending.

Nothing could stop that, though, and as Connor often reminded the others — they weren't romantics.

He couldn't make the night last forever, which meant all he could do was commit as much to memory as possible.

Sunny didn't jump when a hand was set on her back, when it stroked down her spine before grabbing her ass. She didn't know if it was just that she'd gotten comfortable with the men or if she was too far gone to care whose hand it was.

Garrison's dark eyes met hers from beside her when she broke the kiss with Connor, telling her Trent was the one touching her.

Not that it surprised her, especially when a sharp sting occurred moments later, when that hand slapped her ass.

And *boy* did she whine at the feeling, no longer ashamed of it, of her response to it. It was some strange gift they'd given her, an ability to accept a part of herself she'd feared before.

Garrison's lips curled into a smile, as if he liked the sound she made. "I thought we'd try something new," he explained.

Right then, Sunny was pretty sure she'd agree to anything they wanted. They hadn't steered her wrong thus far...

At least, that was what she thought until Trent used his thumbs to spread her cheeks, the point clear.

She swallowed with a loud gulp.

Garrison caught her chin, his grip as solid as his gaze. "You said you weren't sure before. You can still say no."

She took her lip between her teeth. Memories of anal being a very bad thing before threatened her, but she forced herself to think through it. Sex had been horrific before, too, but it hadn't been with them. She nodded.

"Sorry, sweet, but you need to speak up. Do you want to? You can always back out if you don't like it."

She refused to let the past dictate her future anymore, and especially since this was her last night with them, she wanted to experience *everything*. "I want to."

Garrison's smile made her feel like she'd just walked out into the sun, as if she'd warmed from it. "Brave girl," he said before leaning in and pressing a kiss to her forehead. He grabbed a small bottle from the nightstand and tossed it behind her — no doubt to Trent.

She shifted, wanting the friction of Connor's cock back, but he set both hands on her waist and held her still. "Relax, darlin', and keep still. Let Trent work."

Work. That word sure held a lot of connotations.

Trent chuckled a moment before something wet and cool touched her. Almost immediately, he smeared the lube with his fingers before pressing against her ass.

Sunny tensed. She couldn't help it. An immediate expectation of pain hit her, taking her back to trying it before and to how horribly it had gone.

"Breathe," Garrison said. "He'll go slow."

She tried to relax, to tell herself that she'd wanted this, but it was hard to convince her body of that. Still, Trent went slow, was careful, and before long her muscles started to unknit. Sure enough, the pressure mounted and eventually Trent's finger slid past the tight muscles there.

It felt…weird? Not good, she didn't think, but not bad either. She closed her eyes and rested her forehead against Connor's chest.

Garrison stroke his fingers through her hair. "You're doing so well, sweet. And as soon as Trent gets you ready? We'll get to take you all at once, fill every hole you have. I've got no doubt you'll love that."

Trent let out a groan from behind her, as if the sight of him fingering her ass was the best thing he'd ever seen. "You are so tight, you know that? Fuck, I can just imagine how you'll squeeze around me. And you may not realize it, but you're enjoying this."

She wanted to snap at him, to tell him he was an idiot. She was pretty sure she'd know if she liked it or not.

"He's right," Connor added before she could. "Your sweet little cunt keeps squeezing down on my dick the same way you do when you're close, when you're wanting to come. Your head might get in the way, but your body knows exactly what it thinks."

That forced her to take a breath and *feel*. Damn it, they were right. Her pussy kept pulsing, and the more Trent sank into her, the more he teased her ass, the more her body responded.

Not that he let her get used to it. Once he'd pressed his finger in far enough that his knuckles touched her, he pulled back and pressed two into her. The deeper he went, the more she wanted. Before she knew it, Connor gripped her waist tightly because she was desperate to move, to feel Connor's cock and Trent's fingers take her.

Everything melted together, the sensations, the wants. Garrison had taken a seat on the side of the bed, his hand around his cock. He stroked it, his predatory gaze taking in her position, how helpless she was. His words came back to her, and she had no doubt what his plan was.

She pictured how it would feel to be so taken over, to feel Connor deep in her cunt, Trent fucking her ass and Garrison's cock between her lips. It was so far beyond anything she'd done before, anything she'd have thought she wanted, and yet she nearly panted at the idea.

"You're ready," Trent said as he pulled his fingers from her. It left a terrible void inside her, and she complained with a broken whine. He only laughed and set one hand on her ass, spreading her open, before the cool tip of his cock pressed against her.

The sting would have terrified her before, but she was too far gone to care. It twisted inside her the same way it did when Trent had spanked her, when he put the clamps on her nipples, and turned to intense pleasure. His cock stretched her, and she dug her nails into Connor's shoulders as she endured it, as she fought between wanting him to stop and begging him to go deeper, to give her more.

Even better were the almost identical groans from Connor and Trent, as if her body had never given them more pleasure.

She panted, little sounds escaping her throat as she took Trent's long cock, as she accepted every inch of him until his pelvis pressed against her, until she had taken him all.

"What a good girl," Garrison said, tension in even his voice, his hand moving quickly. "What do you think?"

The idea of talking right then seemed impossible, yet her lips moved on their own. Her brain had shut off somehow, and her mouth seemed to work on its own. "I need more."

More? Her own words baffled her, because she was pretty sure there wasn't anything else she could take.

Garrison only laughed, that deep rumble that reached inside her and excited her, before he rose and shifted, bringing his cock to her lips.

Yes. He'd known what she'd wanted even if she hadn't. She parted her lips, let him sink his cock into the heat of her mouth, gave herself over to them all, to whatever they wanted.

That was when Trent chose to move, to retreat and thrust forward again. He didn't go far but he didn't need to — the stroke of his cock against her sensitive ass was more than enough to throw her body into chaos.

He didn't stop, though. He kept going, retreating only about a third of the way before thrusting back in, a constant swell of sensation that she couldn't ignore or control. Garrison did the same to her mouth, fucking into it while he grasped the base of his cock, like some extension so his entire shaft was teased.

Connor lifted his hips from the bed, but because of how he held her still, he couldn't thrust much. It was still more than enough.

Each feeling fought with the others, and she understood what Garrison had meant, how he'd said she'd be entirely filled.

It wasn't just physically, though that was true as well. It was so much deeper. Before she'd taken them one after another, or perhaps two at a time, but now? Now there were hands everywhere, their sounds of masculine pleasure, their hard cocks. They had seemed to reach inside her and fill all the space, the hollow areas where she'd felt emptied out by fear and pain.

There wasn't room for anything like that, not when they took her together, when they drove her past those old worries and into a person who just *was*.

Another orgasm crept up on her, spurred on by the way they tormented her body, by the feelings she'd never experienced before, by the surprise of it all.

"Fuck, I want this to last longer," Trent all but growled out behind her, his hands on her hips so tight, they stung. The words were sharp, as though shoved through gritted teeth.

There was no way she was lasting, not long.

She arched her back as the first wave of pleasure took over her, and Garrison pulled his cock free. Good thing, too, because she'd bet he didn't enjoy the sort of pain that might happen if she caught him with her teeth.

And who could blame her? She was mindless with lust, with the way the orgasm battered her, with how they still didn't stop or give her time to catch her breath. As soon as the worst of the orgasm washed away, Garrison gripped her chin. "Mouth open, sweet," he ordered.

Instead of the command frightening her, even with how deep his voice had gone, it only excited her. She obeyed, offering him whatever he wanted.

In this case, that meant her mouth. "You have the sweetest lips," he said. "But I haven't been able to stop thinking about that throat of yours. What do you think, hmm? You going to let me fuck it?"

Just like every other question they asked her, the answer was *hell yes*.

She must have nodded, because he slid his fingers into her hair and gripped tight before nudging his cock forward. She gagged, but he only pulled back for a second.

"Swallow," he snarled, his voice having lost that control he usually had.

She did as he ordered when he tried again, this time slipping deeper. Her throat made the same motion, and he seemed to revel in the way she tightened around the head of his cock.

He withdrew after a moment, letting her take in deep breaths, then repeated it. He kept a rhythm to it, which eased any anxiety she might have had. She didn't worry that he wouldn't pull back, that she wouldn't get to take the breath she was desperate for, and before long it became just another piece the night, of how they owned her, of how they used every part of her needy body against her.

Trent fucked her hard, the lube more than enough to make sure it didn't hurt, and the feeling of him so deep inside her, in a way she'd never expected to enjoy, was filthy. His thrusts were broken, erratic, as though he weren't thinking anymore, just feeling and doing what came naturally. He rutted against her, wild and as desperate as she was.

He came first, the snug fit of her ass clearly throwing him over that edge. He sank in as deep as he could, groaning as his hands cranked down on her hips, holding her still. It made her wish they hadn't used condoms, because some part of her wanted to *feel* him come inside her, wanted to feel it drip from her afterward.

Connor pressed his lips to her throat, to where Garrison was still sinking his cock, before his shaft twitched inside her, before he let out a deep rumble of satisfaction.

Sunny's own release teetered on the edge, so close she could almost taste it. Garrison sank as deep as he could into her mouth, down her tight throat, so her lips pressed against his pubic hair. "Fucking perfect," he said before he came, his hand tangled in her hair, holding her still.

She swallowed as he pulled out, leaving only a bit on her tongue. Something about him coming so deeply that she didn't have a choice about whether or not she'd swallow him was incredibly hot, and made her cunt squeeze down in a plea.

"Poor girl isn't quite done yet," Trent said even as he rested against her, as exhaustion filled his words. He reached down, between her and Connor's bodies, to grasp her breasts.

She knew in the split second before he did it what his plan was. His fingers closed around her neglected nipples, angling so his nails bit in, as if he'd known exactly what she wanted and had no problem giving it to her even after he'd finished.

Her orgasm hit her so hard, it was terrifying. Her body rebelled, the feeling overwhelming and drowning and freeing all at once.

As she came down, surrounded by the three men she was about to walk away from, she forced herself not to cry.

What was right wasn't always easy, which made sense, because walking away from them would be the hardest thing she'd ever done.

* * * *

Sunny sat in the car, her house looking different than it had before. It hadn't changed, yet she somehow felt as though it had lost its magic.

Which was stupid. Connor had checked out the house first, demanding she stay in the car until he knew it was safe.

After finding out that Tanner was in Utah, that no one was after her, she'd admitted...

It was time to go home.

She didn't want to, but the more she fought it, the surer she was that she needed to.

She needed to stand on her own feet again, needed to go home, to get her life back, to stop hiding from everything and making pretend. Her time with the men playing house had been great—no doubt about that.

But she wasn't a fool. It was like a vacation fling. She'd had her fun, but it wasn't a life she could have. She'd worked so hard to get out from beneath Tanner's thumb, and even now, years later, she still wasn't fully free.

She couldn't turn around and risk it all again. It just wasn't the life she wanted.

So Trent, Garrison and Connor had driven her back, not arguing when she'd said it was time for her to go. The set of their jaws and lack of conversation said they didn't like it one bit.

She sat in the front passenger seat, her legs to the side, out of the open door. Connor stood beside her, outside the car.

"So, it's safe?"

He nodded and pressed a new set of keys into her palm. "Good as new. Slider has been fixed, all the locks replaced, and we had a camera system put in."

"And the blood?" She gulped as she struggled to not think about the sight of Spike there on the floor.

"Already handled. Got a good cleaning crew who handles such things to take care of it all. The house looks just like it did before."

She pressed her lips together, trying to talk herself into going in, into doing what she needed to do.

Because she did *need* to, right?

"We could come in," Garrison said. "At least walk you in, maybe even stay the night if you wanted."

And that tempted her so much. She could say yes, lean on them, make everything so much easier. They were always willing to help her, to take her burdens.

Except that wasn't fair, not to any of them. She'd made her choice, and no matter how much it might hurt, she couldn't drag this out any longer.

She shook her head. "It's probably best if I do it myself."

Connor caught her chin, bringing her gaze to his. "You decide what you want—you always have. We'll go, but you know, you can always call."

She nodded. "I know."

Trent spoke from the back seat. "We're at the club most weekends, you know, if you ever want to come visit?"

Connor cut him a sharp look, but Trent looked as sorry as he ever did—not at all. "Just making conversation," Trent said.

Garrison let out a sigh, as if he couldn't blame Trent but also wished he'd behave better. "You want to get back to your real life—I get it. I just want you to remember that what we had wasn't so bad, either. You don't have to give up your life to add us in. Why don't you just call us, huh? Maybe we can stop in, visit? Even go on a date, like normal people?"

She blew out a slow breath, because while she *knew* what she needed to do, walking that path was a different thing. Telling them they were done was something far harder than knowing it in her head.

"You don't have to know right now," Connor rushed out, as if he saw the hesitation on her face and would rather leave with a maybe rather than a no. "We're not going to call you, won't pressure you. It's got to be up to you."

Sunny slid from the car, her feet hitting the dirt and reminding her that Connor was a lot taller that she was. Still, he didn't reach for her, didn't crowd her. She moved past him, forcing herself to walk even though it was the last thing she wanted.

Still, this had all been temporary, right? It had been to try this out, to test something during the time they had to be in her life anyway.

Now she knew.

She refused to look over her shoulder, to see them sitting there, because she knew that if she did, she'd never leave. She would see them and doubt the choice she'd made.

And she really needed to go. Sunny needed to let go of this insanity, to go back to what she'd had planned.

At least this way they wouldn't see how much it hurt her to leave.

Chapter Fifteen

Sunny couldn't get over how empty the house was. She struggled to even call it home anymore. The vet had said Spike could come home in another few days, which was good because the place that had been her sanctuary felt entirely changed.

Each night, when she'd lain in the bed alone, in the silent, empty house, she'd considered calling her men.

They're not my men, are they?

Each time, though, she'd rolled over and closed her eyes. She'd told herself that she couldn't unring that bell, that once she called, she was admitting she wanted that life. It wasn't just a call. It was the entire future.

They'd given her a good taste of what such a future would be from them. Garrison had given her so much pleasure, had made her realize how much she enjoyed sex and exactly how much control she still had over it. Connor had praised her, had chipped away her doubts until she couldn't doubt how he saw her. And Trent? He'd opened her eyes, taught her that she wasn't broken just because she enjoyed pain, that it was okay for her to be who she was and that she wasn't at fault for what had happened with Tanner.

And they'd *all* taught her that there were people in the world who could give her that if she wanted it.

But did she?

She lowered herself onto the couch on her back porch, tired from chasing her tail, from trying to work through something that had two options.

Call them or not.

Admit she wanted a life like that or reject it.

She knew what she wanted but wanting something and getting it were entirely different.

A strange sound made her twist, peering toward the fence. The rustling of plants?

She scolded herself for her paranoia. With Spike gone, she found herself jumping at every little sound, then cursing Tanner for making her like this. There was no good reason for her to act as if the world was after her. The reality was that she lived in the middle of nowhere, so between rabbits, coyotes and the occasional bobcat, there was *always* movement around her property.

She would have normally gone inside a good hour ago, but what was the point? At least the outside, the sky and the mountains, were the same as they'd always been. They didn't feel changed like the inside did, so she'd stayed out.

At least, she did until her eyes started to drop closed, when she admitted she had to take herself to bed.

Alone.

She had to force herself to her feet, a fear inside her that this was it. This was the life she was headed for. The quiet that used to be so ideal to her now chafed.

When she'd first moved here, the silence had soothed her. Without Tanner's overwhelming presence, his yelling, his sharp words, she'd found her ability to breathe again. Now, though, it had become as stifling as it had been freeing. She missed hearing voices, having people around, feeling the part of something instead of on her own.

She went to the slider with the same hesitation she had each time she looked at the new one, at the way the metal was shiny, unlike her old, dulled one. She pushed past the memory and went into the house, the inside dark so it wouldn't compete with the sky.

The hairs on her arms stood up, something on the edge of her awareness that warned her, but this time she couldn't push it off as paranoia.

She went to flip the light switch, but nothing happened. The glow from the house was gone, the electronics that cast digital times all dark.

She twisted around, trying to peer through the dim house, her heart speeding, her head doing that thing where her thoughts slowed because panic had set in.

Calm down. It's nothing. It's always nothing.

She wasn't going to let memories take her down this path, let them steal things from her and turn her into a mess. She'd worked too hard for too long to let that happen.

In front of her, as her eyes adjusted, a face appeared in the darkness. It was like something crawling from her nightmares, features she'd never forget, the ones that had haunted her for years and tormented her for years before that.

Tanner had found her.

* * * *

Garrison stared down at the takeout Trent had brought home.

He didn't used to mind eating food they picked up, but somehow it had lost the appeal. It felt like the ultimate sign of bachelorhood, and ever since Sunny had left, he realized he didn't *want* that life anymore.

It was funny that after so many years of it, of living with just his two best friends, of taking all the different women both together and apart, he'd never thought it would become monotonous. It had seemed like what any man would want.

Then that little fox had walked into his life and brought a sense of fun, of excitement.

Oh, yeah, then she walked right out again, leaving him there, finally realizing what he wanted and knowing he couldn't get it.

It had been a week, and she hadn't reached out. A week of silence, of him pathetically checking his phone every hour, of forcing himself to give her space.

But, after a week, his hopes had dropped to zero. The more time she had to think, the more she'd dig her heels in.

"You want to glare some more at the food?" Annoyance filled Trent's voice.

They'd been at each other's throats, each day worse than the one before. It seemed Sunny leaving had shown cracks they'd ignored before.

"I'm tired of takeout."

"Well, you're welcome to learn to cook," Trent answered.

"Knock it off, you two." Connor took a bite of the food, his gaze down. He treated them like children who were bickering.

Which…they sort of were.

"How could she not call?" Trent asked, finally addressing the topic they hadn't dared to broach.

"She still might," Connor said.

That was a load of shit. "The more time that passes, the less likely that is. She likes to think, and the more she gets wrapped up in her head, the better the chance that she talks herself right out of it."

Trent pushed his plate away and sat back. "What if we call? Or just…show up somewhere? If we could talk to her, she'd realize she's making a mistake…"

Garrison wanted so badly to do just that. It would be easy to go see her, to remind her of what they had between them, because there was something there.

But that wasn't possible, no matter how much he wished it was. "We can't do that. Sunny dealt with one asshole who called himself a Dom, who didn't listen to her, who didn't let her make her own choices, didn't respect her. If we did that, how would we be any better than him?"

Trent blew out a hard breath. He might not like the answer, but he clearly couldn't argue with it either.

Sunny deserved the ability to make her own choices, even if Garrison were sure she was making a mistake.

A cell rang, the high tone telling them it was Connor's. He rose from the table and went back toward his room, where he'd left it.

Trent pushed his plate away. "I hate this."

"Me too," Garrison said. "Trust me, you're not the only one disappointed."

"I just keep wondering if there was something else we could have done, some way we could have made her realize she belongs with us."

"Maybe. Maybe it wasn't supposed to be, maybe we were supposed to just help her realize she might like this, that she's okay, that she deserves better and can have it."

"And you're okay with that? With us being nothing but a lesson to her?" Trent asked.

"I'm not happy about it, no, but sometimes there's nothing we can do about it. Sometimes life sucks and we just have to deal with it."

Connor's heavy steps came quickly down the hallway, drawing Garrison's attention. He'd known the man long enough to tell his moods from a room away, and nothing but an emergency got Connor moving like *that*.

Connor rushed in, then held the phone out, pressing the speaker button. "I'm with Trent and Garrison now — go on."

The voice on the line was one Garrison recognized — Mitch, the private detective working in Utah, the one who had tracked down Tanner. "I think we have a problem."

Words I'm not fond of hearing.

"What sort of problem?" Trent asked. "Is Tanner gone?"

Mitch sighed, the breath creating static against the mic on his phone. "Ever since I did that delivery, I couldn't stop thinking that something didn't add up. I've done this long enough to trust my gut, and something just didn't fit. A man like that, he doesn't just move on."

"So...?" Garrison said, trying to prompt Mitch to get to the point.

"*No one* never misses a day of work in five years, especially the sort of rich prick his record showed him to be. I've found that if someone's alibi is too good, it's a sure sign it's fake. I went back today, sat outside and didn't see any sign of him. Nothing. When he opened the door, I saw pictures on the wall. Didn't know who it was, not until I researched more. They were of Sunny."

Trent cursed, as if he didn't care for the thought of that asshole having anything of Sunny.

"Not a shock he'd be obsessive," Connor said.

"No, you don't get it. I thought they were old at first, but it wasn't until I got back home, and I thought about it. That dog Sunny owns, the one who got hurt, you told me about him. Is he a big black mastiff?"

"Yeah," Garrison said, his throat tight.

"Well, there were a good four pictures up of her with that dog."

Which meant Tanner had been close enough to Sunny in the past few years to get pictures of her and Spike...

"Where is he now?"

"Well, when I went to his house and there wasn't any movement, I bent some rules and took a tour of his place myself. He's not here and everything is locked down like he won't be coming back for a few days."

"If he hasn't missed work, and he hasn't taken any flights, how could he be coming here?" Connor asked. "Even if he managed it, if he drove for sixteen hours out here, spent a few here, then sixteen back, he couldn't have done that and made it back for work after the attack."

Papers shuffled through the line, then the creak of a drawer of some sort. Mitch cursed, muttering about locks, before a metal-on-metal click that sounded like a cabinet opening.

"Fuck," Mitch said, the curse odd from the man. "On his desk is a picture of him and some guy in front of a small plane." More sounds, the rustling of papers. "There are check stubs in his desk made out weekly to someone named Harron Kyle."

Garrison pulled his phone out, typing the name in. *Ah, social media, the easiest way to riffle right through someone's life.* A man showed up in the results with that name. "Gray hair, receding hairline and a hell of a mustache?"

"That's him," Mitch answered.

Garrison clicked on the image, bringing up the person's profile. A lot of it was locked down, but as he scrolled more, older posts showed up, as though the man hadn't learned how to hide things until later.

And eight years ago?

A post where Harron Kyle celebrated getting his pilot's license. It meant Tanner had found a way to get to Sunny. He'd called her, he'd been there on weekends and could make it back home by Monday to keep up appearances. He'd escalated things, going from phone calls to a break-in and attacking her dog, and now he had to be in California again.

Garrison met gazes with Connor as all the pieces fit together.

They needed to get to Sunny.

Now.

Chapter Sixteen

Sunny backed away, unable to stop the trembling that had started up through her whole body. *He is here.* After so many years, after all her work, all the running and hiding and fear, Tanner was inside her house.

It all came together, pieced together as if his presence made it so she couldn't ignore reality anymore. He'd been the one to call her, to break in, to hurt Spike, to tear apart the life she'd worked so hard to create.

"My little Sunshine," he said, the hated nickname making her stomach churn, something she'd hoped to never hear again.

She wanted to scream, to tell him to get out, to do *something*, but nothing came. She was that same woman again, facing off against him, knowing she'd lose.

When she'd run, she'd never actually faced him. She'd just snuck out, terrified to stand against him, to risk everything.

His lips curled into a familiar vicious smirk. "I was worried that so much time on your own would make you unruly but look at this. You're as timid and weak as ever." He darted forward, but even when she yanked back, he was quicker. He wrapped his hand in her hair, a grasp that was nothing like when Connor did it. It hurt, and Tanner used it to drag her into the living room.

She cried out when he used the grip to force her face to his, to make her look at him, into those dark eyes she'd known so well.

"Get on your knees," he ordered. "Back where you belong."

She did as he said. It wasn't with the same happiness she felt when she did it for Garrison, and she felt no better when she took the position. Instead, she felt degraded, trapped and terrified.

On the floor sat an open bag, and beside it, on the table, the items placed there gave her no doubt to what he had planned. Cuffs, a gag, duct tape and a knife were spread out, digging that terror deeper into her.

"Stay," he said with the sharp tone of one talking to a dog before he peered around. "I didn't have any time to check out the place the last time I was here. I knew you had a dog, but I hadn't realized it was quite so vicious. I hope you know we'll have to put it down. I refuse to have dangerous beasts in our home."

She curled her hands into fists on her thighs, her gaze down, trying to hide anything in her head. *No.* She couldn't even consider that. She'd never let him anywhere near Spike, not again. Even if he dragged her back to hell with him, Spike would stay safe where he was.

Tanner kept talking, not waiting for an answer, probably because he didn't expect one. He'd never cared what Sunny had to say, what she thought. "It's been a long time, Sunshine, but I always thought you'd come around. I gave you time because I figured you'd realize on your own where you belonged. You never dated anyone that I saw, never brought anyone back here, so I thought you understood that you were mine — temper tantrum aside. Then, when I came out a few weeks ago, I followed you to that club." He clicked his tongue in disappointment. "A sex club, Sunshine? That isn't your sort of place, and if you were so desperate for that, you should have come back to me."

She kept her mouth shut, even when the words bubbled inside her, a desire to tell him that what he'd done was abuse, that it wasn't what she'd wanted, that she finally understood the difference.

"So I planned to come back the next week, show you the error of your ways, bring you back home where you belong. Unfortunately, your mutt made that impossible. I would have liked to finish the job, but — " He lifted his shirt to show an ugly patch of bruised skin around a bandage, proof that Spike had gotten a chunk of him. Tanner lowered the fabric. "Good thing I'd brought a crowbar for the door, or I might not have been able to get him off me."

She swallowed down the bile at the thought of Tanner hitting Spike with that, at the anger that he had dared to hurt an animal who had done nothing but protect her. It wasn't surprise — Tanner was a monster — but his words forced her to envision it. Instead of focusing there, she whispered another topic. "Your work said you've never missed a day."

"Did you have someone checking in on me?" He asked it as though the thought amused him. "Of course I haven't—I'm always back by Monday. I paid Harron extra, this week, to bring you back with me. I've built a lovely room in the basement, one where no one will find you, should anyone come looking. You'll stay there until you learn how to behave properly, until you figure out what it means to be a *good* submissive." His words came out low, dark and absolutely confident.

He planned to take her back, to the horror of her old life, to the darkness and the pain and the fear.

Away from all the things she'd found, the life she'd built out of sheer determination.

She thought about her life, about the home she loved, about Spike, who had nearly died trying to protect her, about the men who had taught her that she didn't need this, that she was so much more than Tanner had told her.

All the fear remained, but she refused to let it hold her back. She refused to let it make her quiet and meek anymore, especially when it was Tanner who had put it there. Instead, her gaze went to the knife on the table, the one Tanner had there to use against her.

He came back and crouched between her and the table. He grabbed her chin, his fingers pressing in so hard it hurt. "You are mine. I don't care how many you've fucked around with, I don't care that you think you could get away, or that you played with some other Dom—you are *mine*, always, and I'll remind you of that as long and as often as you need me to."

"I'm not yours," she whispered, the first real time she'd stood up to him, the first time she'd told him no, that she'd said anything against him. It felt like a break, like a tree that had grown against a wall for years, digging roots in, making it unsteady, until it finally crumbled beneath that persistence.

He tilted his head. "No? Whose are you, then? Are you trying to tell me you want those other fuckers from the club to own you?"

She shook her head, each violation he'd made her suffer coming back to her. What he'd done to both her dogs, the way he'd stolen her sense of safety, stolen years of her life. "I belong to *me*," she bit out, then flung herself forward.

It was likely only the surprise that knocked Tanner off balance, since he was larger and stronger than she was. Still, it was hopefully enough. It *had* to be enough. He hit the table, making it skid a few feet back, and the items on it toppled to the floor.

He twisted, trying to get a hold of Sunny, but she fought. She writhed, catching him in the chin with her elbow, clawing and kicking and giving it *everything* she had. She wasn't walking away from her life again. She wasn't going to just give up the happiness she'd found — that she knew she deserved.

He cursed, spitting out names that rolled off her, names that didn't matter to her.

His hand struck her cheek, and spots danced in her vision. Even still, she didn't give in. If he was going to win, if he was going to get anything from her, she'd fight him every god dammed inch of the way, because she *deserved* to have what she wanted, and she'd fight for it.

She reached out, the blade in view but just out of reach.

Tanner wrapped his hands around her throat, finally pinning her, his eyes crazy like she'd never seen before. "If you won't have me, you'll have *nothing*." He squeezed, cutting off her oxygen, but Sunny didn't even let that stop her.

She stretched as far as she could, her fingers brushing the handle of the knife, the world getting hazy.

She didn't want to die with Tanner being the last thing she ever saw.

She jerked, her foot hitting the chair in her living room, giving her that scant inch of reach she needed to wrap her fingers around the handle.

The power was off. Garrison had suspected as much when they couldn't bring up a feed on her cameras. He hadn't kept access to them as a way to invade her privacy, hadn't even thought about his administrative access until after she'd failed to answer her phone, when they'd realized Tanner could be there. At the end of her driveway sat a rental car, no driver, and it pushed Garrison to take the driveway even faster, their SUV hitting the bumps hard.

He wasn't a praying man, but he sent up more than a few on the drive over.

There was something so much worse than her not wanting them, than her not being in their lives — that was the thought of her not being in the world at all anymore. It was the idea of her slipping away, of Tanner getting his hands on her and them never finding her. All the terrors coursed through his head, making him yank the parking brake before the car had even come to a stop in front of her house.

He was out a breath later, rushing for the front door, Trent and Connor on his heels. He could have knocked, could have used his keys, but the yell of a man inside meant he stopped and kicked the front door in as hard as he could.

Locks were strong, but wood often wasn't, and the thing splintered beneath his anger and fear.

Inside was darkness, but some light poured in from the mostly full moon, through the front windows to illuminate the room.

A large man stood above Sunny, who was on the ground, on her back.

Garrison rushed forward, not caring what weapon the man might have, not caring about any risk. Nothing mattered but getting this fucker as far away from the woman Garrison loved as possible.

Except the man teetered backward with an uneasy step, then turned. From his side, a black handle stuck out, blood pouring from the wound.

The man—Tanner—stumbled, then collapsed to the floor, the monster of all their nightmares, reduced to nothing by their Fox.

* * * *

Connor hated hospitals, which was funny, since he'd spent plenty of time in one, at least one for animals.

That was different, though. He was the doctor those times, not just another visitor waiting outside a room.

Sunny was giving her statement to the police, but from what Connor had heard, the case seemed open and shut.

Mitch had found all the evidence that Tanner had been stalking her, that he'd been coming every weekend, and the blood from the break-in would be a match. Also, because the cameras worked on battery backup, they'd recorded him entering the house when he'd attacked her, even though the lack of power had meant Connor hadn't been able to access them.

Still, knowing it was over didn't quite reassure Connor as it should have.

Sunny had looked so small there, on the ground, and when the lights had come back on—a flipped breaker was an easy fix—he'd seen the angry red marks on her throat.

The fucker had hit her and strangled her.

Of course, she'd stabbed him. He'd live—Connor was on the fence on if he was happy about that or not—but it had taken surgery to save him and it had, no doubt, hurt.

That was something, at least. Also, there seemed a wonderfully perverse bit of humor in the fact that she'd stabbed him in the same place Spike had bitten him.

The police walked out, nodding at Connor as they passed. "We're good for now."

Connor took a breath, frozen at the threshold, unsure of his welcome, of any of theirs. The ambulance had brought Sunny, so they hadn't actually seen her since the police had arrived at her house. Would she even want them there? Maybe they were too much in that moment, a reminder of something she didn't much want to remember?

Still, *not* going in wasn't an option, not if there was any chance that she needed them there.

Trent walked in first, the one to always act before thinking or worrying much.

Sunny looked small in that bed, in the hospital gown, and the red marks on her throat had started to darken. It made him realize Tanner hadn't been trying to scare her — he'd been intent on killing her. If she hadn't gotten that knife…

Connor couldn't even finish the thought. Her not wanting them, that was one thing, but her not being alive anymore was a far different thing.

She peered at her lap instead of them.

Not a good sign…

"Hey there, sweet." Trent leaned his hip against the bed. "How are you feeling?"

"Not great," she admitted, her finger tracing the designs on the blanket. "I can't believe it's over."

"Aren't you happy about that?" Garrison asked, taking a spot on the other side of the bed.

She nodded. "I just never thought it would be. These last years, I've always been on alert, waiting, you know? But there's no way he'll talk himself out of this. He's going away, at least for a few years. I just…I don't even know what to do with myself now."

"Whatever you want," Garrison said. "That's the point. No more looking over your shoulder, no more worrying he'll show back up. You'll finally get to just do whatever it is you want."

Would they be a part of that? Connor had a feeling he knew the answer. It was part of the answer as to why she hadn't reached out to them, why she hadn't called them, why she wouldn't even look at them.

Not that he regretted doing any of it. He wanted her happy, even if it wasn't with him.

At least, that was what he told himself. It was true, but hard to accept right then.

"Thank you," she said.

"We didn't do anything," Connor said back, frowning. "By the time we showed up, you'd already dealt with him."

She peered up, meeting Connor's gaze. "I never fought him before. I always crumbled because I didn't know I was worth anything. I thought that was my place. He spent so long tearing me down and making me think I couldn't do anything back, that fighting was pointless. The only reason I *could* fight him tonight, the only reason I was able to survive, was because you helped me see that I could, that I deserved something more, that I could have something better."

Connor reached out, wrapping his fingers around her ankle and squeezing once, trying to walk that line between comfort and too much. "I always knew you had it in you."

"He said I was his, that I had always belonged to him, but I told him I didn't. He asked me who I belonged to."

Connor held some stupid hope that she'd said them, that she was *theirs*. Maybe it was neanderthal, but he wanted her to be theirs, to want to be theirs.

"I told him I was my own."

Connor ignored the ache in his chest at that, like a final nail in the coffin of his hopes.

Garrison nodded and took a step backward, as if he'd read it the same. "We should let you get some sleep. Offer still stands, Sunny, just like before. You've got our number — you know where we are."

She nodded but didn't ask them to stay, didn't say she'd call.

And the reason was clear, wasn't it?

Because she wouldn't.

Chapter Seventeen

Sunny peered up at the cobweb in the corner of her front porch, the one with a daddy long legs spider she'd named Bob. She refused to knock the web down, to take the creature's home from it when it hadn't ever bothered her. She knew what it felt like to lose where she belonged, and she didn't plan to do that to anything else.

Her house felt like hers again, like she'd gotten something back with Tanner gone. He could no longer taint it. In the two weeks since the attack, Tanner had ended up in one big snowball of a disaster. His ego hadn't let him stay silent, and he'd even tried to call her from jail, which had landed him in more trouble. In short? He wasn't going to be getting out for a very long time.

Even though her life seemed to be in order now, there was still something missing.

No matter how much she tried to pretend it wasn't true, how much she tried to act as if everything was perfect, she missed Trent's laugh, and Garrison's heated gazes and the way Connor would snort when she said something he knew was bull.

Spike let out a bug huff as he adjusted, and she turned to crouch in front of him. "What's wrong, big guy?"

He turned those brown eyes on hers, sweet as could be. The bandage was still there, on the small stump left from the amputation, but his pain meds seemed to work well enough to keep him from hurting much. Mostly, he slept a lot.

She scratched him behind the ears, then dropped herself to sit on the edge of his large dog bed. "A lot has changed, hasn't it? You're doing pretty good, though." He didn't give up, didn't pout, just kept relearning how to walk, how to play. "How do you do it? How do you keep moving forward?"

He didn't answer, of course, but placed his massive head in her lap. Funny, she could almost hear Connor's voice in her head, as if the group of men were somehow connected with Spike — both scary-looking but sweet to those they cared for.

You just keep moving forward, because staying put won't do a thing for you.

She sighed, petting Spike, trying to understand everything that had happened, to come to terms with it. Spike shifted again, scooting closer so more of him was in her lap, and that was when it happened, when it hit her, as if she hadn't realized it before.

Spike had done what he did for one reason — because he loved her. He'd risked his own life just because she mattered.

She thought back to Garrison kicking in her door, to the way the three men had run into her living room *knowing* Tanner was there, knowing he could have had a gun, that they could have been hurt, but they'd done it because she mattered to them.

Spike opened his eyes, looking up at her, and only one question ran around her head.

What would I do for them?

She took her phone from her pocket and dialed Kat's number.

* * * *

Garrison turned away the third woman of the night who had knelt at his feet and offered herself up.

She was glamorous—long blonde hair, full breasts that were barely contained in her witch costume, and one hell of a 'come-fuck-me' voice.

Still, he'd sent her off with a flick of his wrist, and his cock took no interest in her.

"Maybe we shouldn't have come," Connor said, his face full of the same disinterest.

"What else were we going to do? Mope around at home?" Trent took a drink of the water bottle in his hand.

Yes, that was exactly what they would have done. Still, maybe it was preferable to trying to come to the club on masquerade night, something that now only reminded them of the woman who had left them. They hadn't come looking to replace the memory of Sunny with another woman—he doubted that was possible— but they'd wanted a distraction.

It turned out all the club did was remind them of her.

"Maybe we need to just take a few months off," Garrison said, as much as he hated the idea.

The club was like family, like a second home. Especially without Sunny, it felt like the only thing giving him that feeling. Still, each time they locked eyes with a woman, when they had the chance to taste her, the idea sounded as appetizing as room temperature leftovers that had been left out all night.

They'd worn the same masks from the month before, the idea of finding new ones seeming exhausting. Even with them, the night lacked the fun of before. Where dressing up had made things exciting, it only felt like a pitiful ruse now.

Still, they'd figured the whole 'fake it 'til you make it' thing applied. Maybe if they dressed up, if they showed up, they'd feel better.

No such luck.

A woman slid to her knees between their seats — number four of the evening.

She had her head lowered, some sort of white lace mask on, her hair braided back.

"Sorry, doll, but we're not interested." Connor spoke this time, since she wasn't looking up, couldn't see Garrison wave her off.

She didn't move, her body small, wearing a white dress that showed off her back and fell to just above her knees.

"Hey," Garrison said, trying to keep his voice gentle. Doms could scare subs, and he didn't want his mood to frighten this one. "There are plenty of Doms interested tonight, but we just aren't in the mood."

She lifted her head, her pink lips sweet, the bottom one swollen as if she'd been chewing it, and wearing a mask he would never forget.

Our Fox.

And on her wrist? Not the club's cuffs, but theirs — the brown leather padded ones, with silver buckles and their initials monogrammed on them. He frowned, glancing toward their bag to find it open, and there, across the room? Kat staring, telling him who had put her nose into their business.

Still, Garrison didn't move, not sure what to make of it. "What are you doing here, sweet?"

She chewed that lip, the best thing he'd seen in days. "I wanted to see you," she answered.

Connor leaned forward, his elbows on his knees. "You made it pretty clear in the hospital. You told Tanner that you belonged to yourself, and that's your choice to make. You don't really want this."

The words hurt to hear, the truth that had kept Garrison up, the one he couldn't get past.

She didn't want this, but they needed it.

It left them at an impasse.

She shook her head. "I *do* belong to myself. That's what I needed, what you taught me. I am mine." She paused, as if searching for the way to explain herself. "See, Tanner, I never gave myself to him, but I *felt* like I still was his. I'm not, though. You made me realize it."

"I'm glad," Garrison said. "I really am happy we helped you figure that out. It doesn't change things, though."

"It *does*, because now that I understand that, now that I'm sure of it, now that you've proven you aren't going to try and steal anything I don't give you, that's why I can give myself to you. I couldn't before." She lifted her hands, their cuffs around her wrists, and set them in Garrison's lap.

It was an offer like he'd never seen before, like the only thing that mattered.

"You're sure?" he asked. "Because you have to be sure. You have to know this is what you really want."

She swallowed hard, a tremble to her hands. "I'm sure. I've been terrified for so long, afraid of what I want, or the world, of myself. I'm not afraid anymore, though. I trust you. I *know* you. Garrison, I've never met a man who can make me feel like I'm the center of the entire universe before, who can drive me crazy, make me totally lose my mind. You make me feel safe, and like I have a place." She twisted to look at Connor. "And you? You're always making sure I know I'm important, and it wasn't until you I realized I *am* important, that I'm not what was done to me." The last look was to Trent, and she hesitated before talking. "And, Trent, you frustrate me so much, forcing me to realize that what I was sure I hated, I don't, that it's okay to not be like everyone else, that I can be who I am and to hell with anyone who doesn't like it."

Garrison didn't speak, letting her sit there in silence for a moment, letting her words sink in.

Her shoulders dropped. "But…maybe I'm too late? Maybe this wasn't a good idea…?" She blew out a soft breath. "Maybe you realized you want something else?" She pulled at her wrists, clearly planning to withdraw.

That woke Garrison up.

Fuck that.

He wrapped his hands around her wrists and pulled her forward, into his lap. The little gasp she let out was the final wake-up call his cock needed, as though it had just realized it was Sunny there, not anyone else, and now it was interested. "You really think we'd let you get away that easily, little Fox?"

She smiled, an honest one, and Garrison knew that even though they were all dressed up, even though they were all pretending to be something else, Sunny had put all her cards on the table.

They'd been looking for something for years without realizing it, and he never would have figured it would be the sweet little fox who had walked into their lives.

Epilogue

Sunny laughed as Trent pulled her into his lap at the men's house. She'd spent so much time there, she'd started to question keeping hers at all.

Somehow, her place felt empty when she went back, which led to her sleeping most nights with the men in the weeks since the party at the club.

Well, and she'd spent many nights *at* the club with them, too. Her cheeks heated at the thoughts of all the things that had happened there.

"What's the surprise?" she asked.

Trent wrapped his arms around her waist. "Nope. You aren't getting that out of me, honey. You'll have to just wait."

She squirmed, rewarded when he groaned, and his cock perked up at the friction. It was bratty, but she'd discovered she had a bit of brat in her, once she'd gotten comfortable, once she wasn't fearful.

There was something about teasing her men that she loved — especially because it often ended up with her bent over something and coming hard enough to make her forget her own name.

Garrison sat across from her, a smile on his lips, the way he always did when seeing her with the other two. He seemed happier, calmer. Maybe seeing everyone content eased some part of him.

Then again, the entire thing had felt odd. In her experience, relationships were full of strife, of fighting, of drama. The fact that there was little of that felt strange. For a while, she had been waiting for the other shoe to fall. It had taken time to realize there was no other shoe.

They argued, now and again. She recalled when she'd driven over in the middle of the night without calling first. She'd thought they were mad that she had surprised them, that she wasn't welcome without advance notice, and she'd tried not to show how deeply that had cut. Garrison had sat her down, using that stern voice he had, and explained the reason was that if she'd been in an accident, no one would have known where she was, would have known where to look, and that it was a concern about her safety.

Once she'd calmed down and understood, they'd come to a compromise. If it was after dark, she would let someone know — it could be her friend, Kat — where she was going.

That was the surprising thing — for as dominant as they were, as controlling as they could be, they always listened to her concerns. They didn't always agree or give in, but they made her feel heard and respected.

Trent put his hands over her eyes, the entire present thing something they'd been giddy about all day.

She had no idea what they'd planned, but she couldn't deny the excitement. Even if she hated it, the fact that they loved it was enough.

"Okay," Connor said, telling her he'd come outside as well, probably with whatever the surprise was. "Now."

Trent moved his hands, and as soon as her eyes took in the sight, Sunny felt as if she might cry.

Standing there was Spike—Connor must have picked him up from her house—on *four* legs. A black prosthetic ran from the stump to the ground, wrapped around him, and he was standing on it.

Spike's tail wagged, Connor's hand on his collar, and the moment he let go, Spike barreled forward. The run was awkward, but in the few steps he plunked his large head into Sunny's lap.

"He's still working on the gait," Connor said. "I've been sneaking over during the day to get him used to it. We've got a few adjustments to make, but he's taking to it well. Another few weeks and it'll be like he's used it his whole life. I've never seen a dog so ready to get back to running."

Then it happened. The tears came, wetting her cheeks as she wrapped her arms around Spike's head and hugged him.

It was one thing for the men to take care of her, to look after her. She appreciated it, of course, but *this* was something else.

Trent rubbed his hand over her back. "We know how sad you were about not being able to walk with him anymore, about him not getting to play fetch. It took a while to find a place that could make something, to get it done—" She turned and pressed her lips to his, ignoring the fact her face must have been a disaster.

The men cared about things that were important to *her*. They loved Spike because she did, took care of him because he was a part of her, and there was no bigger way to show her they were serious, that they loved her.

She slid off Trent's lap and shifted over to Garrison, leaning down to offer him a similar kiss, to try to explain how much the gesture meant to her. He wrapped his finger around the collar she wore, the one she had on each time she went to stay with them. He rubbed across it as he deepened the kiss and reminded her of what other talented things his tongue could do.

"Hey," Connor said, a pout to his voice. "I was the one to actually fit the thing."

Sunny laughed and turned to find Connor with his lip curled up, clearly enjoying the game. She wrapped her arms around his neck, letting him grab her ass and lift her against him as he took his kiss.

"Thank you," she whispered. "I don't know how I can ever thank you for this."

"I've got some ideas..." He pulled her tighter against him, rubbing his cock against her through their clothes.

She laughed, the sort of real laugh she hadn't realized was a thing before meeting them, before getting her life back, before finding a safe place to fall where she could be happy. "Well, I think I've got a pretty big tab to repay, so maybe we ought to get started."

As she was surrounded by three men who had terrified her only months before, three she would never have gotten involved with, she recognized how lucky she really was. She had walked into that club ready to put this life behind her, ready to close to the door on something she'd convinced herself she didn't need.

Instead of the monsters she had expected, she'd found safety and happiness and a home she'd been missing. And in the end, she owed it all the being a fox who had dared to play with wolves.

Want to see more from this author?
Here's a taster for you to enjoy!

Dark Sanctuary:
Trapped by Doubt
Jayce Carter

Coming May 2022

Excerpt

There was something about the courthouse that Ell both loved and hated. She loved its clear rules and the regimented way in which the place ran. There was never a question about what the next step should be or how a person went about those steps.

However, a part of her remembered coming as a child and the crushing disappointment that seemed to follow, no matter what. Being there as an adult gave a person a sense of power, but as a kid?

She remembered sitting beside a social worker, trembling, never sure exactly what would happen. Would they hand her over to her mother? Her father? Some relative she'd never met but who wanted good karma points for taking in the poor, destitute child? Or would she take the gamble that was foster parents?

It was terrifying — always.

Which was exactly why Ell handed a closed cup of hot cocoa to the boy sitting on the bench in one of the many long hallways.

Donnie Denton, the first case she'd ever been assigned on her own. He'd had a black eye but was ready to take on anyone he needed to to survive. It had broken her heart to see him like that, to know he'd lived a life where he'd needed that hard edge.

He took the hot cocoa and offered a rough thank you. While other case managers had had trouble with him — they claimed he lied and was disrespectful, and labeled him a lost cause — Ell had taken to him right away. She still got a smile each time he went to respond with cursing but stopped himself, as if he knew it wasn't appropriate in front of her.

One time, she'd gone to pick him up in a bad neighborhood, when he'd called her because the aunt who he'd been staying with had passed out at whatever drug dealer's house she'd taken him to and he'd had no one else to call. She still remembered how he'd pulled his shoulders back and walked beside her as if he were the adult, the protector, despite being only eight at the time.

Now, at thirteen, Donnie stood taller than her and had started to put on more bulk. Even still, she couldn't help but see that kid he'd been when she'd first met him.

"I'm sorry," he muttered softly, holding the cup between his hands.

"You don't need to apologize," Ell assured him as she took her seat beside him.

"Yeah, I do. I fu — I screwed up. You shouldn't have to waste your time cleaning up my messes."

Ell shook her head. "I know you — if you got into this fight, you had a good reason, right?"

The color leeched from his lips as he pressed them together, the universal signal for 'I'm no snitch,' that he made whenever she questioned anything. Then again, he was going to have to go back to that life, to those streets, and Ell knew very well that the sorts of people who existed in that world didn't forgive betrayal.

"I'm not trying to find out who it was," she pressed, gesturing at his split lip and black eye, all signs he'd taken a hell of a beating. "I'm just saying, I know you have a good heart. You wouldn't be out there attacking random, innocent people. So for this to happen, you had a good reason."

He let out a long breath before taking a sip of the drink. He held it in his mouth for a long moment, as if thinking, then swallowed. "Someone wanted me to do a job, but they didn't tell me the real job. When they did? I told them to fu—I told them no. Well, he didn't take no very well."

Ell set her hand on his back and rubbed, knowing there wasn't much she could do for him. Donnie was one of those hard cases, the type that broke her heart. He'd been screwed from day one, born to an abusive criminal of a father and a mother who cared more about drugs than she did any of her children—and there had been a few. It was like his path had been made for him before he'd ever been born, and no matter how hard she tried, she had no idea how to get him off it.

The creaking of a door caught Ell's attention, and sure enough, Jeff Jadzen, a district attorney who she'd been waiting for, walked out of his office.

Ell rose to her feet after nodding at Donnie, her way of assuring him that she'd handle it.

Jeff took one look her way and walked faster.

Too bad Ell was perfectly fine with running in heels.

"Jeff, I need a minute—"

"Sorry, Ell, but I'm really busy. Set something up with my secretary."

"I tried. I haven't heard anything back in a week, and I've called every day."

"Like I said, very busy." He reached the men's room, then smiled as if he'd won some prize. "It was nice to see you. Call the office, and we'll try to get together next week." He ducked inside, his voice floating out as the door swung closed.

Next week would be too late. The pretrial was set for Friday of this week, and if Jeff insisted on pushing any further...she shuddered to think about Donnie ending up in juvie, of how quickly the rest of his options could float away.

Which was the exact thing that had her walking into the men's room. She'd been in far worse places in her life for far less noble reasons. Then again, there was a reason she did what she did — because it was important. She had no problem with tenacity getting her what she needed.

"Please tell me you didn't follow me into the men's room." Jeff spoke through a closed stall door, his annoyance palpable.

"I wasn't finished talking with you. At least now, you can't leave."

The longest sigh came from the stall. "Which charity case are you here about this time?"

"Donnie Denton."

"*Him* again? Come on, Ell, you run yourself ragged and for what? Donnie isn't some six-year-old who needs you to save him — he's basically an adult in his world. Stop seeing him as something he isn't."

"He's thirteen — that's still a kid. He isn't a bad kid, either."

"You say that because you didn't see the other person from the fight. Donnie shattered his eye socket with a bat."

That took her off guard, the level of violence new. Still, Ell shook her head, reassuring herself that she knew Donnie. He didn't lie to her. If he didn't want to tell her something, he just wouldn't, but he didn't lie.

"You know what it's like for people who live in that area."

"Yeah, I know, because I see what happens to the victims."

"Some victim. They wanted Donnie to do a job that was bad enough he turned it down once he knew the details."

"Is that what he told you? Well, his 'turned it down' moment ended up being *inside* someone's house as they robbed it. Did he leave that part out? That the woman walked in and saw them there."

Ell cringed at the little detail that Donnie *had* left out. Still, it didn't change the rest. "Well, did Donnie touch the woman?"

Silence let her know she was right.

There was the flush of a toilet, then Jeff walked out and headed for the sinks. "No. According to her, Donnie's friend pulled out a bat, and when Donnie objected, the two got into a fight. Scared the poor woman half to death, and when Donnie won, when the other man took off, Donnie said sorry and escaped through a window. We caught him down the street."

"You see? He was trying to help."

Jeff dried his hands, then turned to face Ell. "You see the best in people, Ell, and that's great, but it's going to get you killed. These kids you help, they aren't innocent and fragile. By the time they hit their teenage years, a lot of them are already killers. They're dangerous and they're manipulative, and if you're not careful it'll end you."

How many times had she heard that sort of warning? People who told Ell that she should pick a safer job, that she should do something else?

It didn't matter. She knew exactly why she did what she did. "Donnie has a shot. If you throw him into juvie, you're just going to solidify this path for him. Prison doesn't rehabilitate kids. It just makes them into better criminals."

Jeff rubbed the corners of his eyes. "What do you want me to do? He broke into a woman's house and put someone else in the hospital. I can't just look the other way with that."

"Community service."

"What?"

"He needs to see there are options for him, that there's a life he can still have that isn't on the streets. Assign him community service hours, and I'll make sure to find him a place to work them where he can do some good, where he can see a different life is possible."

Jeff's expression twisted the way it always did when he was deep in thought, when he was trying to see all the possible outcomes. His job had jaded him, but he wasn't a bad man.

Finally, he nodded. "Okay. I'll get it all drawn up and present it to his public defender. Make sure he understands that this is it, though. This is his one big shot. If he gets involved in something else like this, you won't be able to save him again."

Ell agreed, thanked Jeff, then exited the men's room. A quick conversation with Donnie outside let him know the details, and even though he wasn't the sort to admit to being nervous, the shuddering breath he released said he had been. He thanked Ell, then took off.

She would have driven him home, but Donnie was used to using the bus system. He always refused when she tried, saying he'd meet her wherever it was.

A glance at her watch told Ell that she didn't have another appointment until later, which gave her time to gather herself. When she slung her bag over her shoulder and turned, however, she ran directly into someone else.

Hand grasped her arms to keep her upright, and Ell glanced up to find a familiar face grinning down at her.

Ethan Jaymes, a detective she'd dealt with more than a few times. He was tall, dark and handsome—all the things that made her certain he was also trouble, especially when he smiled at her the way he always did.

"Aren't you in a hurry?" he said, his tone laced with amusement.

She pulled away, extracting herself from his strong grasp. "You were the one standing far too close."

"I said your name, and you didn't hear me. Distracted?" He lifted an eyebrow.

"Well, believe it or not, my world doesn't revolve around you."

He let out a soft laugh, the way he always did when she soundly rejected him. It was odd, because sometimes it seemed the meaner she got, the more Ethan liked her.

And, just like clockwork, Ethan's shadow came around the corner.

Clint Faire, Ethan's partner, and an unnerving presence who had always made Ell fidget under his intense stare. He peered at her, no pleasure or surprise showing in his expression. "Ms. Hayden," he said, his tone as respectful as always.

Ell nodded back, still trying to calm her racing heart from her surprise at seeing Ethan. It shouldn't have surprised her that much — the two detectives were often at the courthouse — yet they always managed to make her feel out of control.

Which was the worst feeling she could fathom. Ell was the sort of woman who preferred everything in its place, everything well-regulated and scheduled. Ethan and Clint made her feel the opposite, as if she couldn't quite get a hold of all the pieces of her life, as if she couldn't make sense of it all.

Why, she had no idea.

She'd known the two men for years, though she wouldn't call them friends by any stretch. They'd worked together from time to time — both on the same side and not so much.

"So, who are you harassing today?" Clint asked in his matter-of-fact way that always made Ell's cheeks heat. He managed to reduce anything down to a simple statement that embarrassed her often.

"I wasn't harassing anyone. I was doing my job."

"And who did your job require you to harass today?" Clint pressed.

"No one." Ell crossed her arms and tapped her foot, trying to make her annoyance as clear as possible.

"She followed me into the men's room," Jeff answered as he walked past, not slowing down to talk, seeming more than happy to rush across the hall so he could hide in his office again.

Ethan let out a hard laugh at that, and the way he accepted it without question annoyed Ell. Yes, she was dedicated, but he could have had a second of 'are they being serious? Would she really do that?' doubt.

Instead, he took it as fact, as if he knew she would absolutely do that.

"I needed to discuss something important with him, and he wanted to hide in the bathroom."

"You're going to get yourself into trouble one day," Ethan said as he caught his breath from his laughter. "It's good to go to bat for your kids, Ell, but be careful that you don't put yourself in a position you don't want to be in."

His words ran through Ell like they always did, tinged in something she tried so hard to ignore. Why was it that Ethan got beneath her skin like this? His voice was honey, something sweet enough to draw her closer, but also sticky enough she feared it might trap her.

All the reasons it was a bad idea had gone through in her head on nights when she stayed up thinking about him, even about Clint. She had her life in order. She'd perfectly crafted each part of it, fitting the pieces together, making exactly the picture she wanted. The idea of anyone else coming into that, of them possibly tearing apart everything she'd worked so hard to put into place terrified her.

Life was hard and scary and dangerous, but if she kept the pieces in their spots, if she made sure everything went where it belonged, she could avoid the pain and fear she'd known so well as a kid.

So, Ell offered a quick goodbye before she risked falling any further into either man, before she risked everything she'd built.

The last thing she needed was to let any man knock down the perfect little life she'd cultivated.

About the Author

Jayce Carter lives in Southern California with her husband and two spawns. She originally wanted to take over the world but realized that would require wearing pants. This led her to choosing writing, a completely pants-free occupation. She has a fear of heights yet rock climbs for fun and enjoys making up excuses for not going out and socializing.

Jayce loves to hear from readers. You can find her contact information, website details and author profile page at https://www.totallybound.com

Home of Erotic Romance

Sign up for our newsletter and find out about all our romance book releases, eBook sales and promotions, sneak peeks and FREE romance books!